BF127048.3.

258

Barnardos
Reg. Ch. No.216250

SYBILLE BEDFORD

…as born in Germany which she left for good in her early childhood. She was educated privately in Italy, England and France. Sybille Bedford started writing at sixteen — literary essays, critical work and fiction. Her first book, *The Sudden View: a Mexican Journey*, was published in 1953 and later republished as *A Visit to Don Otavio*. Her first and most famous novel, *A Legacy*, was published in 1956 and televised in 1975. *The Best We Can Do*, an account of the trial of Dr Bodkin Adams, was published in 1958, followed by *The Faces of Justice* (1961), a report on law courts and judicial procedure in England, France, Germany, Switzerland and Austria. The novels *A Favourite of the Gods* and *A Compass Error* appeared in …63 and 1968 respectively, and her two-volume biography of …ous Huxley was published in 1973 and 1974.

… distinguished literary journalist and law reporter, Sybille …rd has covered the Auschwitz Trial at Frankfurt, the … of Jack Ruby at Dallas and the Lady Chatterley and …n Ward trials at the Old Bailey, London. She has …buted to numerous magazines and papers both here and … United States, and as a journalist and critic is most … for her travel writing, her articles on wine and food, … her book reviews. A Fellow of the Royal Society of …re, an English Vice President of P.E.N., she was … the O.B.E. in 1981.

… Bedford married in 1935 and has lived in France, … the United States and Italy. She now lives in …here she is working on a new novel.

WITHDRAWN FROM BROMLEY LIBRARIES

D0229585

A Compass Error

SYBILLE BEDFORD

With a New Introduction by
Peter Vansittart

Virago

Published by VIRAGO PRESS Limited 1984
41 William IV Street, London WC2N 4DB

First published in Great Britain by Collins 1968

Copyright © Sybille Bedford 1968

Introduction copyright © Peter Vansittart 1984

All rights reserved

British Library Cataloguing in Publication Data

Bedford, Sybille
  A compass error.
  I. Title
  823'.914 [F]   PR6052.E/

  ISBN 0-86068-388-5

Printed in Finland by Werner Söderström Oy,
a member of Finnprint

ODB

BROMLEY
PUBLIC
LIBRARIES HOSP

CLASS F

BF1270483

INVOICE DATE

HJ

WITHDRAWN FROM BROMLEY LIBRARIES

TO EDA LORD

CONTENTS

IST GENT.   Our deeds are fetters that we forge ourselves.
2ND GENT.   Ay, truly, but I think it is the world
            That brings the iron.
                                Middlemarch Chapter IV

Le passé est une partie de nous-même, la plus
essentielle peut-être.
                                            Victor Hugo

'You are young, sir,' he said, 'you are young;
you are very very young sir.'
                                        David Copperfield

Introduction

A Favourite of the Gods introduced Flavia, daughter of Constanza, 'the favourite': granddaughter of Anna, the Principessa. Both are still living, though in the background of the novel. It is not essential to have read the earlier work, though it will help. When Flavia exclaims 'Strike me pink!' to a handsome stranger, the unlikely exclamation echoes her father's first meeting with her mother. The two books are close-knit: through them we see the steady coarsening of Europe, the heartaches and missed chances burdening the older characters, the subtle play of Time. People not only arrange the future but alter the past and, so doing, alter themselves.

This novel I rate less complex than its two predecessors. The locale has narrowed: old sophisticated assumptions about morality, manners, style, quotidian decency are gone, or exist only in daydreams, often of those unentitled to them.

At seventeen, in the South of France, Flavia is still cool, self-possessed, informed, enjoying as much as possible of the life that comes her way and seeking to enlarge it, through hard work as a student and by keeping her ears open. She loves swimming, reading, eating and drinking alone in cheap restaurants. Sybille Bedford is admirable at showing people by themselves in the half-moments of wonder and fear, incredulity, numbed inarticulate yearning, unexpected inexplicable fits of sadness, stabs of loneliness inflicted by a marvellous party. Those moods when we seem to find ourself like a stranger, staring from the window into December dusk or at a lighted street: or when a dear friend is ascending the stairs. Flavia is receptive to random delights, chance misgivings, drifting insights, while sunlight lies on a petal and wave, shadows cluster, colours deepen, fade, clouds and trees suggest patterns, and the mind breeds pictures, analogies and, with luck, more. She delights in the simple yet richly organic. She

had loved wine from childhood on. She loved the shapes of bottles and of course the romatic names of the pretty manorhouses on the labels, and she loved the link with rivers and hillsides and climates and hot years, and the range of learning and experiment afforded by wine's infinite variety; but what she loved more was the taste — of peach and earth and honeysuckle and raspberries and spice and cedarwood and pebbles and truffles and tobacco-leaf; and the happiness, the quiet ecstacy that spreads through heart and limb and mind.

But shapes and tastes, life's brightest toys, will not permanently suffice. Anna and Constanza, targets for well-flavoured legend and anecdote in several countries, are well-read, accustomed to entertain artists and politicians, but have always been too occupied, socially, emotionally, to practice an art themselves — though their eclectic parties have given Flavia far more than the small talk of dilettantism. Constanza, at last involved in a love genuinely serious, is now assisting fringe anti-Fascist politics in Italy, so that, when the novel opens, Flavia is living alone in a small French sea-village, reading, reading, hoping one day to review for the New Statesman, then write Huxley-like novels, on the premise that ideas are more interesting than people. A novel, nevertheless, is not her ultimate challenge, merely the preliminary test demanded for sterner intellectual disciplines. More strenuously, she wants to write

books of essays, proposing changes in government, economics, law and general conduct; rational changes effected by goodwill, technological advances and the lessons learnt from history, and conducive to increase in happiness, non-violence and ease. Utopia by consent. (Once that attained, one might give oneself some day to the attempt of creating a work of art; but that, to her, was still as remote and veiled as death itself.)

A low-voiced, earnest prig in a novel worthy but dull, yet another report about a writer exclusively for other writers? Nothing could be more untrue: it was untrue of Huxley himself, as Sybille Bedford showed commandingly in her biography of that versatile and generally appealing figure. Flavia is touchingly vulnerable, she speaks for the youth of most of us, inwardly lonely and, again like most of us, unwilling to admit it. Her nature, her body, both seek more than ideals and ideas. Like her mother, the Favourite of the gods, she has the weaknesses and perils that beauty, charm, unsleeping curiosity attract to their fortunate possessors. Flavia shows herself unlike her grandmother, for Anna has always expected too much, thereby losing too much. She retired too early from emotional contests but for Flavia a passionate involvement with living people is needed to deepen her awareness, colour her personality, extend her resources. It will toughen her, weaken her, just possibly destroy her.

Flavia had the kind of ear that picks up languages and makes a mimic, and she was much more curious about people and better at taking them in than she was aware in her bedazzlement with systems and ideas. Whether she welcomed it or not, the novelist's touch was there.

She needs, then, to attack life, and at the source. Eager young men, older women perhaps only apparently eager, will appear with their various temptations, in sumptuous Mediterranean settings. Flavia is young enough to accept gratefully Southern France of the late twenties and thirties, which promises freedom, work, friendship, play, learning, civilization itself. Also, the intricacies of early love, fruitful even when most agonizing, indeed particularly when most agonizing.

The beautiful rich she has met, and will soon know further, whatever their politics or lack of them. Though their disagreements can be vicious, these people are mostly aware of the public responsibilities of private life, however much they may neglect them. They can accept the need to look beyond the immediate, now that the European sunlight is darkening. Riches cannot hide the mountebank trio, Mussolini, Hitler, Stalin, who are indeed receiving fulsome praise in the West, particularly from leisured intellectuals who would be amongst the first to be destroyed should their heroes win the field. Meanwhile, in many households, bookshelves are filled with the books, plays, manifestoes, of Constanza's set, and Flavia's new friends.

Always, for mental ballast, a test of moral form, she uses less them than the personality of her mother's lover and putative husband, Michel Devaux, who demands some attention.

In her trek from her husband, Simon, to Devaux, Constanza has not only travelled, but progressed. Simon had been unusual in style and lack of scruple — doing one's own thing, as a later generation put it, too frequently entails doing in other people — but she always tended to be attracted by those with a strain of opportunism and buccaneering. An old family friend, Mr James, reflects, 'Never to miss a pleasure in life, at whatever cost to someone else, was an almost philosophical concept with Simon.' With Devaux, it is to do one's duty whatever the personal cost, and that duty he always sees clear, 'which is of course more clearly than one's duty ever can be seen. Oh, he has his faults, or if you prefer, his dangerous qualities.'

His charity and honesty can sometimes disconcert or irritate more conventionally ambitious associates, but cannot be evaded. Mr James has said that a French agnostic intellectual with a non-conformist conscience is a force of nature. Here, Devaux is more often described by others than seen in action, though involved in some of the major contemporary issues. I myself would have welcomed a more direct approach, though this might of course have upset the balance and destroyed the novel's inner compulsion. Anyway, fastidious, with outstanding political and moral integrity, he contains something of Aldous Huxley in his moral concerns, polymath strength, anxiety about pollution, over-population, reckless squandering of natural resources, science without conscience: about greed, short-cut and quack notions of government bawled at their most grandiose by dictators of Left and Right, frequently interchangeable. 'To Utopia' all too often turns into 'to the scaffold'. Constanza and Flavia must both ponder his obsessions, notably the classical problem of how to affect necessary social change without ruining society and contaminating personal life: also, the dangers of tolerating corruption, the incompetent and anti-democratic in the name of democracy. Problems of the times and of all time. But here I must emphasise that Sybille Bedford is not paraphrasing glib or boring manifestoes. These ideas clink about in the heads of her characters, forcing them into personal choices, sacrifices, adventures. Ultimately, lives will be at risk.

Much of Devaux percolates through Flavia, despite the increasing pace of her social life. She broods on the relation of self to habit, environment, genetics; the effectiveness of pacificism against political thugs; the causes and nature of crime; the tiresome fact that undeniable social advance has witnessed and perhaps entailed tortures, moral outrages, state hooliganism and idolatory that would make the statesmen of her grandmother's girlhood — Lincoln, Cavour, Gladstone, Franz-Josef, Louis Napoleon, Bismarck — gape with incredulity. 'The invention of anaesthetics, the rule of law, yes indeed. But secret police, Lenin's Kulaks in the cattle train, Mussolini and the castor oil . . . '

This should never be forgotten. Faithful, erudite Mr James, easily though wrongly considered unproductive for never having been published, though profiting greatly by making no immoderate claims on life, says to Flavia, 'the worst we can do towards the past is to let it go by default'.

'The future of society,' Constanza muses to her young daughter,

had it made an irrevocably false start? The compass error that gets harder to correct with every mile you go? How simple and shining it had all looked when she was young and Mama was preaching democracy, and she went one better with her faith in Fabian Socialism. The influence of private individuals on events was negligible — and yet they must keep on. "One thing I learnt in England: public opinion, the sum of private opinions, does matter, can matter often for good."

However, with Anna far away, and Constanza and Devaux re-setting their lives, and the larger society of chancelleries, cartels and paranoics beginning to totter, Flavia's self-contained existence, the books, letters, swimming, her self-assurance, even her bed, have been invaded by the wealthy, popular Theresa, wife of a successful though artistically problematical painter. They inhabit a nearby villa glittering with the good things of life. Flavia, once invited, becomes a fascinated and sought-after initiate. Day follows day in dazzling repartee — days of picnics and boating, lobster salad and hock, libraries, lively argument over finely calculated dinners and, particularly for Flavia, flattery — flattery candid, flattery subtle, unexpected tricks of love. Flavia takes what she is offered, parties and flirtations, love and appetite are at one with the sea and sun. Momentarily, Therese's gifts enchant. Here is the realm of the fairy godmother and magical garden. Flavia's independence, so vital for herself, and indeed the novel, is threatened, not by the lurking, watchful children, both caustic and vulnerable, but by fairytale charm, beauty, novelty. Yet, as later she would swiftly recognise, a fairytale is no prettified version of life, an alternative culture, an escape into fantasy: more properly, it should be translated *fate tale*. Fate tales make sense of personal life, in which strangers in deceptive disguises, the ugly and the beautiful, the animal and dwarfish, appear with riddles, temptations, initiation tests, ambiguous gifts, which are all invitations to obstruct or fulfil one's potential, to complete oneself, and thus win the ultimate kingdom, or fall away into failure and loss. Oneself, the youngest child, Flavia, existentially struggles for identity, by overcoming 'they', so powerful and destructive in Edward Lear's verses. 'They' are the malicious giants, cruel or indifferent parents, the conventional and impersonal, the plausible, pretentious, and venomous. Perhaps Flavia herself confirms John Fowles' observation: 'single children are always intensely self-absorbed. But also they can't quite imagine that anyone else might ever actually need them.' Perhaps not, but however this may be, she has always known, yet is now tempted to renounce, that heroes and heroines can win through, riddles be solved, family complexes be transcended, malignancies escaped. Fate lies not in magic, the twists of Party politics, palaces too lush and helping hands too grasping, but in considered choice and personal integrity, displayed rather than taught, by a Chekhov, Nansen, Curie, Michel Devaux. Nevertheless, a more perilous riddle, a literal survival test, is soon posed, by a second fairy godmother, Andrée, more stylish and powerful than Therese, and far more enigmatic. Flavia develops a passionate obsession with her, drifting towards hazards which, despite long discussions about life, her readings of Constanza's favourites, Racine, Stendhal, Balzac, Forster, Huxley, Waugh, she is almost totally unprepared for. Andrée is the dark priestess, foremost amongst 'They'. A dramatic, almost melodramatic coup, unusual with Sybille Bedford, described without irony, shows Flavia that the brutal, merciless, and disgusting are not literary inventions of the civilised for the over-civilised. 'You look disapproving? Time you were told a few facts of life, you slobbering little moralist.'

Flavia, astounded by this abrupt revelation of identity, Andrée's and her own, must recognise that she is trapped in a sordid conspiracy, and that not only is she herself menaced but also the happiness and security of Constanza and Devaux. The impeccable Michel, seemingly invulnerable in his principles and reputation, had himself, long before, made a choice signally imperceptive and unwise. He too had been misled by magic.

Andrée is both less and more than Flavia had imagined. She is no Kate Croy, delicately evil, but coarser, blunter, more cunning than subtle, and Sybille Bedford knows just when information must be explicit. Andrée remarks to the hapless Flavia, 'the exercise of blackmail, isn't appreciated nearly enough, it's almost its own reward'. She is impelled by resentment, envy, revenge, the least generous human nastinesses, though remaining credible and various. She is not consistently repulsive and may disclose pathos. Her story too is scarcely complete, and Sybille Bedford is not one to pronounce the inexorable and damning.

Flavia listens to Andrée's precise and disarming lessons.

Very young people are perfectly capable of love, they are sometimes capable of a sensually adequate affair: they are very rarely capable of managing the two together, the *whole* thing is too much for them. And there's something else I don't mind telling you about — to show you that I'm neither unfair nor biased and only harp on your bad points — I want to tell you something about your looks. I can safely do so as I've noticed that you don't care about them yourself one way or the other, and I don't think you ever will. People can take or leave them as far as you're concerned; conceit or indifference it comes to the same. You want to be liked for other qualities. So a compliment from me at the point we have reached is not going to boost your morale. Well, your looks, my dear, are charming; they're not exactly conventional and I'm not going to predict what they will be like in twenty years from now with your guzzling all the way, but for the present they will do, they will do very nicely for any man, boy, or girl.

Can she but retrieve her independence, Flavia could learn as much from this woman as from Michel Devaux. Andrée is intelligent, though for her it is sterile and, for many others, destructive. She has set up a fateful crossroads, at which Flavia can choose, if she will, to advance, fight back, gropingly, resolutely, at last putting her own intelligence to more than the literary and sexual dreaming.

As in all Sybille Bedford's works, there is movement and no deadlocks. The Second World War divides Flavia's life as the First had Constanza's. The Favourite of the gods passes in a way all too earthy; but war renews, or initiates, Andrée's needs for a proper life, shifting her energies to enemies more acceptable, eliciting indeed a certain splendour. For Flavia, whether in war or peace, there abide questions which, as a middle-aged celebrity, she will still have to tackle. Answers remain provisional but they provide the solid gist to her life.

'The mere business of telling a story interests me less and less,' Huxley once confessed. In her biography, Sybille Bedford italicises this, but without comment. Her own interest is different, appropriate to one so concerned with law and procedures, where drama exists and outcomes must result. These can be just yet unfair, often non-proven, occasionally rankly unjust but with poetic rightness. All is liable to be surprising. She knows that evidence can be untrustworthy, even if submitted on oath. In her narrative, witnesses are more important than judges — if judges there are. Wittingly or unwittingly, they betray secrets, let cats out of bags, produce extraordinary memories, and details too plausible, together with much gossip. Few of us are immune from the lures of gossip, which can, of course, also contain a certain validity. This is sufficient to make an engrossing novel, for the true novelist is neither prosecutor nor judge, and has no more need to sum up totally than a painter has to fill his canvas with everything in sight. Human beings evade strict analysis, just as 'love' or 'loneliness' receive inadequate treatment in dictionaries, accurate statistics may add up to woeful error, and a guess illuminate better than a police report. Such trials as Flavia's have no end and can be debated long after their formal conclusions. They show, I suggest, that the written word can still, better than any other art, hint at what it is like to be someone else, an impossiblity, yet ever worth pursuing, and incessant, whether we like it or not. The young Flavia had wondered what goes on behind skulls. Her adventures illustrate a conviction 'that life is good and learning infinite — that this can never pall'. I recommend with confidence a novel neither tragic nor comic, though with ingredients of both, and which is yet marvellously real.

There she went. A foolish girl, a brave girl, a single human creature in first pride of its unique existence. Ignorant, as we are all of us, in youth, in health, untired, taking possession of the world, ignorant of its workings and that of our own natures; ignorant, arrogant, generous, self-enclosed, yet visited, however briefly, by a flash of intellectual passion.

Peter Vansittart,
London 1982

Prologues

The relevant questions, as it happened, came by chance.

The man from the newspaper said, 'The Twenties were your period, Miss Herbert? It is *Miss* Herbert?'

'Well, Mrs, actually,' said Flavia.

'You knew many of the writers of the time?'

'Goodness, no. I was a child. Living with my grandmother most of the year. In Italy.'

'Then shall we say the Thirties?'

'I grew up in them. I grew up in the Thirties. I came of age the year Hitler went into the Rhineland.'

'Is that so?' said the young man. 'But you have written about the Twenties?'

'Other people's past. That always seems more clear.'

'Is it true that your grandmother was a duchess, Mrs Herbert?'

'Not true.'

'Your readers would be interested to know.'

'*Your* readers.'

He said earnestly, 'Mrs Herbert, our readers are your readers potentially.'

'What a delightful prospect: you have so many.'

'Thank you.'

Flavia gave him a look, teasing, detached, friendly. 'My grandmother was an American lady.'

'Oh, yes?'

'She was a Miss Howland and came from Rhode Island, New England.'

'Yes?'

'Yes.'

'She must have got married.'

More firmly, Flavia said, 'She's been dead these thirty-five years.' Then added, 'Oh, she was married.'

'I'm only trying to fill in your international background.'

Flavia said nothing.

He looked insistent.

'As a premature European?'

'But you were *born* in England?'

'Born in England. I had to cross the Channel.'

'Your father?'

'Was called to the Bar and became a member of Parliament, *if* that describes him. *He* can hardly be news now. He died early. Much too early.'

'Wasn't it he who left those pictures to the nation?'

'Yes, they went to the nation.'

Something made him ask, 'You knew your father? You were old enough?'

'No.' She did not add, I was old enough.

'And where were you educated, Mrs Herbert?'

'At home. Not that we had one. There were . . . interruptions.'

'Is that so?'

'I had the luck to have some bright friends.'

'University?'

'No university,' said Flavia.

'The bright friends——?'

'Older than myself.'

'How did that come about?'

'Accidents of time and place.'

'I understand you lived in France as a girl? The South of France.'

'Yes, in France.'

'It must have been quite the life.'

'You know, in its own way, it was.' Flavia got up, crossed the room, sat down in another chair. It was a habit she had.

'There was an illusion of freedom, the French used to be good at providing that. And there was one thing one didn't think about then in that corner of the shrinking West— who called it that?— we never thought that life as we knew it could change at such a rate, that the quality of life would change.'

'Yes?'

'And there was the place itself. . . .' She was talking rapidly though with sudden hesitations as if she were picking her way, 'The countryside down there was so very good— austere, uncluttered: olives and rock. And *light*. Always light. And of course the sea. It got under your skin, you became part of it, until you came to feel that you could live nowhere else. It was like love.'

'You had a French stepfather, Mrs Herbert?'

'You might call him that.'

'He also lived on the Riviera?'

'In retirement, withdrawal rather than retirement. He wrote. Sociological home-truths. Nobody listened much. If they did today, they'd probably tear him to pieces. He didn't think much of the common man and he foresaw a great many things that have happened since. He held no false hopes. By the way, it was not the Riviera, not by a long chalk. The unsmart side of the Coast: Provence, a fishing port and a handful of people.'

'But you left?'

'By Munich it was all over.'

'After the war, you didn't go back?'

'I didn't go back.'

'Didn't you want to?'

'There's nobody left there and the place must have changed. Besides I rather dislike my younger self. Don't ask me what it was like.'

'What was it like your younger self?'

'Young.'

He said, 'That's no crime.'

'Ah, well.' Flavia picked up a paperweight, put it down, lifted her hand. 'One does odd things. You see, when one's young one doesn't feel part of it yet, the human condition; one does things because they are not for good; everything is a rehearsal. To be repeated ad lib, to be put right when the curtain goes up in earnest. One day you know that the curtain was up all the time. That *was* the performance.'

The young man said, 'When did you publish your first book?'

Flavia told him.

'A late starter?'

'A late starter. Though not a late vocation.'

'Was that the first——?' he supplied a title.

'What homework! It must be a pretty thin book— it was a kind of an echo.'

'Echo of what?'

'Oh, many things; other people's ideas. Things one liked to believe in.'

'Would you mind checking this list of publications for me?'

'Not at all.' And presently she said, 'And now I must give you that drink.'

'If you can make it a quick one, I have another assignment.'

'What will you have? Scotch——?'

'Please.'

She made him one and gave herself a brandy and soda.

While they drank she said, 'I'm afraid this has been rather a dull interview for you. But if I may say so, you're a bit to blame as well. People in your trade have so little curiosity.'

'Oh, come on!'

'It takes two to tell the truth.'

Before he left the man from the newspaper produced a book in a vivid jacket. 'It's by this author I'm going to see now,

American. It's coming out here this week, it's supposed to teach you how to change.'

'Seldom a bad idea.'

'You know, how to cope with life by doing all sorts of stunts to yourself——'

'Do let me have a look,' said Flavia.

'It's all in recipes.'

'Recipes?'

'Here's one that tells you to sit down in a chair and ask yourself a question and give the answer; it's usually a bad one so you go on asking day after day till you get it right.'

'And what's the right answer going to do for you?'

'Search me.'

'What kind of questions?'

'There's a whole collection, you've got to get the right one too.' The man from the newspaper read out, ' "The life of what person, real or fictional, did I try to lead between the age of sixteen and twenty-one?" '

'Easy,' Flavia said, 'the first answer, the bad answer: My own.'

That same evening, late, Flavia once more found herself talking to someone who was practically a stranger. It was the end of a dinner party. Those who had stayed had settled down and there was a sense of lucidity, detachment, ease.

'It's going to happen to me next year,' he said. 'What does it feel like?'

'Like the last days in December, the end of a page in the ledger. An accounting day.' For the dinner tonight had been given for Flavia. It was her birthday. The fiftieth.

'A conventional accounting day,' he said.

'Oh, quite. But compelling.'

'I'm surprised at *your* observing it.'

'I observe a few conventions; don't you?'

He said, 'But then I am a reasonably conventional person and I'm certain that you are not.'

'Conventional according to the light of our generation, or our times?'

'One tries to arrive at some compromise.'

'Isn't that conformism? The French say, *être dans le vent* for being with it, it sounds more free but it's the same thing.'

'And you don't try?' he asked.

'To conform? No. Not really.'

'Those conventions——?'

'Eclectic. A pretence of fitting somewhere.'

'Pretence to whom?'

'Oh, myself; only myself.'

'And do you?'

'Fit? I feel at home in a good many places.'

'At home on a visit?'

He had a long, leathery face and small, friendly eyes, this man whose name she had barely caught, who was sitting next to her, sitting back in the armchair glass in hand at this late hour, and Flavia, who was taking a liking to him, said, 'That's it. More or less.'

With seeming irrelevance he said, 'I bet you get away with things?'

'Do I? I never think about it.'

'*That* is the way to get away with things.'

'My family did— they got away with things, poor darlings. Up to a point, *up to a point*. I suppose it was a mark of their time? The high-handedness?'

'It could have been a mark of your family?'

Flavia said quickly, 'You couldn't have——?'

He said, 'I could, but I didn't.' Adding, 'I'm in Rome a good deal.' He looked at her. 'They still talk of your mother.'

'They do? I'm so glad!'

He did not take it up. 'So you actually draw a balance sheet at the end of the year?'

'I don't say that I read it. Anyway, it's never so bad after a writing year.'

'And today?'

'Today is worse. Today is fifty 31sts of December come home to roost.'

'Is it age you mind?'

'Who wouldn't? Actually I don't think much about age— yet— or that thing about looks and losing or not losing them. One would prefer to be young of course, in working condition young, but *youth*?— isn't real youth *unimaginable* now?'

'But you do mind?'

'*Yes*,' said Flavia.

'What do you mind?'

'Time,' she said at once. 'Loss of time. Time wasted or not wasted— gone. Over. Gone. Having reached the point where the slice in front *must* be less, *is* less, than the slice one's had.'

'The best part's gone?

'Very likely. The largest, certainly.'

'Does sheer quantity count?' he said.

'Of course it does. Just as in money.'

'Would you like to have it all over again, your time, if you could?'

'Yes,' she said, 'Oh, yes, *yes*.'

'For love of life?'

'*Indeed*. But mainly . . . to do things differently.'

'You would like to tinker with your past?' he said.

'More than that!'

He waited.

'I should like to have been better, to have behaved better.' She diluted it, 'As who does not?'

He still waited.

Lightly as if without volition, Flavia said, 'I made a wrong start.' She heard herself say, 'It got me off course.'

When nothing further came from her, he threw in, 'What did?'

Self-possessed again she shook it off, 'One says these things.' Her tone had changed.

'My dear,' he said, 'does one?'

It brought her back. 'I have not before this minute.'

He said reasonably, 'You have now.'

'The accounting day,' she said. 'And perhaps you. I know what you are not asking, Do I want to talk about it? It's only for memory— a series of incidents.'

'Incidents of consequence?'

For the second time that day, deliberately now, Flavia said, 'It takes two to tell the truth.'

'One for one side, one for the other?'

'That's not what I mean. I mean one to tell, one to hear. A speaker and a receiver. To tell the truth about any complex situation requires a certain attitude in the receiver.'

'What is required from the receiver?'

'I would say first of all a level of emotional intelligence.'

'Imagination?'

'Disciplined.'

'Sympathy? Attention?'

'And patience.'

'Detachment?'

'All of these. And a taste for the truth— an immense willingness to *see*.'

'Wouldn't it be simpler,' he said, 'just to write it down?'

'Postulating a specific reader-receiver?'

'Casting a wider net: one or more among an unknown quantity of readers.'

Quite cheerfully now, Flavia said, 'You forget that I am a writer. Writers don't just write it down. They have to give it a form.'

He said, 'Well, do.'

'Life is often too . . . peculiar for fiction. Form implies a measure of selection.'

He pleased her by catching on, 'At the expense of the truth?'

'Never essentially. At the expense of the literal truth.'

'Does the literal truth matter?'

She thought about that. 'To the person to whom it happened.'

'Even if that person is a writer?'

Round them there were signs of breaking up. People were standing, someone was dialling for taxis. Flavia too stood up, put down her glass. Before turning away, composed now, smiling, she flicked out an answer, 'Then, there might be a clash of intentions.'

Much later that night, in fact in the small hours of next morning, Flavia woke. Instantly acute, formed sentences, unprompted, unthought, sprang into her mind, flashed by in continuation, in parody of the many duologues of the day.

I don't want to look at that place. I don't want to tell about that time. It was a good place. What happened cannot change that.

On a slower, a more deliberate level, she recognized the compulsory nature of her state, the enforced wakefulness, the pseudo-lucidity, the distortion—the mill-race inside the mind; on another, the torrent carried on. I don't have to go on dragging that child. Cut it out? Cut it out of my biography. It's got nothing to do with me now. It need never have existed. *It did exist.* Would . . . she, would . . . Constanza have told about it if it had happened to her? The question does not arise: it could not have happened to her, she could not have behaved in that way; it was not in her nature. At that point Flavia thought she heard herself say aloud, It was in my nature. I did behave in that way. Next split second she was fast asleep.

CHAPTER ONE

A Day

The clarity of those mornings of spring and early summer, the second year at St-Jean, the sense of peace, slow time, the long day to come, the summer, the year; the years.

Wide windows, not yet shuttered at that hour, opened from the circular white-washed room on slopes of olives and the distant shimmering bay. The air still light and cool already held the promise of the dry unwavering heat of noon. Flavia turned seventeen, alone, entirely alone for the first time in her life, was at the long table stacked and neat with books. She was working: playing at work, hard at work, immersed, yet alert to hour and place and her own joy.

She read; marked a passage, attempted a summary: six keywords and a date, handled another book with deliberation and pleasure in pursuit of that magic rite a cross-reference; read on. All was grist, discovery. If speculation delighted so did concrete fact: infinity and bureaucracy, appearance and reality, the tree or non-tree in the quad, the supply of drinking water on the road-marches of Imperial Rome. How rich the world, how interesting— I am learning— There is no end to learning— Application— One foot before the other— This is the door of the feast and today is as good as tomorrow.

Mid-day was marked by another stillness, different in quality. Flavia shut her books. Quickly she left the room, ran downstairs, left the tower. Outside struck the full noon blaze of Provence. She walked down the hillside, the last part a bit of a scramble; the air smelt of hot stone and thyme. The bay was empty, the French had gone home to eat. Flavia went to a rock-shelf and pulled off her simple clothes— linen trousers, polo-shirt, much washed, much faded, white briefs— and put on a child's cotton bathing-suit. Flavia, then, was a lanky girl, long-legged, small-hipped, thin though not bony, who carried herself with a tall person's slouch. Compared to her Mediterranean contemporaries, she *was* tall; in England she would have been regarded as above the average but not as tall as she felt herself to be. Her hair was very light both in colour and in texture and it was bobbed; her skin was slightly freckled and her face was changeable. She had heard her father, Simon Herbert, described as a stooping young man with a rather ugly, rather charming face, a bit like Boswell and a bit like a bright pug's mug; her maternal grandmother had been an exquisitely pretty woman. Flavia had her colouring and a version of her features with the porcelain left out, and some of her father's ugliness and much of his charm. As far as visibles were concerned she appeared to have been concocted from the Anglo-Saxon elements in her descent. There's nothing of Constanza in the girl, people often said, some adding, perhaps not such a bad thing. And indeed there was no trace of that Giorgionesque, that dark and golden beauty, Flavia's half Italian mother. The only indicator of Latin blood, apart from a generous mouth and splendid teeth, was a certain swiftness of gesture: from childhood Flavia used her hands when talking.

The feature that was most her own was Flavia's eyes, blue eyes, and they too were changeable: at times screwed up against the sun or in concentration; at others, large, dilated, almost dark.

She had already slipped into the water— she was not one to waste unnecessary minutes on dry land— swam, swam out, went still, went under, floated— solitary— struck out again, let herself drift. Now the little wheels inside the skull had ceased to spin, there were no more words, only weightlessness, mindlessness, that cool fluidity and the sky.

Afterwards she clambered up the hill, groggy, sea-sodden.

At her mother's rented villa the key—a custom of the country— was under a flowerpot. Here, too, there was not a living soul in sight. The woman who came to clean and wash had gone home hours ago. In the ugly dining-room, blinds down, it was reasonably cool; a cover had been laid for Flavia on the oil-cloth, and a dish, some mess of vegetables, rice and egg, left on the stove. Flavia lit a flame under it and went to comb her salty hair. When the food was hot she carried the earthenware pot into the dining-room, poured a splash of red wine into a tumbler and filled it up with cold St Galmier water— scholars do not drink in the middle of the day— propped up the week's *New Statesman*, helped herself and ate. She ate ravenously and with pleasure, and she did not leave a scrap. There was also a platter of boiled arti-chokes, a fresh white cheese and a bowl of fruit. Flavia mixed herself a pool of olive oil with pepper and a squeeze of lemon, and attacked the artichokes. They were meant to have come first but she was usually too hungry to begin with anything so fiddly and besides she liked artichokes too much. (Flavia was still capable of saving up some treat, a habit she had been able to form during the suppers of her early years eaten on empty hotel terraces and off trays in upstairs rooms, nursery suppers of not exactly nursery food and without benefit of brothers, sisters or a nurse.) As she ate, leaf by leaf and one by one, she began to read y.y.'s middle. At the fruit— cherries and green almonds— she had reached the novels. Flavia read the *New Statesman* from editorial to weekend competition without haste or skipping, rationing herself to make it last for several days, and she paid for the subscription out of her own allowance. She regarded that paper much as Christians of solid faith used to regard heaven, the place one hopes to get to. The concept of personal salvation is indeed of august magnitude and it is not easy to think of oneself as worthy. The alternative, however, is damnation; the dwelling in outer darkness ever after instead of walking in the company of the elect. Thus Flavia was privately hopeful of becoming (in the fullness of time) a contributor to the *New Statesman and Nation*. The book reviews, while she found the political leaders more interesting, fascinated her particularly; she had heard it said— she hoarded such tags of information— that the fiction bin was the comparatively humble gate through which one entered the kingdom. Down from Oxford with a good degree (so the fullness of time had not so many years to go) one was given (if one wrote well enough?) a batch of novels to review. For that chance one was paid and it might come to as much as two pounds ten a week. (Some made an extra guinea by selling the books themselves in the Charing Cross Road, but Flavia was not convinced that anyone could really bear to part with their review books.) With those earnings added to the small income (one somehow managed to have) there was time and freedom for the next stage on the road to the literary life, the writing of one's first novel. Not that Flavia had much impulsion to write that work. She envisaged it as a discipline, a part of the novitiate, and had no notion what it was to be about, except, she promised herself, that the novel would be as little as possible about people and of course not personal. She had even less desire to write autobiography than straight fiction; she did not see herself as a future novelist; ideas were what she believed that she was after. Aldous Huxley, and also Michel (the man my mother is going to marry), professed that ideas were more interesting to them than men and women, and Flavia was sure that she agreed.

What she hoped to write (talent and acquired knowledge permitting) were essays, books of essays, proposing changes in government, economics, law and general conduct; rational changes, effected by good will, technological advances and the lessons learnt from history, and conducive to increase in happiness, non-violence and ease. Utopia by consent. (Once that attained, one might give oneself some day to the attempt of creating a work of art; but that, to her, was still as remote and veiled as death itself.)

Meanwhile, to learn, to think, to write (when properly trained) about public affairs was a good and sane and useful way to spend one's life, and of course a very happy one. Meanwhile, one must work hard.

Flavia carried her luncheon dishes into the kitchen, rinsed them, a precaution against ants, stacked them tidily. Then she made herself a minute quantity of intensely strong black coffee in a little Neapolitan tin machine. To muttons. She locked the villa and walked back to the tower through a few hundred shadeless yards. There inside thick walls she found, at the tail end of the siesta hours, a deeper coolness, another dimension of peace, and she was buoyed by the sense of her own solitary wakefulness. She loved that time of day as she did the early morning and sometimes the night— to *feel* oneself alone, what source of energy, what balm! Perhaps after a childhood that although also essentially solitary had been much exposed to grown-up human emotions such abeyance of pressures satisfied an instinctive need. With a will she settled down again to her tasks.

By six o'clock Flavia shut up shop. She went back to the sea—the sun had gone from the rocks—for another, shorter, bathe, a sustained fast swim to wash off indoors, books, the heat. When she got back to the villa it was evening. All the rooms except dining-room and her own bed-room were unused and shut up. Flavia rather quickly went upstairs to tidy herself for going out. She changed into another pair of trousers, freshly laundered and beautifully pressed— the cleaning woman whom she scarcely saw did her very well— a light blue shirt of Egyptian cotton and a silk neckerchief of conventional design. Rope-soled shoes, stiff chalk-white, dark blue jersey over the arm and she let herself out again, put the key under the pot and walked down the hill. It was still broad daylight. She carried a book.

She did not carry a bag. One of her trousers pockets held loose money, notes and coin, the other a comb, a clean handkerchief and an automatic pencil. She also carried on her the weekly letter from her tutor, a man in London whom she had not met, as a kind of talisman. At this hour Flavia had to hold on a bit to her morale; she became conscious of sticking to a part. Reading and swimming were things she had done and loved as long as she could remember. Now was something else.

The much painted waterfront of St-Jean had not become a car park then. The boats in the harbour could be seen: fishing-boats and sailing-boats and some trawlers, and the line of pink-washed, blue-washed houses with four cafés almost in a row. People on the quay-side were doing things with ropes and baskets, clusters of men were standing huddled over that static game, there were plenty of people in those cafés, but there were no hordes.

Flavia bought herself a French newspaper at the kiosk and firmly made her way to a single café table. She ordered a Cinzano, watched the waiter slide a lump of ice into her glass and working the trigger of the soda syphon. The syphon spluttered, gurgled, shot dry air. The waiter shook it and produced another. Flavia thanked him, took a sip and unfolded *L'Oeuvre*. She read the opening of Madame Tabouis' column and looked up again, looked about her at the boats so quiet on the water, at the comings and goings, at the evening sky. She was conscious of not enjoying any of this as much as she might. In her mind she rolled over one of the phrases with which she used to amuse or scare herself as a child: The situation is fraught with perils.

Presently a man a couple of tables away caught her eye. He was middle-aged. '*Toujours seule?*' he called.

All alone. Flavia had become used to dealing with that opening over the last months.

'Indeed, yes,' she called back cheerfully.

'I hope you have good news of your mother?'

Some said, *maman*, some said, *madame votre mère*. He had used the latter. Her own preference depended on the speaker. Flavia had the kind of ear that picks up languages and makes a mimic, and she was much more curious about people and better at taking them in than she was aware of in her own bedazzlement with systems and ideas. Whether she welcomed it or not, the novelist's touch was there.

She said, 'Yes, fairly good news, thank you.' A postcard with a view of Ronda, sent from somewhere else; a poste-restante address. A letter, a nice letter, from Michel, some time ago.

The woman who was with the man, and was in fact his wife, put in, 'Still with her family in Italy? Her father is not improving then?'

Fraught with perils. 'Not really,' Flavia said.

'And she doesn't send for you?' They were residents, not summer people, retired and come South from some other part of France; their name was Fournier. Flavia's mother during her first winter in the place had spent some evenings playing cards with them.

'I've got to go on working for my Oxford Entrance.' She had learnt the uses of French banter, so she added, 'I'm nursing my career.'

They laughed. 'Come over and join us.'

Flavia said that she was just finishing her drink.

'Then you must come to lunch on Sunday, you must, you're not working Sundays.'

'But I do work on Sunday.'

'In St-Jean that well-known academic centre?'

A satisfactory answer to that Flavia felt could not be shouted across a row of tables, and a satisfactory answer it had better be.

She went over and accepted a chair. 'Well, you see, I'm not supposed to have distractions, and then my course is set for me in England and it would mean a lot of fuss getting the books sent to Italy, they're always getting held up in the

customs by the fascists.' Lewis Carroll's Message to the Fish:
I said to them, I said it plain, It would better to Explain.
Was it?

'But if your mother can spare you and the books are in
England— why stay at St-Jean?'

A piece of logic. Flavia volunteered more information.
'My mother hopes to be back here some time later in the
summer; she will want me with her then.'

'Oh, she *is* coming back then? Do you hear, Albert? Mrs
Herbert *is* coming back. So it must be true about the house?
She *has* taken that old *mas* inland?'

'Yes, we've taken the house.'

'But it isn't ready— *you*'re not living in it?'

'There's a good deal that will need doing,' Flavia said,
'that's why we kept on the villa.' Last thing she wanted
brought up was her own living arrangements, was Michel's
tower: was Michel's name.

Mme Fournier said, 'Are you making a start getting work-
men in? We'd only be too glad to be of help. When did you
say you were expecting your mother?'

Her husband cut in, 'How can the poor girl say? Doesn't it
all depend on the old gentleman's health?' It could have
been meant kindly though irony, that staple conversational
prop of the French, was lurking in his tone.

'Oh, quite,' said Flavia.

Back at her own table, she remained safe from further
intrusions; and after a few more minutes it was decently
time to put money into her saucer, bow once more and go.

In the back-street restaurant where she ate her dinner six
nights a week, Flavia was happy again. The hour of con-
straint was over. *Chez Auguste* was a place that flourished also
as a cookshop, and children and old women kept pushing
through the bead-curtain with bowls and dishes to be filled.
Customers who ate on the premises were working people
and a few unmarried clerks. The atmosphere was respectable
but not cheerless. Flavia was looking forward to her food and

drink. She was a boarder, which meant that she paid weekly in advance and a franc was knocked off the price of the set meal and they kept a napkin for her in a numbered ring.

Dinner usually started with some substantial and high-flavoured soup, fish soup, bean soup, mussels; the other courses were made dishes, Monday— pot-au-feu; Friday— aiouli and brandade de morue; on other days, according to what was cheap and good (not necessarily best) in the market, tomates farcies, friture de poisson, gratin d'auber-gines, paupiettes de veau or civet de lapin, the kind of menu that these days is commonplace in every other London bistro. At *Chez Auguste* the cooking was honest and without attempts at elegant variations; it was cooking meant for people who ordered, ate and paid for these dishes because they knew them, liked them and knew what they were en-titled to expect. The wine provided was good wine of its kind, a red eleven degree of last autumn's vintage, decently made, that came from a family property in the Var.

There Flavia sat on her wooden chair behind her thick white plate, open book in front of her, but she did not read. This was the time of the sounding thoughts, the flow of words in the mind. She spoke to herself of the great mundane issues— that was the term she used— of peace and war, violence and political choice; of the curable ills of humanity, uncured for these thousands of years. Crime was not neces-sary, hunger not necessary, nor war, the infliction of pain. . . . She thought spoke of remedies— change of institutions by individuals (experts, detached, disinterested), subsequent change of individuals (in the mass) by changed institutions; she spoke of controlled finance (no more profit motive), capital punishment (abolished), disarmament (total), elec-toral reform; she spoke of her own life dedicated to such glories, and saw it, her whole life, stretching before her, the order, purpose, tranquillity; the pleasures; and she was over-whelmed. Oxford, the word made flesh— tutorials, poetry read aloud, going on the river, learning to make a speech, a glass of wine in my rooms, sitting for Pass Mods., a gown. And later, much later, dual *summum bonum* publications and a fellowship in one's college, goal and beginning— a lifetime in the company of one's peers and betters, hard work and leisure, books, more books and talk for ever, the common-room, mellow evenings, the year divided into terms and long vacations, by the Mediterranean (in my mother's house), finishing a book; travel, architecture, painting. The life of the mind and the sensual life (again her terms), the sensible choice of what existence has to offer. To offer to those in luck. Luck of disposition, abilities— heredity, then? *Is* it immutable? Luck of environment, a modicum of privilege— well, yes. Minimal privilege that could soon be made, one would work to make, universal. The rest, the personal life (I shall never marry), the emotions, are delusion, wasteful indulgence, a futile cross. Emotions can be disregarded. Surely the personal life, also, is not necessary? So Flavia, seventeen, told herself at *Chez Auguste*, eating slowly, re-filling her glass. Domination, jealousy, possessive love: in the world they lead to war; in private to . . . confusion, misery, embarrassment. One can be civilized, one can be free. One will have friends, one will have lovers. These were part of Flavia's vision of the sensual life, disembodied future ap-paritions, urbane, agreeable, vague; what the sensual life spelt out for her most vividly were picnics, lobster salad, hock and selzer, and going to the opera, in Italy, in summer.

Even in the monastery, even in prison, there is a break of routine within the routine. Once a week Flavia gave herself a half-day off. On Thursday afternoons she took the bus into Toulon to do errands. She chose Thursday, the French schoolchildren's half holiday, because she liked the day and because it was one of deliverance for her, on Thursdays she sent off her weekly essay and work report to England. The essay took all Wednesday, was all effort, anguish, agony. It meant writing, the *real thing*, and she experienced an almost physical impediment to commit a sentence to blank page. The choice scared her: nothing seemed good enough, nothing that could not be made clearer, better, richer. Thoughts, words, arrow-strong, flew in all directions; they did not flow into sentences and paragraphs. Pacing the circular room, Flavia suffered and despaired. The discovery that writing was extremely difficult for her had come as a surprise and shock. She believed that it was merely some form of beginner's cramp, a thing one can overcome from one minute to the next like ceasing to wobble on a bicycle; she could not believe that for herself it would be permanent. (There, as in how much else! she was wrong.) The work report, by contrast, she was able to dash off on Thursday morning in a rapid personal telegraphese.

At Toulon she collected a supply of money. Being under age, she was not able to have an account with a French bank. 'Can't she keep it under the mattress as you are all supposed to do?' Constanza had asked, but Michel got round the difficulty by arranging for the use of a safe deposit box which Constanza stuffed with cash. 'Take out what you need, darling, and don't forget to pay the rent.' But Flavia did not choose to run it in her mother's way. She insisted on a fixed sum for her keep (boarding *Chez Auguste* was her own idea) and on sticking to it. Learning to handle money, as she put it to herself, learning to do well on relatively little is part of the training for a life of independence. No weight of overheads, no clutter of possessions— no pot-boiling, no uncongenial work. So at the bank she counted her personal allowance off a wad of franc notes; this was the pocket and book money she had enjoyed, increased every few years, almost as long as she could remember. As naturally she was not expected to pay for her school-books the arrangement provided opportunities for nice decisions. 'Mummy, I've ordered the new François Mauriac and *Those Barren Leaves* and I'm putting them down to education. I hope that's not too unfair? I am paying for the *Guide Michelin*.' Into a second envelope went the living allowance which did for the cleaning woman's shopping bills and wages and her own dinners. She locked the box again, and after the bank there was the post office, a quick haircut, some soap to buy (good soap, one cake), and the day was hers.

Bookshops. A stroll on the port (When are we going to scrap all those battleships?). And presently it was time to give herself the treat of the week, dinner in a good restaurant, a classic French restaurant (once more, her term). She experimented now and then but her steady choice was *Le Sourd*, gilt, white and quiet. Elderly men dined there alone, unaccompanied young girls did not. As it had not occurred to Flavia that eyebrows might be raised, eyebrows, probably, were not raised. Even on her first appearance no one had tried to fob her off with Barsac and meringue. Flavia got on with waiters, they did not smile on her quite in the same way as they did on her mother, but they smiled. At *Le Sourd* the waiters were old; they talked menu to her and gave advice which she took willingly if not every time. Her aim was to strike a balance between trying out new things and having what she already liked. If she ordered a sole with an elaborate sauce she might follow it with a cut of red meat, straw potatoes and watercress; if a grilled Mediterranean fish, by a fowl done in cream, going on to a piece of roquefort or brie and ending with wild strawberries. All of it was lovingly enjoyed but the big interest of the evening was wine. (My one expensive taste.) That once a week Flavia drank half a bottle of good claret; nothing that she would have felt to be outrageous, nothing like Haut-Brion or Lafite, but something in the order of a third or fourth growth of the Médoc. She *had* tasted Lafite, pre-phylloxera what's more; Anna always insanely hospitable had fetched it up one day perhaps for love of Flavia's father. (Anna . . . the principessa . . . my grandmother . . . she thought of her dodging between these names, she hardly thought of her, so recently estranged, so recently among the dead.) She had heard much of her father's great fondness for wine from an early age, and of him she did think as she sniffed her '26 Chateau Beychevelle or Pontet-Canet. Flavia, too, had loved wine from childhood on. She loved the shapes of bottles and of course the romantic names and the pictures of the pretty manor houses on the labels, and she loved the link with rivers and hillsides and climates and hot years, and the range of learning and experiment afforded by wine's infinite variety; but what she loved more than these was the taste— of peach and earth and honeysuckle and raspberries and spice and cedarwood and pebbles and truffles and tobacco leaf; and the happiness, the quiet ecstasy that spreads through heart and limbs and mind.

Variety presented difficulty when one ate alone. The fish course. (Fish and red wine, she had tried this out for herself a long time ago, did not taste good at all.) Would it not be unworthy, wasteful even, of the dinner, the occasion, the claret to come, to make do with a sip of water or just nothing, spoiling the ship for a halfpenny's worth of tar? What she finally did was order a half bottle of some modest white, a Cassis or Muscadet, drink a glass or two and simply leave the rest (someone else will finish it). What she did not know for once was that her father at a similar age, dining alone and confronted by the same dilemma, had come to a similar solution by the same process of reasoning; the only difference being that he had not left a single drop in any of his bottles. Simon never did.

When it was over, Flavia paid, tipped, shook hands, caught the last bus and windows open to the wind and stars was rattled through the night with lines of sonnets flashing in her head. Put down at St-Jean she walked home, as she did every night, not up on the hill but the long way through backcountry and olive groves, past their future houses and down to the sea once more by the other bay and back again and often twice. It was now that thoughts were words and words soared and all was splendour, meaning, ecstasy, and she was overwhelmed once more by certitude: Life is good and learning infinite— this can never pall.

There she went. A foolish girl, a brave girl, a single human creature in first pride of its unique existence. Ignorant, as we are all of us, in youth, in health, untried, taking possession of the world, ignorant of its workings and that of our own natures; ignorant, arrogant, generous, self-enclosed, yet visited, however briefly, by a flash of intellectual passion.

At last she let herself into the dark house. She did not turn on the lights. She would have liked to see herself as putting in more work, but she was too exalted; besides, up since first light now all at once she was dog-tired. In near darkness she undressed, washed, folded up her clothes; as her head touched pillow she wished herself a nightly incantation, Same tomorrow! Before the smile had faded she had dropped into sleep.

CHAPTER TWO

A Week

I

During those years it did not rain in summer. Rain was not expected between April and October, and no rain came. There was no fresh green and thus there was no change. The months were monochrome; nothing appeared to move; dryness, heat, was the dimension in which plants and beasts survived or throve; there was no other time in sight, life was now and now was long.

The feast of St-Jean fell at the end of June. There were fair-booths and dancing-boards along the waterfront, and everywhere, wafted into back-streets, wafted across the bay, the drawn edgy sound of the calliopes, the quick round pops from the rifle range and the hot synthetic smells of *frites* and boiling sweets.

There were new faces. Houses opened inland and on the hill. The arrivals were not tourists; thirty-five years ago few people and certainly no French went all that way for a couple of weeks. The summer people were professional men and tradesmen from places like Perpignan, Nîmes or Valence, who lived in the same kind of climate and liked giving their children a holiday by the sea. They stayed at one of the two or three modest hotels or occupied, often owned, the same house year after year and they brought car, cook, dog and of course the entire family. It was only quite recently then that people from farther afield had begun to think of the South of France as inhabitable in summer at all, and these pioneers— Americans, American writers, South Americans, Cosmopolitan rich— did not go to St-Jean. The new wave there, the beginning of one, was French— publishers and intellectuals from Paris, writers (such as Michel Devaux)— and a few first English: elements if more sophisticated than the notary from Tarascon, a good deal more staid than the Americans.

On the night of the fireworks, as Flavia was about to finish her *cœur-crème*, a party of seven or eight swept into *Chez Auguste:* They looked like strangers, indeed strange birds, in the place but they made themselves at home calling for tables to be put together, calling for olives, wine and bread, shouting inquiries about the progress of their bouillabaisse. All were sun-burnt and the men wore the same kind of clothes that Flavia wore with the northern town-dweller's delight in summer ease; and so, with some individual ornamental touches, did the women. They were painters, literary journalists and painters' wives. Flavia, who thought that she was able to put a name on one or two of them looked and listened.

Artists were part both of the old and the new wave of inhabitants. The two or three great painters who early in the century had in fact discovered St-Jean were no more; good painters of the Twenties and the Thirties would as soon have roller-skated across their canvases as painted once again the famous waterfront. They painted in their studios in Paris, and occasionally in their studios at St-Jean. For the painters still came. They still loved the country and the climate and the life; essentially, it was their place; some in their first hour of prosperity had bought a piece of land; when prosperity held, they built.

Those who ate and drank at *Chez Auguste* that evening past the halfway mark between two wars had reached a platform of their lives; they had done, all of them more or less, what they set out to do, had got to where they wanted and could now— in their own thirties— look forward to a reasonable period of slower development, of enjoyment. They were gay that evening, after the heat of that and other days, in high spirits, bubbling over from one subject on to the next. The women were pretty and fragile, each man had a face of his own, but the person who dominated their party, whose eye was sought, who was listened to, was a woman of entirely startling appearance. The large colourful head, sitting on powerful bronzed shoulders and a strong neck, the features as hard-cut as those of an Aztec chief, gave a sense of rock and jungle— and at the same time conjured up a cockatoo. The nose was a fine beak, the very large, prominent light eyes were heavy-lidded and boldly lined with kohl and blue, the wide forehead was divided by a triangle of fringe, and the hair, originally honey-coloured and worn half-length, was extravagantly bleached and streaked by sea water. The great handsome monster had a smile of serene, archaic sweetness; she wore sailor trousers, and little scarlet singlet that left bare the back and athletic arms, shells on her ears and more shells about her neck. Now and then she gave sound to a fine barbarian's laugh, a laugh that reminded Flavia of Constanza who, too, used to be capable of laughing with such force and unconcern. The monster's Christian name was Therese, and Flavia, who had once briefly met her in the winter, knew that she was married to a well-known French painter who was just then at what may have been the peak of his artistic reputation. In a dozen years he had gone, and she with him, through the cycle of obscurity, gradual recognition, success, large success, new pressures. Together they had, in that curious phrase, *mangé la vache enragée*, that is, experienced poverty, the extreme poverty endured by Modigliani and Juan Gris, of the unheated studio and the unpayable rent, of food giving out and the credit at the *crèmerie*, days of actual hunger. Help traditionally came from the Sunday collector shop-keeper down the street who would take a canvas in exchange for a bag of coal or rice or a supply of paints. Loulou had also had Therese. All who knew them even if they did not know their exact history— had she really taken in washing? Did they *know* anyone in those days who had washing to send out? Had she really slept with the landlord?— agreed that she had been a source of strength to him: Therese had pulled him through. She certainly had sat as a model, to him and to most of his group; today from Chicago to Sydney her head is as much an international monument as the waterfront of St-Jean. In due course he had been taken up: by a dealer, a critic, an art-review, a salon; miraculous plenty was followed by near affluence, real affluence, opulence; praise by applause, hangers-on, réclame. Now he drove an American car and she drove a Bugatti, they had built a house at St-Jean and they sent their children ski-ing.

Flavia very much wanted to know which of the men he was. She was in for disappointment for Loulou was not there. He was staying at a villa at Cap-Ferrat doing a woman's portrait; he was due for another at Venice. He was in fact on the threshold of that stage of his career when his sitters were rich or famous (and often beautiful which his critics argued was not his line), his prices high and those who had first admired him were loud with second thoughts.

Therese was speaking, and the sound it made was unexpectedly delightful. The voice, like the laugh, was low, but gentle, fastidious even; Flavia had not dreamt that French could sound like this. Therese was telling them about having been out to sea at dawn, she talked about an apricot tree, her cats, a white jug she had bought for cream. What she said was brief and straight, clear of *tournures de phrase*; to Flavia there seemed to be a flavour to those transparent words (something, it crossed her mind then, one would be hard put to translate) and she wondered if she was right. Of course she was unable to place her geographically and otherwise, except that she did not sound as if she came from the South. (In point of fact Therese, whose diction *was* admired by her compatriots, was the child of a rural postman brought up in a fertile province who had run away from home and school at an early age to seek her liberty in Paris.)

Therese did not call from the table, Therese got up, crossed the floor, put a hand on Flavia's arm (she always remembered that moment though at the time it only startled her), spoke. You're all alone my dear, do come and sit with us.

All alone, the disliked phrase again, but it held no curiosity or offensiveness, and the actual words of course were not my dear, but *mon petit*, not you, but *tu*, and Flavia who had already got on to her feet felt obscurely flattered as if this did not so much signify her own young age as some bond with these superior beings. 'I should like to very much,' she said with almost equal directness and picked up her book and pocket torch. Therese turned over the book in Flavia's hand, glanced at the title. It happened to be *Candide*. Therese said, 'How sad.'

II

The rest of the evening became merged in memory with many others. Flavia retained a sense of sitting for a long time on a chair beside Therese (they were eating and she had finished), of Therese at one point hand-feeding her with a half-lump of sugar dipped into her own glass of eau-de-vie, of talk flowing about her, of contentment in her insider's outsider's part. When they broke up Therese told her that she must come to dinner the next night, You know the way, come early and bring a bathing-suit. Surprised and unsurprised, Flavia went.

The house she remembered well. It was on what everybody called the other bay and just above a beach. It was an hour or so before sunset and the Loulou children were swishing about in the sea. They were three small pitch-brown terrors with little to choose between them in size or looks. (In fact two of the three boys were twins.) They informed her that *maman* was still out in the boat, pointing to a blank horizon, then ignored her. When later they went in for a few show-off aquatics Flavia retaliated by swooping into a dive that left them well behind. '*Maman* can do better,' they called after her.

Presently the boat came in with Therese at the helm, and they all went up to dry and change. It was a new house, essentially simple but built on ample lines. The dining-table in the living-room that ran the whole length of the front looked as if it could seat twenty, all the bedrooms were large and square and all the beds were large; mosquito nets hung limp and white from ceilings and there were windows everywhere. The floors looked bare and cool, made of old, unpatterned tiles, highly polished. Everyone had a bathroom and of these Loulou's was the most resplendent (it was shown to Flavia the first day) with a sunken tub and a row of outsize bottles of eau-de-cologne in a niche.

'Papa rubs himself down with a whole half-litre every time,' the little boys said.

There was not much furniture and what there was was very fine and plain, and there was a luxury of built-in cupboards, shelves, pantries, storage space. Everything was exquisitely kept. There were few pictures, a couple of Pasquin drawings, a ravishing small landscape of Derain's, nothing by the master himself. Loulou was always too much in arrears with his dealer, Therese said, to have anything to spare. For books, there were a few new novels in their white covers with the imprint of Bernard Grasset and the N.R.F., and a long row of Colette. The garage was vast, and one could not fail to notice the enormous refrigerator, an object of leviathan build one would never have expected to find in a French private house. Therese gave her big laugh and said it was for Loulou's fish.

It was a house, obviously, that was what they had wanted it to be. (Flavia had yet to learn which were Loulou's touches and which Therese's.) It gave a sense of a great deal of fresh air and of almost voluptuous cleanliness; it was a house that was used certainly, where people slept and made love and put on fresh clothes, but in which they did not often sit; where food was cooked but the dishes were carried outdoors. Much of the life went on elsewhere. Loulou worked in a studio at the other end of the property, the children lived on the beach or roamed St-Jean; the three or four women servants did not sleep in. As for Therese, Therese was out in the boat, in the sea, out to market, out in the garden, out in the Bugatti, out in full sun, in mid-night, out along the coast with her friends to find other friends, other places to dance and eat.

As on the evening before there was a crowd at dinner— a long table under an arbour, some new faces, introductions, by Christian names only: Giles— Jeannine— Bobbie (Bobbie was a woman)— Paul— Flavià. Again there was the same sense of heightening, of being *en fête*, of shared intimacy, and for Flavia of self-suspension, of being— happily— part mascot, part onlooker, the now visible, now invisible mouse at the edge of another world. Two things were different. One was the place— the immense delight of being where one was, in stillness, under leaves, above the sea, the perennial delight of a warm night in open air. The other was Therese; here she was unequivocally the giver, she was the master of that board, the fount of hospitality. How she looked after her friends! How your glass was filled; your plate was always warm, your chair turned to the view. The food itself was beautiful, there is no other word. Simple, right, with an exquisite refinement in the simplicity, food such as can only be achieved by love, skilled care and a true taste.

They had sorrel soup— sharp, frothy, refreshing— and after that, Therese told them, they were going to have roast duck with peas. The English, she said shaking her monster goddess' head (how quickly one came to accept that blend in her of the wholesome with the exotic), were fond of duck with peas. Ah well, it was seldom right: the duck kills the peas; young peas are too delicate against a full-grown bird, peas ask for butter— unsalted— and duck often wants no butter at all but needs some active flavour to stand against it or something neutral and robust.

Flavia decided to become audible. 'A cassoulet?'

The duck tonight were young birds without a half-ounce of fat on them and their crisp skin and rosy melting flesh went perfectly with the light sweetness of the peas barely out of the pods.

The man who had been named as Paul, who sat next to Flavia and had heard her, said, 'You like cassoulet?'

'It's the other extreme: the beans kill the duck.'

He said to the table at large, 'Fancy, it eats.'

'What next?' said Flavia.

Therese looked across. 'Of course she does.'

'Three helpings of soup,' said Bobbie.

Flavia giggled.

'An English girl that eats!'

'Were you brought up in England?'

'Only part of the time. I spent years in a place,' she addressed herself to Therese, 'where the food is second best in the world.'

'Ah?'

'Catch'em young.'

'*Where?*'

'In Tuscany,' said Flavia.

Paul lost interest. 'Spaghetti.'

'*La pasta asciutta.*'

'Not at all,' Flavia said with some warmth.

'You mean they *don't* eat spaghetti?' Bobbie said.

Flavia who had meant to tell them about Italian truffles decided to let it go; she had no great wish really to impart anything of her own. The talk turned to events of the day, plans for the next one, to motor cars. She listened, waited. Seduced though she was, her thirst for the general was not in abeyance. At the age of nine one stops asking Do you believe in God? Only a year ago she would have asked them, Do you believe in the Republican form of government? How high would you place Balzac? What *is* your idea of life? It was no longer possible.

She felt her youth as well when Therese told her— in the

nicest possible way— that from now until her mother's return she must have dinner with them every night: the house was open, her place would be laid. 'I think your mother would prefer you to come here.'

Flavia, shedding further years, said gravely, 'I'm sure she will think it extremely kind of you.'

Therese said, 'You shouldn't eat by yourself in a place like *Chez Auguste.*'

'Why not?'

'It isn't suitable.'

Flavia saw that Therese meant it and was a bit shocked in her turn. She leapt to Constanza's defence. 'She doesn't know about it' (nor mind, bless her), 'and I don't only eat at *Chez Auguste.*' She explained about the classic restaurant.

Therese was not impressed. 'From now on, *mon petit coco*, you are having dinner here.'

The others were still on the Citroëns.

'Take the new Eleven now, years in advance— it's going to be the model T of the decade.'

'The Americans will never catch up again, they've missed the boat with front-wheel traction.'

'Not everybody wants it— too hard on the steering.'

'Does hold the road.'

'So ugly.'

'All cars are. They have to be out for a year or two before one doesn't see them.'

'I always say, a new cheap car and drive it for all it's worth; sheer madness nowadays to hang on to great big old thing like Michel Devaux's Delahaye——'

There was a fraction of silence, noticed by Flavia and filled by Therese, 'Ah, but that's such a fine car,' Giles, who apparently had not noticed, went on, 'By the way, where *is* Michel? I haven't seen him this year.'

The second silence was longer. Flavia had a giggly impulse to put the cat among the pigeons by naming what everybody here (excepting Giles) appeared to know. She could hear herself say with an exaggerated English accent, *Michel voyage avec ma mère.*

Therese said, 'Michel's had a lot of trouble again lately with his wife.'

'Can she do anything— haven't they been divorced for years?'

'That's what people think. They're not. She said she would and then refused to sign the papers. She's supposed to have told him that she never will.'

'But surely he could now? After all these years, he can get off on desertion.'

'Now he could. If all goes well.'

There was a third silence. Flavia's impulse had passed.

When everyone went home Giles and Jeannine offered Flavia a lift. She said, no thank you, she would walk. They were standing in scented darkness by the gate facing the road.

'It's on our way, don't be polite, hop in.'

'I mean it,' Flavia said, 'I always walk, I like to walk at this time.'

'That little girl's got a will of her own,' Giles called to Therese as they drove off.

Therese and Flavia stood alone. Therese said, 'You know what you want— that's good.' She gave her a light tap on the cheek, 'See you tomorrow, coco,' and turned towards the house.

The very next night an incident occurred. It was a banal incident, an evening incident such as will occur and one which, with those particular undertones, must have been exploding then among people dining together throughout the world. There was a newcomer, a man who had arrived earlier that day on his way to somewhere else and was spending a night or two in the house. Flavia had seen his car at the gate and he had joined them on the beach for a bathe. He was a big man, well-built, perhaps a touch out of condition but

well-built all the same. The others addressed him by his sur-
name which sounded like Clary or Clarin.

They were cracking langouste shells when he said, 'You'll
be interested to hear that I've persuaded the *Crédit du Nord* to
give those murals to Loulou.'

Paul said, 'But Loulou doesn't do murals.'

'*He will*. When he hears the price.' He looked at Therese.
She said nothing.

'He will, won't he?'

She said, 'You must ask Loulou.'

'He ought to do them if he knows what's good for him.
You don't turn down the *Crédit du Nord*.'

She said again, 'You must ask him, it's his business.'

Clary or Clarin said in loud tones, 'I am asking *you*—
we all know who wears the trousers here. I came to ask
you.'

Therese turned her eyes on him, then lowered the hooded
lids. Flavia thought, how right expressions are: her face *has*
turned hard.

The mouth-piece of the second most important bank in
France bent over his plate. General conversation picked up,
drifted. The new ministerial crisis, the slump, the franc,
America, Tardieu, Camille Chautemps, Poincaré, Pierre
Laval, Herriot, half-hearted talk of people who have heard
it all, said it all before, who haven't got much confidence,
hope or inside knowledge.

'*Vieille fripouille*——'

'*Lui, alors, quel con*——'

'At least *he* has what it takes——'

'Mark my word, he'll be back next month——'

'He's getting soft——'

Not analytical, Flavia thought, *not* the historical view.

Melons were brought. Therese sniffed them, cut them,
handed out the crescents impartially.

Clary, who had recovered, tilted back in his chair and said,
'I have it on good authority that the National-Socialists

will be in by next year, with the right backing they'll get Germany on her feet again in no time at all. And not a bad thing either. Economic stability and a strong government in Germany can be turned to good advantage for France; what we want now is a policy of rapprochement.'

The atmosphere changed. Clary, encircled by a current of hostility, went on in his loud voice. 'Like it or not, that's where the future lies.'

Flavia piped up, 'But they're fascists.'

'That's the last word, is it? You're all afraid of labels. It's a *dynamic* movement, something *we* don't seem to be capable of any more, and all you can think about is that a few Jews will get rubbed out.' The actual word he used was *Youpins*.

Therese rose.

In a smaller voice he said, 'You can't make an omelet——'

'No. *Not Here!* Not in this house!' In one fluid movement Therese strode round the table, was by his chair (his face had turned red, now he picked up his spoon), seized that big man by the scruff of his neck— literally, lifted him clear, propelled him on to the path, down the drive, into the dark. That swift ejection completed she returned, sat down. Nobody spoke a word.

It was, one must repeat, a banal incident; what made it indelible for those present was Therese: her strength, her un-hurried speed, the inevitability with which she had moved in—Medusa, the statue in Don Giovanni. That, and the power of the emotion that united these people round the table.

From below there came a tiny sound, a tinkle as though a thimble had struck pebbles.

'My spoon,' said Therese.

Then they heard the car starting up. Flavia sat big-eyed and shaken. 'Eat up your melon,' said Therese.

But they could not keep away from it.

'What worries me most,' said Giles, 'is where he must have picked up those pretty thoughts— considering the company he keeps. If the bankers have started singing that tune, God help us all.'

Paul said, 'Therese— *his things?*'

She said with complete brutality, 'He can buy himself a tooth-brush— at a night chemist's.'

'Oughtn't one——?'

'I'm going to pack his bag in the morning and dump it into the sea. He can well afford it.'

'Those silk shirts.'

'No, waste,' said Therese, she turned to the maid who was clearing. 'Tomorrow you will pack up the stuff and take it to the *Asile des Vieux*. An anonymous gift.' She laughed.

Presently someone said, 'Loulou won't like it.'

'No more he won't.'

Therese did not respond.

'That swine's done a lot for Loulou.'

Later on Jeannine said, '*Ma* Therese, I believe that story about you must be true.'

'What story?'

'That when you were first married to Loulou you took a job in a circus.'

They broke up late. Flavia's walking being now established, the cars drove off. Again, as twenty-four hours ago, they were alone. Flavia put her arms round Therese and kissed her on the mouth. Once more she was surprised— never remotely, consciously, had she envisaged anything of the kind— and unsurprised by her impulse. It happened. After a fraction of hesitation Therese responded. Flavia mainly felt an overwhelming sense of triumph. Therese ran a hand through her soft hair, 'Do you want to stay the night, coco?' Flavia, who had foreseen, did foresee, nothing, leapt to a decision, Yes.

That lovely orderly house: how right it made everything. Therese went up the white staircase, Flavia following her.

'Do you hear something?' Therese had stopped.

'No,' said Flavia, lying.

They reached the landing. Again that whimpering sound. Therese said, 'Listen. It's Pierrot.' (How the devil can she tell?) 'I must go to him.'

Left behind, Flavia waited, paced, waited, rigid with bafflement, suspension, will. Something— what? but she shut off thought— was in danger of being snatched from her; something, a chance, a cue, an opening, of huge importance to herself, something that had been offered, now, like that, free, that must not be missed (strangle the little brute), might not come her way again: she had to have it, have it now, have it over. Her perceptions were shut to anything but this. For one so avid to learn, those moments might have provided a startling lesson. She merely prayed; Please let her come back.

Therese appeared, Pierrot had got a stomach ache. Too many green figs though he would not admit it; he had been frightened, poor kid, waking up with a pain. 'He wants some mint tea.'

The vast kitchen at that hour had an almost shrouded look. The great pots and pans were scoured and hung up, the charcoal range was lidded. Pierrot's mother got busy. Flavia stood tense and alien.

'Have a cup?'

Flavia scowled.

Unhurriedly Therese bore off the tea and tray. 'I'm going to sit with him till he's asleep, you had better go up to my room, coco.'

Later Therese found Flavia standing by the window. She went to her, 'Now is another hour.' Flavia's resentment vanished. And then this forceful, simple, subtle, many-sided woman in a manner compounded of protectiveness, sensuality and a great ease took her into her bed.

To the young, so much is known and unknown. Before: the mystery, the blue-print, the half-imagined, half-refused.

Once on the other side: the always-known, the click into
place, acceptance; the unthought unthinkable turned fact,
the plunge accomplished, the ship afloat. (*Or:* revulsion;
recoil; regression.) For Flavia the shock— the double shock—
of recognition was in the heart (pleasure itself still eluded her
that day), was a lightening, a light slight puff of happiness
such as persists sometimes after awaking from a serene although forgotten dream. She told herself (the mind would
not turn off) how cosy, how reassuring, how *nice*.

As usual she woke at cockcrow. Time to go to work.
Therese, who must have willed herself awake for a few
moments, said, 'Why don't you swim on your way back, it's
the best hour.'

'I will. All hours are best.' Therese muttered some approval. '*Bain à toute heure*,' Flavia said; not much of a joke,
but she did so feel like making one.

'Have a good day, my coco, see you at dinner-time.'

'How not!'

Practically asleep again Therese said, 'That's not French.'

Flavia, leaving, said, 'Course not. Italian. Straight translation. Constanza language.'

Swinging home she was still lifted by that sense of lightness,
that sense of some puzzlement, some latent uncertainty, some
ambivalence, cleared. The grown-up future now looked safe;
the faces of those lovers hitherto so obstinately veiled appeared at last revealed. Arrived at her own bay she did as
she had been told; swimming, the phrase that poured into
her mind was French, *Tout rentre dans l'ordre*.

Back in the tower, back at her desk, she was filled with a
renewal of love for those books and what they held. Cheerfully, with concentration, she set to work. Only once was she
intruded upon by a spark of the irreverent Italian mood, as
poor Anna called it who had deplored it so, first in her own
daughter then in her grandchild. In mid-Gibbon, Flavia
looked up and giggled: The sensual life is in the bag.

III

Quite soon, of course, Flavia required a hundred and one definitions; but Therese was not one to be drawn at will into human intricacies. The analytical talk, the literate gossip about behaviour and events to which Flavia was accustomed from her mother who had spent her formative years in articulate London, would have been dismissed by Therese as superfluous. Flavia had to wait and do with such scraps as came her way. Indeed almost the first thing she learnt from the older woman was that it is possible to get to know people first and ask questions, if any, afterwards. One evening Therese came out with at least one casual answer.

'Oh well, you know, it doesn't really matter very much which of one's friends one goes to bed with.' Thus she disposed of the problem, if to her problem it was, of bi-sexuality.

Flavia drank it in. She found the attitude enlightened, generous and nicely debonair. All the same it did not take one all the way.

'Any kind of friend? Regardless——?'

'If one is attracted.'

'But there are preferences?'

'Evidently,' said Therese.

Flavia longed to ask a personal question. Absolutely did not dare.

After a while she ventured, 'Aren't some . . . preferences more usual than others?'

'Usual?'

'Well, to most people, the majority? All the people who get married.'

'We weren't talking of marriage.'

'What I mean,' Flavia said, 'even outside marriage, isn't it *more* usual? or isn't it?'

Therese gave her some attention. 'One needs different things at different times,' she said.

Flavia considered this. After another while she said, 'I think I'm pretty sure about mine.'

'Your what, coco?'

'My preferences.'

Therese got nearly angry. 'You are too young for such idiocies. You have a life in front of you.'

Aping the tones of a glib Frenchwoman, Flavia said, 'You must look out for a boy of your own age.'

'Certainly. Some day. At present you need older people.'

'I only like older people.'

'There you go again, coco. One changes.'

Again Flavia would have liked to probe. It was the first time that she knew anyone at all well without at the same time knowing about their past.

Therese said, 'Paul?'

'Paul?'

'He finds you attractive. *Tu lui plais.*'

Flavia had not thought of herself in that light in one way or another. She felt flattered. 'He *is* a very good art critic, isn't he?'

'My poor child.'

Therese combined the principle of not meddling— very much a principle with her— and a sporadic sense of responsibility. She also had intuitions. Now out of the blue she asked, 'Coco, does your mother know that you have been quite on your own all this time?'

The question or at least the meaning of the question that Flavia so resented had always been, How *can* your mother leave you on your own so long? not, Does your mother *know*? She simply blushed. Then she giggled. 'Well, as a matter of fact she probably thinks that a maid of ours is with me.'

'But she isn't?'

'Well . . . no. You see, she went to Italy for a rest. She's got a bit of land in the Udine and she means to settle it on her nephew, that's a lot of paper-work, *chez nous*. And she isn't very well, you know— she had that shock, poor Mena—

so she does rather want to keep away for a time. She thinks it's all right because an old friend of ours has come to stay near me at Bandol.'

'But *he* never came?' said Therese. She said it without irony; for herself she was quite devoid of that Gallic strain; she simply wanted to know.

'Well . . . no. He's not awfully well either, he's quite old. That journey and only for me. He would have come but I rather think he thinks that Mena is still here. His name is James. Initials and James; we call him Mr James. My mother and I have known him since we were born but we never call him anything else, not Uncle James or anything like that, perhaps because to us he is unique.' Flavia could hear herself becoming garrulous. 'He's very intelligent; when I was a child I thought he was the most intelligent man in the world. He's an American. Now he's old.'

Therese said, 'Your mother believes that your maid is here; your maid believes that your American friend is here; your American friend believes——'

Half guilty, half pleased with herself, Flavia said, 'There's been some hankypanky.' She said it in English of which Therese was supposed to understand a few words.

'What?'

'I was the go-between. Oh, I did forward the messages and all that, only I allowed them all to . . . form impressions.'

Therese said quite sternly, 'I don't like that.'

'I thought you did when Giles said I had a will of my own.'

'That is not the same.'

'I only did it because it is what everybody really wants.'

'How can you be sure?'

Flavia met this seriously. 'I know. What *is* for the best? But sometimes I think one knows.'

Therese repeated, 'I don't like it.'

IV

Flavia alone brooded over it. Like that other time, she told herself, the first time (I keep mum about for ever and ever cross my heart), then it was for the best. I did it for her. And surely it was right? It was Anna's last will, her last act of will, an act of love, 'To my beloved daughter.' Morally it was valid. The earlier one was an impulse to leave waste, to bring the pillars down, writ in anger. The Church says that the last thought counts. I would do it again. But it was easy— a bit of paper burnt, a drift of ash rubbed out, a word here lightly: and so much changed by so little. *Deus ex-machina.*

Flavia did not giggle. Am I becoming a . . . manipulator? 'My beloved daughter Constanza'— and she all right, with the money she is used to. *That* was not wrong. She had said to me, One only lives once. She might have taken the law into her own hands; I did it for her. But I must not get the habit. It is not how I want to live; not really.

CHAPTER THREE

A Night

She came back to it all a few nights later. Therese, so un-
curious, so immersed in the moment, set it off. In that voice
of hers, that warm low voice, she said, 'I know you must be
feeling sad so often, that was a bad thing your grandmother
dying so soon.' Flavia's reaction was, Oh God, she knows too.
And it did not happen here, not at St-Jean, it happened a
hundred miles away and more, across the border, at Alassio,
in another country, in my country, one of my countries.

She found herself answering quite reasonably, 'It was bad
for . . . for Constanza."

She was not unaware that Therese disapproved of the use
of her mother's Christian name— the French had it all
straight, about the family, about death, and how to talk
about it; and they did talk: familiar with death.

'They parted in anger. The last time they saw each other.'

Flavia herself had an impulse to talk— now, to Therese, to
this Frenchwoman, this new, this alien friend she liked
immensely. 'The last time they met on the face of this earth.'

Therese stroked her hair.

'They had been against one another for a long time. That
day it all came out. Constanza tried to follow her out of the
hotel— as she was very very upset, my grandmother— but
Constanza was too late. You could say that she died of . . .
moral shock. But then, she had wanted to before. Mena told
us. Our maid, her maid really. She was with Anna for forty
years. It is sad, sad, sad for Mena. She loved her so. I must
tell you how it began: Mena got to Rome when she was
young— her people were very poor— someone had promised

her work but there wasn't any. Then a woman in the
street— the Via Monserato, between the Tiber and the
Farnese Square, they talked about it so much, Mena and my
grandmother, when I was little, I think they talked about it
every day: *Il Quartiere Papale*, it does have a magnificent
sound, hasn't it? and so much of it a slum; the rich live above
on the *piani nobili*, the ground floors and cellars are rented out
to artisans; my mother, who was brought up in those streets,
says to know them you must have breathed the air in the
evenings when the wine-shops are full and they are lighting
charcoal braziers on the pavements; she says I will go one
day, but I think I know already— well, a woman in Mena's
street who sold salad greens knew the cook who worked for
Anna and the prince round the corner and Mena was given
things to do in the kitchen. One day Anna came down,
Eccellenza as they call her there, and saw Mena. Mena says
Anna liked her face. Don't think that Mena is pretty, she's a
tiny woman: shrivelled. Perhaps she wasn't then, it was before I was born, even before Constanza was born, when they
were still happy. Mena's everyday face is just stubborn, you
could call it proud— she's a countrywoman from a good
province as they say— but Anna took to it, she did take to
people— her infatuations Constanza says— she took to my
father when he was a very young man and he wasn't so good-
looking either. Nothing like the prince, her own husband,
who was so *bel uomo*.

'With Mena it lasted. Anna taught her and made her her
own maid and they lived together ever after. She had her
own room in the palazzo on the same floor as Anna's which
wasn't at all the usual thing then: In 1892. Not that the
Roman aristocracy didn't look after the people who worked
for them— though people nowadays don't like it when you
say so— servants didn't sleep the way they did in Tsarist
Russia or at Versailles before the revolution, but it still
didn't seem good enough to Anna— I told you she was
American?— so Mena always had a nice room of her own;

later on too, at Brown's Hotel. Brown's in Dover Street, they went there straight after it went wrong, my grandmother and my mother and Mena. I know Brown's, I stayed there myself.

'I never saw the palazzo. I have never been to Rome. That's all part of the story. I've seen them at Pisa and Florence, they're only large houses really, rather grand all the same, so much stone and ceiling, hard to keep warm in the winters. Anna put in heating, it was almost the first thing she did. The prince always let her spend her money in any way she liked. She spent a good deal on the house; well, it was his house, she kept it up for him, even afterwards. That was one of the things we did not know. She kept up the palazzo for twenty years— two decades. *Imagine* that. And she never saw it again . . . alive. Mena knew it all and how Anna loved that place. As for Constanza, she says she left it, she left it behind and that is that. If she had stayed, all would have been different; it wasn't in her stars to stay. She does talk like that. Not that she believes in anything, religion and so on— and nor do I of course, though I was brought up a little as a Catholic— but she goes by omens, *auguri*. Romans do. Mena didn't mind leaving either. She didn't mind anything as long as she was following the Signora principessa. Goodness when I think of the moving they must have done, the trunks they must have packed. And when they were travelling it was Anna who looked after Mena, you know, ordering in languages for her in the wagon-restaurant. She spoilt her, people said. It was Anna's way. She spoilt my father, too.

'When he came to see them, Anna and my mother, the first time in London, 1914, the war had just begun, Anna had some rather good Sauternes on the table. She told me she never saw a man so pleased by a glass of wine. He never forgot it. She spoilt me too, when I was little, and Constanza had everything when she was young. Only she doesn't care much for things or what she eats, what she wants are people,

action. Mr James says that she is unbribable. It's a thing to
be. I shall be in my work, I hope.

'Well, Mena had the best of it— Anna *was* good to her.
"Never a harsh word, in all those years," that's what Mena
told us, "how many can say that of themselves?" *We* can't,
Constanza says.

'I don't mean that Anna didn't go on the way she did in
front of Mena, but it wasn't directed *at* Mena and she knew
it; she only minded her being unhappy. When Anna raved
in front of me, I did mind. I used to sit under the table and
pretend not to hear. When I was older I often left the room.
It made me feel horrible: unkind and strong. Mena always
stayed it out. Oh, *she* was good to Anna. She got up at night
to look at her asleep, to see that she lacked nothing. That was
how she found her . . . that night at Alassio.'

When Flavia spoke of all of this, it was also night. They were
in bed, Therese and she, and they did not know how late it
was. It was only their second week and Flavia, a little
puzzled, a little awed, at times, was at ease now with the
alien friend, the tender and exciting alien she was beginning
to love a little. Things were going well. Flavia was working;
the long days in the tower were intact, only in the evening
she set out for the house on the other bay; the difficult hour
at the café was cut, even writing became bearable. Often
she stayed the night. Not inevitably. Therese had implied
other claims. Benevolently, she exercised a check, kept a
light hand on their relationship.

That night there had been much wine at dinner and
Flavia, though far from drunk, felt warmed, free. As long as
she could remember she had *heard*— servant's gossip;
visitors' cluckings; her grandmother denouncing the past;
Mena explaining away; Mr James rationally doling it out;
Constanza's open dissections. She had heard; she had not
thought. Her mind had been occupied with things like the
freezing point of soda water or the melting point of cheese;

later on it became the non-revolutionary redistribution of the means of production and the alternate vote. She had not thought, perhaps she had felt? For now she found that it was there, an entity— not quite picture, not quite story— demanding sense and shape: expression. This rather reserved child, this self-styled future utopian essayist, found herself rattling on about unhappiness and happiness, found herself possessed by a desire to comprehend and convey what had happened, was happening, to a handful of people near her.

The windows were open and the sky was dark. Lying on Therese's shoulder, staring into near darkness, speaking to the dark ceiling, she went on. 'Anna was Mena's life. Yes, we counted; we are the family, she looked after us too. Now it's no longer the same— for her, it's all over; she's worn herself out and she's through with us, we remind her too much of her. She wants to go back to her own people with her savings and what we have given her and cut a bit of a figure. It was because I felt this that I . . . interfered. Can you see now?

'Mr James? Anna certainly wasn't *his* life. We don't know what that was. One didn't ask. He liked to tell one that he was a dilettante, "I've never written a line for publication nor put brush to water-colour, in short I never did a stroke of work, except for those few years teaching at Harvard, and I must admit that I enjoyed every moment of them—in retrospect." That was a set-piece. *I* believe he was a real bachelor with a ravishing mistress tucked away. He always had plenty of time for us. He was very fond of Anna, though she often maddened him. He knew her as a girl when she first came to Rome. She was so pretty then, he says, and full of hope and plans. She had a way of never doubting other people or herself, it was headstrong, he says, and naïve and infuriating, but it was also touching and one let her have her way. Losing her like this must be a blow to him. She wasn't his life: she was his youth; Constanza says they had the same kind of public behaviour and as one gets older it counts. It's begun to count with her and she's still young. Your generation. I don't know what I shall have to share with *mine* when I get older? The members of it I knew had all sorts of behaviour, public and private. Resort children. It had more to do with their nationalities than their ages. I could tell you a lot about resort children. I used to get a pretty good idea of what was to come just from the way they shook hands with a grown-up. They are all living on some-where in the world. This very minute. Hard to take in.

'Anna and Mr James didn't meet at a resort, their families were connected, vaguely. Her father was a lawyer who wrote, he was quite an eminent man, of great intelligence; erudite. That's where Constanza's got it from, her mind; and her conscience, her *touch* of New England conscience as Mr James says. The Italian side were mostly ninnies. He— my maternal grandfather— made a stand against war, all war; he wasn't very popular and retired early from public life. A bit like Michel, Michel Devaux.

'Mr James only got to know Anna well in Italy. In the 1880's— two Americans living in the country of their choice. That's where Anna's story began. Only that for him, being a man, it was a matter of choosing. One fine day he decided to take an apartment in Rome. Anna had to get there by marriage.

'He did explain that to us quite often, when she had fallen in love with Europe and the prince proposed, she saw herself in Rome; the Eternal City, it was always that to her. He, Rico, the young man she met on Lake Garda, was the means to an end.

'That, Mr James says, was her first mistake. Her not seeing it as what it was. She would not allow herself to see it. It had to be a love match. Life had to be what she believed it ought to be; she had no sense of reality. It never crossed her mind— that was the bad part of the mistake— that for the prince as well the marriage could not be an end in itself. She knew that the prince was not well off, he never made any bones about it. It was obvious to everybody in Rome that he had to marry money. He had his widowed mother living with him and two sisters who had to get husbands; both Mr James and Constanza say that it would have been considered an almost monstrous act of selfishness if the prince had insisted on marrying one of the Montecativi or Roccarosa girls for their *beaux yeux*.

'That didn't mean the prince wasn't pleased to get Anna. He would have turned down millions if the woman had been ugly or ill-bred or disagreeable. He *liked* Anna; he thought she was charming and a credit to himself, and he meant to look after her. But the point that Anna failed to grasp was that without the money it would never have occurred to him to marry her.

'Anna didn't *have* millions. At least she didn't think so; she used to scold Constanza for saying they were rich, when of course they were for Italy. She spent a good deal— she always did that. Her trustees kept writing to her, she never paid any attention. They kept writing to her about retrenchment till her dying day. She didn't spend *very* much on herself, she spent on houses, and during those early years she entertained— people lived differently, you know, dinnerparties for English visitors, musical parties, charity affairs; and she spent a lot on other people, on her new family and the poor. It was natural for her to give people things; making them comfortable, she called it. Oh, always in the material sense.

'She never brought it up. Curious thing— she who held on to so many grievances, never spoke twice about the money she kept pouring out on all of us. Constanza never had a penny of her own, we were Anna's dependants you might say; well, we never felt it, she never made us feel it. It *is* curious.

'As I told you, Anna adored her new Italian life. *They* adored her— that did count. There was the prince's mother, mamina, the old principessa she was called to tell her apart from Anna. Mr James remembers her well, she was a sweet woman, all good nature, not a thought in her head, who asked for nothing but to love and cherish (*her* husband had been spectacularly unfaithful to her, even for Rome—it runs in that family). And then there were Constanza's aunts, the prince's sisters. Well, Anna transformed their lives. They had been sitting at home (unheated, before Anna put in the plumbing and the armchairs) with cousins and priests coming to black coffee now and then while the prince was out on his horse or at the club. Suddenly there was Anna doing a hundred things a day: the house wide open, parties and picnics and streams of presents. It wasn't only that. They loved her. You must see it— there was all that freedom, so new, so different from what had been dinned into them before.

'And for them it was exotic. One must realize that they didn't travel. The women not at all. The prince had come over to London to be married— from the house of Anna's sister who was settled there— he hated every minute of it. He carried on about crossing the Channel for years. It was diabolical, he said. I think he was just very sea-sick. But it stuck in his mind that getting to England was something perilous and rare like rounding the Horn, it must have had something to do with his allowing himself to get so wholly cut off from Constanza later on.

'But I mustn't confuse you. In those early years the horrors of travel merely reminded him what a long, long way Anna was from her own country, and he used to say that they owed it to her to make up for it. "Poor woman— let her have her head."

'Anna wasn't really pining for America one bit. She did care about American democracy, that was one of her great ideals, she looked forward to the ultimate conversion of Europe. The prince used to tease her about her efforts to get people taught to read and write; it became a household

joke, Constanza joining with her father, though she herself
was much taken by Fabian Socialism as a girl. The big
difference between her mother and herself, she says, was that
she, Constanza, was a realist. The Romans are realists. It's
the one thing Constanza had always been proud of (although
she is a total internationalist of course). Being a Roman.
Oh I can understand it. It is something. I am one quarter
Roman myself, you know. I often tell myself, but I can't
quite feel it. One quarter Roman, one-quarter American,
one half English. Only modern Rome, anyway; Constanza
won't admit that when I point it out. Romans like her believe
in an unbroken line to the Antonines.

'Where was I? The prince teasing Anna. You see, it
appears that they got on well enough. She rather patronized
him, but he was impervious to that; it amused him— he was
not unsubtle, Mr James says, but didn't bother to show it—
he was amused by her American independence which served
him just as well as Italian docility. They each came and went
as they pleased. For her it was art and her circle of friends
and admirers. I should have explained that she was an
intelligent woman. She was well educated; she had the good
memory we all got from her, and she really did get to know
about pictures and architecture, more than most dilettantes.
At least my father thought so. The prince himself was not a
stupid man, basically, according to Mr James, but he had
let his mind go and he didn't care. He was equable and a
pessimist and very gay in everyday life. He was quite determined to let sleeping dogs lie. That meant ideas, under-
standing people, searching for motives; he didn't want to
change the world as Anna did and Constanza in her early
years. He was an all-change-is-for-the-worse man.

'Anna didn't have to go to her museums alone, there were
plenty of young men and older men hanging about. Anna
was quite a flirt in those days, Mr James insists on that, it is
quite the hardest part to imagine. She always seemed to
loathe it so . . . what flirtation leads to. That was what she

used to rant about, Men. *She* didn't hold with going to bed with one's friends.

'You see, she, didn't even hold with going to bed with a husband. That's perhaps why things began to go to pieces when the boy was born. But that was years later. She didn't appear to mind the first time. Constanza. She talked of her duty to give the house an heir. Constanza wasn't an heir, she was a girl. That didn't seem to matter either.

'It's time I began telling you about Constanza. Chronologically. She was born when they had been married a few years. She always says it's easy to remember her age as she was twenty-one in 1914. She was married in that year, too. To Simon, to my father. And divorced before the end of it. The war, not the year. But I said *chronologically*. Rome in the 1890's then. Yes, Constanza was born in the nineteenth century.

'From the start she was something quite exceptional, they all say that. They never saw a child who could read and ride so early. I mean *ride*, not write. Horses. Constanza was mad about horses during her first twenty years. She had complete physical courage. I have not. She says it is only because she knows when it's not in her stars to be killed in a ditch. And there were her looks. Well, you've seen her. She *is* beautiful. Simon used to tell people she was a Giorgione toned down by Gainsborough; there is something lighter than pure Italian. She says she had a perfect childhood, an almost miraculous childhood. It might so easily have turned otherwise. Without Anna for her mother she would have been brought up like an Italian girl of the time, like her aunts. Anna believed in children being free, she *trusted* them, and she saw to it that Constanza got a proper education. At home. But by the most brilliant people; even Mr James took a hand. Constanza loved to learn then; like me.

'Apart from the education she was allowed to run wild. She played with the children in their street when they had the time which wasn't often and with diplomatic children, a cosmopolitan lot, like mine, only that Constanza was gang-leader. She *was* wild. In spring she was sent to their country place with mamina and some nice English tutor and they stayed all summer. That was Castelfonte. The house was so run down that even Anna couldn't afford to do anything about it and she never liked it much. The prince came often, he and Constanza loved the place. She lived out of doors and often went to work in the fields with the *contadini*.

'She says she looked up to her mother, her father was her own flesh and blood, they understood each other, they were allies. In no particular cause, just for the fun of it, the bond of it, like baiting Anna about democracy. It was all good-natured, Anna made no scenes then that one knew of. There were no demands on Constanza, real demands, grown-up demands. She was aware, she must have been aware, she says, of the deep affection her father bore her, but alas she took it for granted.

'The prince was affectionate by nature, he was devoted to his mother and to a majordomo of his parents' days, a man called Socrate, and there was one horse, Archimede, he could never do enough for, but his love was for Constanza, Castelfonte and the Marchesa Giulia. Constanza doesn't know in which order the other two came but she knows now that she was first. He didn't show it when he let her go.

'When they had that first trouble, Anna finding out about the prince and carrying on as if it were the end of the world, Constanza must have been about five or six; she doesn't even remember; Mena does, every minute of it. It was she who took up the trays Anna wouldn't touch when she kept to her room and had sent for her trunks. The prince was shaking and the women in the house, the old principessa and his sisters were blaming him, you see they all thought that Anna was going to take Constanza away with her to America. Well, in the nick of time they realized that all that Anna was wailing about was some French floozy the prince wasn't even particularly attached to (a crony of Anna's, a

censorious old toad who lived in hotels and got everything
half wrong, had spilt the beans to her). So the women got
Anna to open her door and the prince was pushed forward
and asked her pardon and promised never to see the French
girl again and they had a great drama and Anna consented
to be reconciled.

'Even so they had to send her half round the world. The
prince scraped up the money they had set aside to repair
the roof again and Anna went off to India with some English
acquaintances and stayed with the viceroy and came back
with a ruby. That stone has had a curious history. With us;
I've no idea what it did in India. In the family rubies mean
luck. I really do believe that without it we wouldn't have
got here, without that silly ring I should not be here with
you now, Therese, now this moment.

'Of course it had nothing to do with the ruby itself, the
real cause was their all being so insanely superstitious. When
Anna brought it home— some thirty years ago it must
be— the prince put it in his pocket. It was unset then, just
the stone. It was his protector, his charm, you know, he
touched it, turned it over in his pocket when he saw an
omen.

'After Anna's return the good years went on. Constanza
says she was sure that her mother was happy. She could be
that; even later on. She always would have liked to have let
herself be happy. It was probably after the old principessa
died that Anna became . . . unsettled. There wasn't much
scope actually in Rome for Anna; they never let her *achieve*
anything. Nothing changed. Women don't vote even in your
country, they told her. And she couldn't do anything about
Castelfonte, she couldn't even get them to attempt making it
profitable— she never understood about the land, that
wasn't in her blood.

'Then one day she found that she was going to have
another baby; she was so wretched that she tried to keep it
secret at first. Constanza was getting on for fourteen and

everybody had forgotten about an heir. Even the prince
wasn't particularly pleased, he said that times had changed,
there wasn't going to be a place any more for the likes of him
(he detested United Italy). They had Constanza. Let *her*
make some splendid new beginning, let her start a *new* line
(in all but name).

'Anna did get better once the boy was there. (It turned out
to be one: Giorgio.) She rather spoilt him now and again;
but when it showed that he wasn't intelligent like Constanza
she didn't like it. He has turned out badly, my young
uncle, a delinquent practically. Mindless, glib, conceited,
all out for number one.

'And now I really must come to what happened, to what
... put a stop to it all. It's hard to tell it as it must have been,
it was so unexpected. Out of a clear sky, or so it seemed to
them. You might say that this thing had been brewing up for
a long time, that the threat was there; they hadn't seen it.

'Anna and the prince had been married, well, if not for
twenty years, not much short of it. Constanza was growing
up and knew it. She was giving herself another two years,
then it would have had to start for her, the conventions and
the frills. She was not looking forward to her coming out as
an Italian girl, but she was determined not to let herself get
married early. First she wanted to learn and see, she wanted
to wait for a man who did things and was something on his
own. Oh, she liked boys then, *she* liked boys of her own age,
she had love affairs quite early. At Castelfonte. With
neighbours' sons. They knew that she wasn't going to marry
any of them, she wasn't going to marry an Italian like her
aunts' husbands. Her mind was open as long as the man had
great quality; she saw him as an explorer possibly, or an
English statesman. . . . She told herself she was going to
wait— *as long as it took*— then choose.

'You see, if there was one thing they felt sure of it was time:
time in front of them. They were a family living in Rome
for better or for worse, that wouldn't change any more than

the world would change. The world before 1910. I often
think of it. My grandfather saying that everything was going
downhill, my grandmother talking of progress, but neither
expecting it for that year or the next, they didn't dream *of
real* change, not in their lifetime nor their children's.

'One morning someone tipped the truth to Anna. The old
story, the old truth, the facts. He wasn't a Roman; the
Romans didn't talk, didn't go tale-bearing. An American
told her, a young man, one of Constanza's tutors. He had
taken it that Anna knew like everyone else, he was half in
love with her and wanted to show his allegiance. He said
something unconsidered, Anna pounced on it. When he
realized what he had done he panicked and she had it all
out of him. The Marchesa Giulia.

'Thirty years of it. . . . The prince going to see her every
day. . . . A love of his youth begun long before the marriage.
Rome looking on them as a devoted couple.

'She learnt it all— the Marchese himself tied by his own
attachment to a married woman married to a man who loved
an opera singer: perspectives of liaisons, sensualities, *com-
binazioni*, everybody having their place in the chain. Everybody, not Anna. She turned white as paper—the young
man fled.

'When the prince saw her standing in his door, he would
not take it up. For him it was an ordinary morning. He said,
"Oh, Anna, what is it *now*?" She asked him if it was true—
the long lie? He didn't bother to deny it. Mr James said
afterwards that this was the worst mistake he made. They
might have been saved if Rico had met tragedy with drama.
That morning the prince felt merely tired and repelled. It
was the wrong day.

'He made use of what Mr James calls the great masculine
resource: leaving the house. He went off to a shoot. He stayed
away two days. It was fatal.

'When he came back Anna refused to see him. She had
locked her door. Mena was helpless. On the other side of that

door was Anna, alone. She had driven herself into doing what would hurt most; she had decided to take Constanza from her father. For herself it meant leaving Rome. On their way to the station she would not throw her coin into the Trevi Fountain.

'She had planned it all. The Church permitting no divorce, the way open to her was separation. She had sent for lawyers. They had made her realize that even with proved adultery it would be a long and uncertain fight before she would be allowed to take away both children as the Italian courts would be reluctant to let the prince's son be brought up outside his own country. Anna cut it all short, She offered a compromise. She gave up Giorgio in return for custody of the girl. The lawyers fell for it. They called her generous.

'The prince's entourage did their best to stop her, the sisters, the brother-in-laws, his own lawyer, the priests. The prince himself was ready now to shake her out of it— he was fond of her, even then, always was; breaking up a family seemed inconceivable to him, a form of hell, a madness. Anna remained frozen. She sent him a message saying she would never see him again as long as she lived. (That came true.)

'The others hatched plans for him, like abducting Constanza and hiding her in the depth of Calabria. The prince turned it down. When all had failed they decided to send for Constanza herself— it was the autumn and she was still at Castelfonte. She was nearly sixteen; if *she* refused to go and told her mother so herself, Anna, they reckoned, would not be able to go through with it. Constanza was tough and had a will of her own like Anna. They asked the prince what his daughter would choose to do. He knew. When I asked her, now, twenty years after, "Whom would you have chosen to stay with, Constanza?" She answered, "*If* I had been told the true facts, my father, there could have been no doubt about that." The prince never asked her.

'They couldn't persuade him. He wouldn't let them tell

her. He forbade it: he would not have the child put in that
position. It was Anna who sent for her finally. Constanza
found the house in gloom and confusion. The prince
appeared briefly. They were alone. Your mother has been
difficult again, he told her, best for her and you to travel for
some time— Papa, where are we going?— The tickets are
for England. Be good to her, look after her, bring yourselves
back to us soon.

'That was all. An hour later they left.

'That was how the prince behaved. And Constanza
never knew it.

'And then they were in London, the three of them. Anna
kept to the hotel room; she had told Constanza something
unspeakable had happened, Never question me. To Mena
she said that her life was over. I have seen her like that myself. How we dreaded it! We used to duck and wait. I can
see now that she was really very unhappy, terribly unhappy.
I think she must have longed to be coaxed out of it. We didn't
help her much. Mena did in her way, it wasn't enough, she
needed an educated person to put her case to— everybody
ought to be allowed to put their case— we didn't even try
to hear hers, we only heard the tone. There she was, pacing,
pacing, like something locked in. We hated it. I often hated
her. I couldn't bear her judgements, I didn't agree, I don't
agree, with her values. But, Therese, she was so unhappy,
unhappy. . . .

'Perhaps she wasn't so wrong when she felt cheated and
outraged and alone? Perhaps what happened to her was
really bad? But jealousy *is* wrong? *is* bad? Perhaps it's real
too and makes people suffer? On Therese, is it? Must it be?'

Flavia fell silent. She reached for a sip of water. Much of
what she had been telling had been brought out raggedly

at first, there had been hesitations, intervals, while she was trying to see, groping for a piece in the jig-saw; and then it all seemed to come to her, she only had to keep speaking. She had long given up the tussle with French and lapsed into straight English (which Therese, damn it, was supposed to understand). During the last minutes she had been talking with extreme rapidity in a light high voice.

More calmly, she went on, 'And what about Constanza? Now we come to the ironical side of it all.

'She had never been out of Italy before— now there she was without as much as a full day's notice at Brown's Hotel looking on top hats and umbrellas out of a window that worked like a guillotine. Well, they had hardly brought her up a tea-tray (with the most delicious things to eat) when she was told that there was someone downstairs to see her: it turned out that most of the young men, her one-time tutors, were dons now or curators or secretaries to cabinet ministers and apparently asking for nothing better than to take her about, and there were Anna's English friends, all those people who had dined or wintered at the palazzo. Anna refused to see them but let Constanza meet their boys and girls and go down to their houses in the country. From that minute she was in a whirl. She began to hunt, she says, she loved it. She loved everything, her new-found friends and her new friends, the intellectual ones and the sporting ones and the jokes they made and that kind of life in England and everybody being so accomplished and gay. It all came at the right time, she said, at exactly the right time.

'Her mother still didn't tell her the reason for leaving home: she implored Constanza not to ask and made Mena promise not to talk. Constanza did ask, Anna simply repeated, Something too dreadful to speak about. And when she kept on asking, When shall I see papa? Anna never said, Not before you are twenty-one; she didn't tell her about the legal arrangements she had made. She said that if Constanza went it would break her heart.

'Constanza says that she felt so much for her mother, even if she did not understand then what it meant to her to be cut off from Italy, from Rome. She couldn't bear things like Anna refusing to keep house or giving any pleasure to herself. She felt that it was up to her now to protect her mother: Mama, do come to the House of Commons with me. Mama, won't you give a luncheon for my friends?

'They lived like that for about two years. Then Constanza made another leap. She had become grown-up and again she was lucky. She was able to slip into a place in an adult society. She didn't have to go through the debutante stage. She was able to manage it because Anna fancied herself as having renounced the world and because of their rather special position in England as accepted outsiders not subject to the letter of the rules. Before her marriage Anna had been taken up as one of the handful of pet Americans and now, although they did not know exactly what had happened, everybody in London sided with her. The kind of friends she had were loyal by definition, and they liked her, in their eyes she was a woman who could do no wrong (she was only separated, mind, not divorced), they were ready to do any thing for her and when she would not let them they did it for the girl. They liked the girl, too. *That's* not beside the point.

'Anna wasn't rich for England, far from it. Mr James says the yardstick was the multiplicity of houses in full running order. Two isn't *multiplicity* and Castelfonte never was in running order, and now they were living in hotels. So (for all her personal extravagance) the principessa was regarded exactly as she regarded herself, just decently well off.

'Constanza belonged more than Anna. A matter of language. What with those tutors, hers is English English, her friends' English; she did the same things and made the same jokes and had the qualities they admired— the post-Edwardians, the young new Georgians of her set, her sets— dash, courage, brilliance, intellectual freedom. *And* there were her looks, nobody could forget them, nobody except herself; she never did a thing about them, as women do these days, she never gave a damn: as my father used to say, she wears her beauty lightly. Oh, she was an insider in London, she belonged. At the same time she *was* a foreigner, a foreigner with privileges, a rare bird— catch Constanza not having the best of both worlds.

'It was the time when so much began, the new writing, painting, the ballet coming to London. . . . She had two years, in the centre of it. Everything was right— the place, the time, her own age, the excitement in the air and the capacity to feel it. Many of her friends were in politics or belonged to political families, it was the era of the Liberal reforms and that was what fired her most: she went to dinner-parties where she sat next to men who were going to make a speech that night and there were weeks when she went to the House every day, it was what she had always wanted, it was history, it was important, immensely important and she was seeing it, seeing it happen and *that* was important to her.

'There is little of that left now, she says. *I* hope she is not right. Possibly, she says, there will be other years like those— for other people. And that is sad, too.

'She had love affairs. Less pastoral ones. (No more afternoons in the mulberry groves of Castelfonte with boys like Donatellos.) It was young men now, older than herself; she liked them tough and full of talent; she was not ambitious directly but found that life with the obscure is less interesting. And she was careful not to be found out; her recklessness, she says was only apparent: she always thought of Anna. Only fools— she says, she thought then— overpay.

'Then it was 1914. First of all she came of age, as I said, in the spring of that year. She had known the truth for some time by then more or less, and the legal position, but had never quite managed to have it out with her mother. Anna had recovered to the extent of running a house again— a furnished one in Regent's Park— and of going out a little. She had good days and bad.

'There had been one flare-up. According to the agreement Giorgio, Anna's little boy, spent a couple of months each year with his mother and they used to send him over with a nurse-maid and a courier. He was due again and suddenly they heard that the prince himself was bringing him. Mena says that Anna was convinced that he was coming to fetch *her,* and Mena swears that she was ready to go back. Perhaps he only meant to see Constanza, at any rate the lawyers messed it up. Next thing they got through the grapevine was that the journey was off.

'It was then that Anna started on the sleeping stuff, taking too much, erratically— a sort of Russian roulette. Mena coped with it.

'There is one other thing that makes it all so odd, so difficult to understand. This. When Anna was first told about it in Rome by that ass of a young man, when she learnt about the old truth, the long lie, she cried out it was a bolt from a clear sky shattering her life. But was it? After she was found dead and there were so many questions and Mena told so much, she said to Constanza— oh, I can give you the very words, I shall never forget them— Mena said, "One day many many years ago, when the old principessa was still alive, she opened a door and saw them, the prince and the Marchesa Giulia, in the long room at Castelfonte." Anna shut the door again, she did not know that Mena had followed her, and walked round the house and came in by the terrace, a smile on her face. What do you make of it? What can you make of it?

'As I was saying, Constanza was twenty-one. The day after she went to Anna. "Right or wrong, I must go now and see my father." Anna's answer was, If you go to him the instant you are free, what will the world say? That really shocked Constanza. That one sentence, it made her see something about her mother. She also remembers her own answer (we do seem to have words to remember), "The world, mama, will say what you tell it; it always has." She felt hostile enough to be able to press going to Rome that week. Then: bathos— Giorgio, yes, the little horror was with them once more, got the mumps. Quarantine. By the time that was over Constanza was in a fatalistic mood, she agreed to wait until the autumn. Reluctantly, but then she still loved Anna, although she had begun to judge her. Only it was the autumn of 1914.

'The war drew them together again. To Constanza it was an end, an end then and there— the sole fact that it happened, that people consented to it happening, men sent out, actually going out to hurt and kill, *systematically* destroy one another's homes and lives and loved ones, the folly of it, the beastliness, the *pain*; the strange mad illusion that any of this, under any aspect, any theology, any ideal, could be right— the staggering, inconceivable, immediate, ultimate, concrete wrongness of it all. How they felt it! How right they were!

'They all did war work. One can always try to do something for individuals. Anna became very active and efficient running charities and committees; Constanza took a shift at a canteen, and after Italy was in the war she got a job in a ministry, real work, and she did it; for what it was worth. She always does— without much faith in what she is doing, like those anti-fascist chores she used to take on until recently (I shouldn't talk about that really). Whenever she turns her hand to something, she says, it is trivial.

'Funny thing happened about money during the war. Anna decided that she must not profit by it in any way and consulted Constanza— she always did: You are my chief heir and it will affect you— Constanza told her to go ahead.

So Anna bullied the trustees into changing her investments, she made them get rid of large blocks of French loan and Russian railways and go into something pacific and domestic instead like American soap companies. Later on she forgot all about it. But you realize the result? We are living on it.

'In that same first year of the war, Constanza met Simon, my father. He turned up at a party one night having just managed to get back from Italy where he'd been supposed to be studying and it came out that he'd been to Rome, too, and had actually met her father and knew their story— better than she did— and had sat at the feet of the Marchesa Giulia. He took them all off and that made Constanza laugh at once, but she didn't have much time for him, she was in love with someone else and he had enlisted. However, Simon came to call at Regent's Park, he had the perfect excuse. The prince had asked him to take over a small present; Simon had stuck it in a pocket and thought no more about it, only when he saw Constanza he decided to deliver it in person. She unwrapped it and it was the prince's ruby, set for her in a ring. The prince sent it to her with his love, just like that. Well, it shook her. And it made her look at Simon again, he was the messenger, he was a link, it had to mean something. One cannot understand Constanza's actions without taking into account that side. She still did not have much use for him personally; he, too, was twenty-one, they were exactly the same age take a week or so, and very sure of himself, too sure, even for her taste. He was what Anna called an impertinent young man.

'Only this time she didn't. Anna adored Simon from the word go.

'They clicked, as they say. She found him charming and stimulating and good company. *She* was charming to him. On that first visit he told her quite a bit about himself. Younger son, very much so; brothers Army, one already out in France; chilly place in Northumberland; little money to go round; parents chilly too, as well as proud and stiff. No cosy warm Italian family life for him, he told Anna, school, university, crammers, lodgings, his happiest time had been a couple of years recovering from pneumonia with an uncle, the British padre, on the Ligurian coast. The future? To be free. To have an interesting life. To have the good things. How? First of all turn one's back on the bloody war, then qualify for some career. One of his main interests was Italian art, but he rather felt he'd like to keep that for himself, not muck it up with money and degrees. He supposed he had better start reading for the Bar, quick and easy. "*Was* it?" "Oh, yes, certainly for me." One thing he did want was money, enough of it, and pretty soon: "Without money you miss most of the pleasures and lose most of the time, and don't let's pretend otherwise." His people kept him monstrously short— "I can't wait till they discover the debts I've made; though as a matter of fact I can wait, it would be wiser too."

'On his second visit he told her that she was like the favourite aunt he had never had, or better still— Americans make such wonderful parents, will you not adopt me, please? She did. He *lived* at Regent's Park. Constanza was out most of the time but when she dropped in to change, there they were, rattling Italian to each other, poring over Anna's art books— "Bet you've never been inside Sant'-Agnese in Oscurità?" "But I have, dear boy, and I know the tomb you mean though it is *not* by Taddeo Duodecimo as attributed." Anna prided herself on setting a good table; now, in wartime London, she put her mind to it: great lasagne pies, Virginia ham, as well as all the best fish, game and vegetables her friends in the country sent her. There was always a supply of the two things Simon liked to consume at all hours, fresh fruit and very good brandy. And of course every wine he would name. Speak to my wine merchant, dear boy, he ought to have some of that left. She was so animated again, it was a joy to Constanza.

'Then her own young man was at the front. It was total anguish, she told me, not for herself, but for *him*. She thought that he might get killed. She didn't exactly pray, she kept up some kind of attention, a vigil, the whole time; she never dared let up. Simon was a help to her, keeping the surface going, making the hours pass when she was not on duty at her canteen. They walked in the park, it was winter then, endlessly. He discovered that as a girl she had had a passion for Stendhal, so had he, and they talked about Julien Sorel and Tolstoi and Rimbaud.

'One day her young man was home, invalided out of the war with nothing really bad. Constanza found him uncouth and a bore— that was one of the things being with Simon did to one— she broke it off and went to parties again. With Simon now.

'Her mother looked happy, and for a while all was good. Then she was in love with Simon. She says she has never again felt so close to anyone, he was like an accomplice and brother. So she judged him— she always felt impelled to judge Simon, measure him— he was a grabber, but then he had never had anything so far, and also he had daring and enjoyed himself so much, so very much, he loved the suppers *and* the singing. So all was still well; they were happy (in spite of the war). Only Mr James worried, he was afraid of what was brewing.

'Simon played a trick. One day Anna came in, all emotional, but beaming this time. Wonderful news! What the devil? Your engagement of course! Simon has told me he asked you and you have given him hope.

'Constanza was furious. Anna became agitated, Don't tell me it isn't true! He *has* asked you? As a matter of fact he had, Constanza giving him short shrift. Simon hasn't a bean, she told her mother, besides I am much too young. Anna turned all American, What can be nicer than a young couple with their way to make, and what was *she* for? *That* didn't appease Constanza. But you love him? Anna wailed.

'She did, worse luck. She didn't approve of him. That was one impediment. It may sound priggish, but she says it's unwise to go against one's nature, its fundamental requirements, she knew that she could only make a go of it, a real go— and that was what she wanted— with some very extraordinary kind of man, and she hadn't met him yet. It occurs to me: Oh good God, was she a romantic, too, in her own way? No more of a realist than Anna? Surely she was clear-sighted? And isn't that what counts?

'Well, she didn't *admire* Simon—the way she admires Michel now; I can see how much she does, that's why I am so for it. And he *is* admirable. The austere ideal, the man who acts out his principles and endures what is— can you imagine Michel Devaux saying as my father so often did, I've only got one life and so much time, I can't afford to stand back? Yet, Simon was right for himself? What would *he* have had if he'd played the stoic? Who can tell? How can one tell?

'After the trick of the engagement Constanza wanted to break it off then and there whatever her own feelings. They rushed out into Regent's Park— out of earshot— and Simon told her, yes of course he was forcing her hand, it *was* blackmail: he did love her so, she was the right one for him and he'd take her tomorrow on five hundred pounds, *if* someone would lend them to him, and he did rather fancy himself as a married man at twenty-one.

'"On my mother's money?"

' "That's my bit of luck— the trust fund thrown in as well as your extraordinary mama. Darling, sweet Constanza, let's do it, let's do it now, we are going to have a jolly life you and I, let's cock a snook at the world and the mess it's in."

'Yet if she insisted he would wait, he would wait for her if he must. You presumptuous monkey, she told him, there's nothing to wait for, I'm not going to marry you. "Yes, you will." "Oh, *caro*— why cannot we go on as we are?"

'For a time she tried to do exactly that. Anna— of course— didn't know that they were having an affair, so now there were awkwardnesses, unfunny lies. And Anna was getting restive, dazzled as she was by the new prospect. Constanza saw it all too well: Anna above all needed a future and here it was, a son-in-law whom she could help to make his way in the world. It was a frightful time, people were dying and dying— how could one hang on, she asked herself, to one's private plan for a life? She loved Simon; too much to set out with him in that way— two pawns in a *combinazione*, a deal, even if partly his own. She loved her mother more. She was married before the spring.

'Simon made a hash of telling his parents— he did hate them so— he went to Northumberland and come back rocking with laughter, Do you know what they are taking you for, my sweet? You and my darling principessa? Adventuresses. Scheming foreigners. Papists! That's the worst for them; they're cutting off my pittance if I ever see you again. "Dearest boy," said Anna, "you must allow me to let you depend on me."

'Simon went to get himself some shirts made. May I order a whole dozen, Anna?

'Mr James was angry (for him) and almost interfered. Constanza agreed with much of what he had to say; but he did not know of any way of not letting down Anna either.

'There might have been a religious question. Simon was not unwilling to turn R.C. just to annoy his people. Constanza shelved it by promising to take him to Rome after the war for some slap-up ceremony; meanwhile they made do before a registrar.

'They settled down— rather well— in that house in Regent's Park. Simon stayed at home working for the Bar Examination, he passed the first part quite soon just as he had predicted. Then I was expected, that was rather a nuisance. They *had* something to worry about then: conscription. Constanza would have liked Simon to have been

a conscientous objector. Simon said goodness knew he did
object to being blown to pieces: but, No. In the end one
had to do as one's friends did. When I'm old I want to sit
and drink my wine with them in peace (poor Simon). So he
went and got himself a commission before conscription
became law.

'He was away training when I was born. Anna had me
baptized by a Catholic priest. Constanza didn't protest, she
had become a . . . subdued agnostic. Simon said it was a
splendid idea, that, on top of my being a girl, would
guarantee his people's keeping their paws off me. (They
have ignored my existence to this very day.) The name they
gave me was the old principessa's, the prince's mother, the
kind one.

'Then Simon was in France (an infantry officer in the
trenches!). Anna was brave. She had changed, what she
wanted then was victory and America to come in. Constanza
told me how alone she felt between her mother and that
baby; only her friends were a support, some of them, too,
turning against the war. Simon away was the first young
man all over again, a hundred times worse. Simon was so
alive. Her existence was suspense, and prayer, this time it
was prayer. For Simon's life. (His second brother was killed
at Verdun. They had that news.) In 1916 Simon was
wounded; one leg was smashed by a grenade. (He walked
with a limp ever after.) But he was home, honourably out
of the war, everybody saying how well he had done. When
they rushed to his hospital dragging hampers, he was
practically levitating with relief.

'He was given a job in Whitehall. There too he did well.
In fact he was quite brilliant and promoted almost at once.
Approval stimulated him and he began to work extremely
hard. He began to get interested in politics, too; Anna had
something to do with that at first. Men who had found him
unsufferable a year or two ago began to see his abilities or
his charm. They still said that he talked much too big, but

they did stop treating him as a scruffy nonentity. He was offered constituencies; it was taken for granted that he would stand for Parliament in the first post-war elections.

'Anna blossomed. Constanza was not sure. He was earning a decent salary and had been made welcome in the Liberal Party. Now she was worrying about motives. To his face.

' "You despise me, don't you?" he said. "I thought I was marrying a fellow immoralist; scratch her and it's a New England Governess."

' "I think I almost prefer you still grabbing at peaches and silk shirts."

' "My poor girl, there's nothing sacred about politics."

' "Perhaps because of people like you."

' "Oh, you do despise me!"

'There was more. Something that she had expected even less than ambition. Jealousy. The Yellow Monster. Simon worked late at his office then went on to places meeting people whom he ought to know, next morning he'd say to her, You were awfully late last night where have you been? Whom did you dance with? She told him. *Twice? What for?*

'It put her back up. It was so against her own code. She warned him.

' "Well, what do *I* know?" (Simon was drinking quite heavily then, even Mr James said she ought to have had allowed for that.) "What about all those other chaps before the war? *During* the war for all I know? How can I trust you an inch?"

'Constanza wouldn't stand for an answer. Simon apologized. Next week he started again. "You don't love me. You're a true American wife: husbands come last."

'Mr James spoke to her. Simon's had a harder war than you realize, he's still under a strain. My doctor tells me that leg of his must still be hurting like the devil.

' "But why *jealousy*? Goodness knows he has no grounds."

' "He may like *you* to tell him that."

' "He ought to know."

' "Dear girl, can't you see that Simon isn't as sure of himself as he likes to appear? He wants *you* to admire him."

' "But I do. I love being with him. I admire his talents; I'm not sure that I trust the uses he will put them to."

' "Yes, you do doubt him."

' "That absurd obsession with infidelity. He's carrying on like mama."

' "And you, my dear? Aren't you being the intransigent wife?"

' "Oh, no," she said. "I hope not. It's only that I cannot stand possessiveness, it diminishes people."

'Then Mr James sighed. "People are what they are."

'Now I must come to this quickly. For me it is the saddest part. It changed everything, *again*. In the last year of the war there was a girl who had a job in Simon's office. I won't tell you who she is because the name is a household word. Constanza and Simon used to call her Miss Mouse because she was so meek and mild and everything Simon did was perfect. The name was their joke because she didn't *look* mousey at all, she was a great flashy beauty— there was some Latin blood there too, just what Simon liked— a mouse in tiger skin. She fell in love with Simon. Constanza gave him an example of how she thought one should behave, never a murmur or fuss. Miss Mouse's father controlled a string of newspapers; he is very rich. Miss Mouse decided that she must have Simon.

'That marriage, too, was founded on blackmail. Simon was made aware that he might find himself obliged to stand down as a Parliamentary candidate if he failed to make an honest woman out of the Press Lord's daughter. If he did, he would have a newspaper empire backing him. And the money— it was going to be the *multiplicity* all right, another kind of existence altogether, power, great possessions. . . . He said it might be fascinating.

'The pressures, Mr James told me, and the prizes were considerable. It was a strange time, with the end of the war in sight, people feeling suspended, nothing appearing very permanent or real. Simon was convinced, or persuaded himself, that he'd been ill used by Constanza, that their marriage had been a mistake, a youthful mistake, the kind of thing one did in a war.

'He casually suggested a divorce. Perhaps he expected some protest from Constanza, a declaration, perhaps he hoped for it. Constanza did not help him, or only in her way. She lived up to what she believed in. "If you want to, *caro*, certainly." She just took it. Nobody saw the blow it was. Such a blow.

'It wasn't even easy. Simon couldn't afford to let himself be divorced; Constanza did some extremely quixotic things and they managed to fix it so that she appeared to be the guilty party. They plotted it together and they were nice to one another during the whole of that time and when it was all over and the lawyers were serving papers, their parting was quite unbearable. Simon wept and wouldn't walk out of the house. But that moment passed.

'Anna? Well may you ask! That was the dreadful side. The present and the future wiped out for her there was no recovery. Simon was merciful, he told her himself and he gave her time. Constanza saw his face as he came out of her room.

'What did he tell her (abetted by Constanza)? I don't know exactly. A rigmarole he made up. No word of the Press Lord's daughter or remarriage— one thing at a time. It was full of holes but at least Anna wasn't obliged to see them. She never understood nor accepted, but her feeling for Simon had not been destroyed. During the months they were waiting for the divorce he came to see her nearly every day. *They* remained friends to the last.

'It was her relation with Constanza that was strained. That, too, never recovered.

'Nobody else was convinced by the official version of Simon's divorce. He blamed Constanza. He couldn't bear people taking her side; he turned his back on her entirely. They never met again.

'It had been arranged that my mother should have me. "What about Flavia? Between Mary (Miss Mouse) and Northumberland there will be no place for her. The bambina hardly knows me, let's give her, too, a start on a clean slate. If she grows up bright and interesting we can renew our acquaintance, *a discrezione.* Meanwhile you keep her, Mena'll look after her." Constanza said, I will look after her, what next?

'It is true— I didn't know him. I can imagine him so very clearly, from his photographs, his words, but I do not remember him *myself*— I should have, I was two years old— it's strange that I cannot remember *seeing* him bending over my cot, as they say he did, glass of brandy-and-soda in hand.

'When the actual case came on the judge said some harsh things about the wife. The father was a busy man, he said, engaged in work of national importance, in the child's best interest he would give the custody to the defendant's mother. So Anna became my legal guardian. I don't know how much actual difference it did make. For Constanza it created a sort of void— no real responsibility; and it tied us all together in new ways.

'As it happened, the war ended a few days after the divorce. Constanza went to Rome as soon as the trains were running. There were no friends; she found her mother's circle dispersed, her father a middle-aged man. She had been away too long, in another country.

'When she came back to England at the end of the winter, Anna with Mena and me had moved again into Brown's.

Constanza took a small flat of her own. In the winter that followed we all had a house together and Giorgio came to stay, and the winter after that Anna took me to Switzerland while Constanza travelled with someone in Spain. And that's the beginning of the life *I* remember. It went on like that, the three of us never quite living together, never wholly apart. I often missed Constanza, but not being with them both at the same time was easier. My grandmother was very good to me. To her, I was Simon's girl. When she read about his new marriage she said, The yellow press have caught him, poor boy. She sent him a wedding present.

'There was often something about Simon in the papers, not only in the tabloids, in *The Times*. His election to Parliament. His maiden speech. His prospects. You see, his cousin, too, had been killed in the war, the only son of the West Country branch of the family. Then Simon had said that his eldest brother was lucky, winner takes all. He didn't as it turned out. He died after the Armistice, dysentry in Egypt. So Simon was now an only son, an eldest son, and he stood to inherit in Somerset as well. A great house. (There was supposed to be a Mantegna.)

'We travelled a good deal. When Mussolini took over in Italy, Anna decided that it was her duty to make her protest on Italian soil as an Italian citizen (a not too vulnerable one for the time being, but she tried her best). So she allowed herself to return at last. Rome, of course, remained forbidden ground. We lived at Fiesole for a while, then Livorno, Lake Como, Florence again. I was not sent to school. Anna had me educated at home as she herself had been and Constanza. I'm afraid it was scrappier in my case— no continuity. We shall see whether I've learnt enough when I go up for those exams.

'That's upon us *now*, upon me. The time I know has gone so fast. Am I skipping? I'm not trying to tell *my* life story, I haven't got one yet (perhaps it began last week?) I'm trying to tell Anna's. I suppose I want to explain— I almost said, find out— about her dying. Her story is complete now, isn't it? It's unchangeable.

'There are one or two more things I must talk about. Come to think of it, not much happened to Anna from the time Simon left us till she died— fifteen years or nearly. Well, her son grew up and not into much; but she had expected that, she had discounted him (when she chose Simon?). Giorgio popped up now and again, with girl trouble, with money trouble, in a new car. He joined the Fascist party. Anna coped with him all right, Giorgio never seemed to cause her any real pain; her tirades, which used to be against the prince, were about Constanza who had ruined our lives by losing Simon. You see, she expected so much, always had, and now she was expecting some miracle to come to her through her daughter. Constanza, living from day to day, refusing to make plans, was letting her down again.

'One cannot tell about Anna without Constanza coming into it. *And* the other way round— during her whole life so far everything that happened to her mother went to shape what happened to herself. Perhaps it is like that in many lives? To *that* extent?

'I said I had come to the time I knew myself. It's curious, I feel I have less to tell about it: I know what it was like, it was daily life; it doesn't stand out, make a tale, like the things they told of the past.

'Constanza always kept her flat in London. London was her base, her friends were there. As you know she hasn't married again. She turned them all down, that was Anna's refrain, no one was good enough. "Right enough, mama. Oughtn't it to be something nice and lawful this time? The kind of marriage my father recognizes when he sees it? It's his turn, poor man. Can you produce a choice of eligible Catholic Agnostics for me?" I think she half meant it, though what she really felt was that this time she *was* going to wait.

'One year, I was still quite little, we were in Italy, in a small place on the lakes. Constanza came up the path from the steamer holding the post, Anna was standing on the terrace waiting, Constanza cried out, "Simon is dead!" Anna threw up her arms and they vanished into the house.

Constanza was stricken. (She even sent away her young man of the time who was staying at another hotel.) She told me that there was nothing to be said for death, nothing in mitigation: it *was* extinction, the end. Anna wouldn't speak of it at all for some time; later we heard about Simon's will— he left her various things, his art library for instance (it's a wonderful one)— and it gave her some kind of peace.

'It happened in Somerset, in that house. Simon's uncle had taken him under his wing, so Simon and his wife, Mary, half lived there. Simon was drinking like a fish; he wasn't getting on with Mary at all; he was working too much, and they said he was worried as he was about to switch Parties. That night there had been a dinner for some of his London friends, they sat up late and there was a kind of wager, they went out into the park, it was a chilly night, and Simon in his evening clothes jumped into the water-piece. Afterwards Mary came to him aghast, "Do change your clothes, darling, I beg you." He turned on her, "Who are you to order me about?" He just sat on dripping, calling for more brandy. Next morning he ran a temperature but insisted on getting up. It became double pneumonia. He died three days later in a nursing home. He wasn't much older than thirty.

'I must tell about the curious will he left. Simon hadn't inherited yet; the house was entailed of course and as there was no direct male heir (my being what I am) it looked as if it were going to some cousin overseas, only later it became known that Mary had had a posthumous son: he's still a minor— here's another member of my family whom I haven't met, I seem to have an assortment.

'Well, what Simon could or thought he could dispose of were the pictures. He'd been collecting, you know, Italian

painting. Oh, *en grand*. Every time he bought one you saw it
in the papers. A Tintoretto, a Titian. Mr Simon Herbert
acquired a Veronese, exchanged his Bellini. . . . It used to
amuse Constanza. How he must adore it, she said. If he'd
stayed with us, he'd never have got further than etchings.
For the money came from his new father-in-law. Prestige:
Simon had told him that he would bequeath the pictures to
the nation. Even so, Mr James insists, it's the first Mantegna
that counts. Without that coming to Simon he doubted if the
Press Lord would have forked out. When Simon's will was
opened they found that he had left the pictures to me. Not
just for life, for good. He even advised me to sell them— I
would find the legacy a great help in getting an interesting
life. Until I came of age he wanted the pictures to be in his
ex-wife's custody. "She will look after them and at them."

'The lawyers wrote that my father's new family would
contest. Both Anna and Constanza let go at once. Naturally.
So the pictures went to the nation after all. I've seen them.
They're in a room of their own called the Simon Herbert
and Lord X Bequest.

'There was an aftermath. One day an enormous crate
arrived at Constanza's doorstep. A letter explained that it
was the pictures Simon had owned before his second marriage and which by rights belonged now to his daughter. It
was puzzling. When Simon first turned up he didn't have
anything at all. They undid the crate and there was a live
Douanier Rousseau, one of his huge bright beast and jungle
pieces pouncing upon the room. There was a second picture,
a Juan Gris, very fine. Who had paid for them? Why? It was
a mystery.

'Constanza put them on her walls. She did look at them.
She loves them. They are literally the only possessions she
has in the world: those two pictures, and the ring, her
father's ring. She doesn't even have a wristwatch. All this
brings me to our getting here, to St-Jean. I'm coming to
that now.

'I told you that Constanza regarded London as her base,
her home if you like. Lately she had begun to feel that things
were changing, or that she was changing. Her friends were
settled, politics infinitely depressing, she came to the decision
to make some break; it was time for her to go. Go where?
Not to live in fascist Italy (it was still all right for her to spend
a month or two, with her British passport, with her mother
and me and carry messages over the border for the under-
ground). She had no plan, except to move— *navigare*; the
price of the future, she said, was to burn one's boats.

'She gave up her flat. That was last summer. A day or two
before she was due to move she ran into a man she had known
as a rather mysterious friend of Simon's who used to turn up
on leave now and again during the war. It was he actually
whom Simon had asked to be the co-respondent— bogus
co-respondent— when they were concocting their divorce,
it was about him that the judge had scolded her and given
me to Anna. Nobody had ever heard of him again.
Constanza's friend's said he was a myth. Now there he was.
He had a new name, a new identity, in fact he was Lewis
Crane, you know, the art critic. He is also a kind of consultant
that's less well-known, he's supposed to run the art market—
lives like a tycoon, but he really loves painting. Simon taught
him. He told Constanza that. During the first days they
talked of no one else: this man had loved my father. He told
her things she had not known about him— good things, acts
of generosity— it came out that it was he who had got Simon
on to my pictures, the Douanier and the Gris; he had
practically given them to him. That gave her a turn.

'Then Lewis Crane asked her to marry him. She said no,
of course; he persisted. For the second time in her life, she
says, he had appeared out of the blue as it were and took
charge. After she had left England, a few weeks later in
Milan, she accepted him. He had to be in Amsterdam next
week, he told her, and Rio in November, so they decided
to get married in Brussels in the last week of October.

Constanza said she would have to tell her mother first, and me.

'Anna and I were at Alassio. We had been there some time. The régime is tightening and she had been warned that they might no longer put up with her outspokenness and propaganda; her friends thought that she would be safer somewhere close to the French border, but she was taking against the place. The Ligurian Riviera wasn't Italy to her; she felt in exile once more; the move had been a failure.

'Constanza asked me to meet her and Lewis at Genoa. I must say I was rather excited to meet him. I have read his books. He is a big man. Not big as a bear, big as a cat. Not my idea of an intellectual, or a businessman; to me he's like a merchant in a fairy tale. I asked him if he had a fur-lined coat, he said as a matter of fact he had. Constanza *seemed* all right, and I could see that he thought the world of her. He said that at moments I reminded him of Simon. I promised to see that Constanza would get to Brussels on time, and he promised to take me behind the scenes of the art world.

'So I went back to Alassio and at the end of the month Constanza came to pick me up and to tell her mother. We were going to travel together as far as Paris, I was to go on to Calais. You see, I had been doing something about my own future, too. Mr James helped me. He found a tutor in London who was going to coach me for University Entrance. I was to live in his house; Anna had said yes. She also said that I was leaving her. She wanted me to say, Please come to London with me. She might not have come, but I didn't want to say it. Some days were . . . difficult. I longed to be off, I wanted to be gone before anything could prevent it. Then Constanza arrived.

'There was a frightful scene. About Lewis. I could have

heard even though closed doors— I stopped my ears. But I heard her cry out, I heard the tone.

'Next morning I asked, "Mummy, we *are* still going? You to Brussels, I to London?" "We are. What next?" But Constanza was tense and cold. "I had hoped it would please her," she kept saying. "I so hoped she'd be pleased." Our train went after luncheon; Anna didn't come down.

'We sat in the train, my mother and I, waiting to get into France. That slow train with all the stops, full of militiamen and police as so few Italians are allowed to go abroad. I wonder how long it will be before we take that train again? I guessed that Constanza was acting courier. (For the last time. She, too, has since been warned.) As we were standing still at the frontier— you know, nonchalant, nervous, not showing it— the compartment door opens and who should walk in? My uncle Giorgio. He was all *ciao ciao* and kissy cheeks; she practically said, Bird-of-Ill-Omen where have you sprung from what do you want? He had missed us at Alassio and followed the train in his car, he had something to speak to her about. I left them, I walked down the platform making faces at the blackshirts. When Giorgio had skipped I went back and thought no more about it. Ten minutes later we were in France— the relief. At Nice we were to change trains: as we're getting up Constanza notices that she hasn't got her ruby, her ring. Naturally she doesn't want to get off before having looked for it properly. There's no time. We stay and the train moves on. The conductor arrives and the head conductor, there's a search, no sign of the ring. They write a report. All the time the train is carrying us slowly but surely up the French coast. Constanza is handling it lightly, but I know how shaken she must be by losing the ring. It's getting later and later. We all share a kind of supper. By then we realize that we've missed all connections up the line. The men tell us we'd better get off now and spend the night somewhere. Constanza hesitates, we don't jump to it, the stops are so brief, the stations look so dark. Eventually they practically push us out. There is still a bus and it takes us to that hotel on the port. Next morning we know where we are. Constanza is able to put a name to it, she has seen that waterfront before but where? She has seen paintings of it: it must be, we are at, St-Jean-le-Sauveur. *We are here*.

'First thing I did was to try to get us organized to leave again. Not so Constanza. Ought we to rush on before doing more about the ring? "Constanza," I said, "we are expected. Lewis is waiting for you." "So he is," she said.

'I couldn't budge her. The weather was delicious; she liked the look of the place, the last weeks had been hectic. Every day it was something else. It was Sunday, she was expecting a detective, the timetable at the café was out of date. "Darling, there's no *hurry*."

'Once he knew where we were Lewis telegraphed every few hours. "What *are* you going to tell him?" Exactly, she said. Then I did ask her, "You haven't changed *your* mind, mummy— you *are* going to marry Lewis?" "I don't know, I don't know," she said, "let me wait."

'*I* don't like waiting. I can't bear it. And there was nothing I could do.

'One morning she had made up her mind. "You'd rather like me to marry Lewis, don't you?",

'Very much, I said.

'Why?

'We are used to giving answers. I tried to tell her. I wanted to have her looked after, have her settled— even if it sounds like Anna— I wanted it for myself. It would be nice for us to have a home.

'She listened to me and said, "I'm sorry, darling, but I wasn't going to do it for *you*. You have your own life before you (rather as you said to me, Therese) and you must make it for yourself. *She* has not. Only when we had that row did I realize how much the wish to please her had come into it. Again! I've learnt nothing."

' "But she was *not* pleased."

' "That's the irony of it. As she sees it, what did I come to offer her (and she waiting all these years)? Marriage to a middle-aged art critic who has turned dealer. I didn't dress it up; no wonder she took it as life letting her down once more. Lewis ought to have gone himself, he is a showman: *he* might have caught her, Simon's friend, as he did catch me.

' "But mama is not the point. The point is that I made a mistake— oh, I do have a feeling for him, that helped to confuse the issue, we do like one another— what I have come to see is that my falling for Lewis was not what I took it to be."

'I did not ask her what she had taken it for. She was cool that morning, detached, brutal with herself— people say that Constanza has such arrogance, well, she also has humility. I knew she would go on.

' "I took it for something inevitable. A link with Simon. I took it for a continuation. Now I see that it was— marginal. It tied up some loose ends." '

' "And now," I said when I had taken it in, "what will you do now Constanza?"

'She evaded that. "Write a letter to Lewis. It's not going to be easy to convince him." (She was right there. Fortunately he's gone to South America.)

' "With yourself? Where will you go?"

' "Go? Why not stay?"

' "What for?"

' "I have a feeling that I ought to sit back— one chooses too often— that the next move is not up to me."

' "Why here?"

' "We are here. Don't you think that fate has given enough hints?"

'She even took this awful villa, it was offered, it was available; and when I saw that she was firm about not letting any of her friends come out to stay with her, I decided to stay myself. She wanted to be alone— she never was before— but perhaps not *entirely* alone. I just told her that it might be interesting for me to get to know something of France, after all I was still young for University Entrance and could probably arrange to do some of the work here. She gave me rather a long look but let it go at that.

'It was she who liked being in France. No memories, no ties: new ground and neutral ground, restful she called it. She found the French mysterious and fascinating and liked to listen to them talking among each other and me to take them off for her afterwards. We did laugh so much during those months— you must have seen us sometimes at the café. We'd never been alone together for so long before. I did a lot of work; Constanza read. Racine, Balzac, new novels. We used to picnic below Michel's tower, it was shut up— they told us it belonged to a French man of letters— it's more sheltered than the villa. And we talked and talked, on our walks and late at night, I sitting on her bed wrapped in a blanket, goodness the place was cold. She did talk about her life— Rome, the war, Anna— all that came up. but so much else besides.

'The future of human society. Had it made an irrevocably false start? The compass error that gets harder to correct with every mile you go? How simple and shining it all had looked when she was young and mama was preaching democracy and she went one better with her faith in Fabian Socialism. The influence of private individuals on events was negligible— and yet they must keep on. "One thing I learnt in England: public opinion, the sum of private opinions, does matter, can matter often for good." How did we get into the situation of today? Economic bewilderment in the United States, uninspired government in Britain, unemployment, gloom, insuperable problems everywhere, unspeakable things happening to men and women inside half the countries in the world. "In our poor Italy on a comparatively petty scale," she said. "Think of Soviet Russia. Yet never make that mistake, Flavia, never take lightly the one man in the prison cell." She believed that there would be changes, a new cycle of prosperity, Mussolini will fall. "But when? How? What about the people to whom it will have cost perhaps a third of their lifetime? What about our tendency to slide into the next trap?"

'Do we know our true needs? She asked herself, Are we inescapably the products of our habits and environment? Are we not already too many, *simply too many*, to be able to change the patterns deliberately? Who should begin? *Quis custodiet?* It is hopeless.

' "Constanza, some things *have* become better? Which do you think are good, entirely good? The rule of law?"

' "Yes," she said. "Where it obtains."

' "What else? The Kellog Pact?"

'She said, "The invention of anaesthetics and the abolition of judicial torture."

'*Where it obtains.* And that would get us back to castor oil and the secret police; Lenin's Kulaks in the cattle trains, Devil's Island, English prisons. Oscar Wilde. Crime. Ends and means. Free will. Character, what makes it, what destroys it. Conduct. She would speak of the necessity of holding on to a framework of belief, a reasonable percentage of belief.

'One thing she often came back to was what she called the great divide in all individual lives. Youth, when death has no reality (she doesn't mean fear of death, children can have that), and our actions and pleasures are for their own sake, for what they are *now* and *new*. Middle-age when the fact of death— impermanence, and our own slackening of impetus— is the dominant, the clef changing the notation; what we do, we do for the nth time. What will it add up to? We are concerned then with the sum not the parts.

'What is achievement? Art, undoubtedly. Religious experience? outside her range. Science? for what ends? Increasing human happiness? another chancy one that. And for the ninety-nine without a vocation?

'Pessimism, she affirmed, is to her the most rational view,

the long-term view. In the present she mostly enjoyed herself, or had so far: "I've been sad so often yet from day to day
I've enjoyed everything that was going."

' "Mummy," I said, "in your whole life what have you
enjoyed most?"

' "Hunting, I suppose."

'And we talked about the books we were reading. She re-
read *Howard's End*, twice, it was so beautifully fatalistic, she
said, it suited her present mood. Among the new English
writers, I am backing Aldous Huxley and she's backing
Evelyn Waugh. Someone sent her *Vile Bodies*, when she had
finished it she cried. She hadn't done that she said since she
was my age and came to the last page of *Le Rouge et le Noir*.

'I said nothing happened. Well, Anna came a few times.
She had herself driven over and never spent more than the
day. She brought us Parmesan and Italian vegetables and
Mena to do an afternoon's worth of sewing, but it never
went right, she disapproved of us dreadfully. The mistral,
the villa ("When I think of Somerset!" "Don't Mama."),
Constanza's aimlessness.

' "What *are* your plans? Your brother is doing very well."

' "All of a sudden?"

' "Giorgio is marketing a new design for a motor car and
they are favourably impressed at Turin."

'She never mentioned my having got stuck here as well,
but I could hardly look her in the face. She wasn't even glad
about Constanza's having given up Lewis. "Mena, *is* she
worse?" we asked. We asked that, we did not ask, "Mena,
what can we do?" Her answer was, "She is tired of herself."

'When she was gone we felt miserable, angry with her *and*
like criminals.

'The rest happened by post. First it was something good,
or so it seemed to me. Constanza was moved but sceptical.
It was late in the day and nothing had led up to it. For the
letter was from the prince. Poor Anna had been very indis-
creet, the *fascisti* were going to arrest her or put pressure on

her to leave the country for good, but he had been assured
that if the principessa were to live again with him quietly in
Rome nobody would touch her. He was offering her the
protection of his house and name. "She is my wife. We are
both getting old. I have missed her."

'I said, "Giulia?"

' "Giulia *is* old now and papa has persuaded himself that
he is; he has allowed himself to slip into old age. Mama has
not done that. *She* hasn't softened, *she* isn't resigned."

'So Constanza went and met her mother halfway at Nice.
She came back defeated; she had not been able to move
her.

'Constanza's next task would have been to get her to leave
Italy . . . without too much pain. "Will it be London?" I
asked. "Do I have to live with her?"

'Before we did anything there was something else. It was
good *and* bad. An envelope arrived with only a receipt
inside, it was for the ruby ring. It was at a jewellers' in Milan
and could be retrieved for a certain sum. Constanza was
stunned. The ruby was coming back to her! It had been
pawned with a discreet firm and the person who had pawned
it was her brother Giorgio.

'It was all too obvious to hindsight. When Giorgio had
descended on us that day in the train he had asked her to
advance him the money to build the new car, and when she
had turned him down he was furious. He snatched the ring.
(Constanza has a habit of slipping it off and placing it on the
table in front of her. She's done it for years.) Now she had to
pay up. She telegraphed Anna to meet her, she couldn't have
put her hand on so much money on her own.

'They met again at the same hotel. An orchestra was
playing and they were served tea. I don't know why
Constanza told me that when she told me so little else. Only
this. When Anna heard, she changed: she became formidable. She cried, "So my son is a thief. *That, too!*" She turned
on Constanza; Constanza lost her head, she struck back,

she said the things she had not said in a life-time, the things that should not be said. Anna rose and walked away, very slowly and stiffly— Constanza tried to follow her but a waiter held her up with the bill. When at last she got out of the hotel Anna's car was moving down the drive.

'Constanza went back to St-Jean. The day after we tried to telephone from the post office but could not get through to Alassio. Four days later early in the morning the telegram came.

'When Constanza got there she was told that her mother had made a mistake with her sleeping pills, her maid had been witness to that. Veronal. The principessa's heart, had been bad for some time. Mena was unshakeable. America cabled that Anna had left instructions to be buried in Rome. And so she was. From her husband's house.

'Afterwards Constanza came back here with Mena. They were both . . . strained. They did not talk about it, we did not talk about it. (At first.) Let her rest in peace, Mena said. Constanza was kept busy coping with Anna's estate. It had to be done through the American Consulate at Marseilles, sixty miles there and back, she was away most of the day; I was glad of that too, we didn't really want to be alone with each other just then. And when that was over, well, since everybody here seems to know about it, there was Michel.

'Constanza has been . . . fortunate. (She doesn't like one to use the word lucky.)

'Did you know that Michel actually turned up on that dreadful morning when Constanza was frantic to get to the station? I thought he was the taxi driver. He came as a neighbour offering help.

'The week before we had noticed that the shutters were open at the tower (no more picnics) and we had seen the car. The French politician had arrived. We used to refer to him as the man of principle. You see we had heard quite a bit about him— the locals boggle at the way in which he doesn't dodge his taxes. We were told that he refused to take his seat in the Chamber of Deputies because there was something he didn't approve of in the campaign. "Mummy, he must be an awful prig." "He doesn't sound like one." She had bought a copy of *De L'Administration*. "That's written by a first-class mind."

'Well, I didn't take him in that morning. When he came back later on to ask if I needed anything, I was struck by his face— the intelligence in it, the structure, it is a noble face, isn't it? Constanza says it's a French period face, Clouet, the portrait of Monsieur Pienne (clean-shaved). And I was struck by his youth, I expected someone . . . ponderous, not a man in espadrilles and blue over-alls who moves like a feather. He is Lewis Crane's generation actually, about ten years older than Constanza. You know that he stopped by the villa every day asking what he could do for me, offering lifts, bringing books, staying to talk. The kindness! And he a writer, not minding about his time.

'I asked (I was trying to fit in what we'd heard of him) about his having passed out of the *Ecole Normale* so high, which had rather impressed me. He was amused, though not very. He said that he was not a *Normalien*, he was *Condorcet* and *Polytechnique*.

' "Marcel Proust went to Condorcet?"

' "Right."

' "But not on to the other?"

' "Right again."

' "You did pass out high? What's the French equivalent of a Balliol double first? And would you mind explaining what is wrong with being *Normalien*? I'd have thought one had to be very bright indeed even to get in?" "Ambition," he said, "*l'amour du portefeuille.*" "*You* didn't take up a profession, you went into politics and gave them up again?" "I gave up front-line politics, yes."

' "Would you call yourself an *homme de lettres*?"

'He laughed and said that nobody under ninety called

himself that nowadays. I said, more's the pity and that I had seen the term both in the *Petit Larousse Moderne* and the *Figaro Littéraire*.

'Michel laughed again and said, "Well, we do have a great many men of ninety. All the same don't believe everything you read, *ma fille*."

'Another time I asked him about his having turned down Parliament on a point of principle. That really amused him. "I've never had the honour of being elected. I stood down well short of it. I see that I enjoy an exaggerated reputation for probity among my compatriots. I can assure you it is wonderfully easy to acquire."

' "But you *could* have?"

' "Become a legislator? That, too, is not difficult." He had come to realize that the technique of politics as currently practised was ineffectual and in the long view immeasurably harmful in twentieth-century conditions. To maintain any form of quality and security in our environment and lives we would have to scrap most of our notions and tackle everything from different ends. "The knowledge is there, it needs to be applied."

'Wasn't that a tall order, I said; and again please to explain. What about democracy, what about that technique?

'Michel said I reminded him of his audience at the time when he made speeches. Democracy, alas, though still far from being universally practiced or accepted, was already out of date.

' "But we know that any alternate system is inevitably worse, much worse?"

' "We might say that democracy, at this stage, is preferable to any current dictatorship and to many periods of absolutism in the past. Can we say that it is preferable to *any* system or order of government that might be devised?"

'I asked him what he had in mind.

' "A controlled hierarchy, selected rather than elected."

"By *whom*?"

' "Controlled by law. Selected by objective tests."

' "What will come first? The laws and the tests, or the hier-archy?"

' "*That* is the crux. There we have infinite moral and political problems. The initial *mise au pouvoir*, the *right* beginning. It may be impossible. It is worth thinking about."

' "My mother says, As we cannot call in the gods, *quis custodiet*?

' "The beautiful lady whom I drove in my car? *A quoi rêvent les jeunes filles?*"

'When Constanza was back, Michel took her into Marseilles every day. I don't think she noticed him beyond feeling vaguely grateful for his kindliness and care. I don't think they talked much in that car; she was still so tense and shocked. He drives fast and she's always liked speed. He seemed to know what she needed, silence, a little small talk to make it natural, transport at the door. When he brought her back he just drew up in front of the villa, jumped out, opened door, kissed hand, "*Bon soir, Madame*," and he was off. I went up to the tower sometimes later in the evening for a talk, he had said I might. We sat in his lovely round room with all the books (little I thought!). I asked him what he did with himself in Marseilles all day long? "Oh, I get a surprising amount of reading done in the car." "Notes and all? I do call that concentration." But did he mean that he actually sat waiting outside the U.S. Consulate? "Well, they do keep her there till all hours," And what did they do between twelve and two p.m.? "I usually drop her at Cintra's Bar, she can get a sandwich there and a glass of port."

' "You *drop* her? You don't go in?"

' "She hasn't asked me to."

' "But, Michel, dear, isn't that what the man's supposed to do?"

'He said very sweetly and tenderly, "These are no normal occasions, *elle a eu beaucoup de chagrin*."

'A few days later he told me that he'd been to Cintra's *with* her. At the door she had suddenly looked up and said, "Don't *you* eat?" He said, "*A coté*." Constanza said, "How absurd, and how perfectly awful of me." I told Michel that was all very well but for goodness' sake stop taking her to that white port-wine place, the sandwiches there— though delicious— are minute. "Do take her to a proper restaurant." From then on she came to the surface more; it wasn't long before she said to him, "This cannot go on, haven't you anything *better* to do than being my chauffeur all day?" "And what did you say then?" "Flavia, you ask too much," he said, and surely I could work that one out by myself. I think I can.

'Then there was the day she told him that she had read his books. *That* shook him, though he made light of it. To please him, I said, "What's more she really admires them. You have such a lucid style. Your ideas disturb her— they are open to misconstruction." He looked dazed— he who is always so unruffled, so controlled— he muttered something like fancy her being interested in that kind of stuff. I bridled (I shouldn't have), "Because she is a woman?" (The other night I had asked him if he didn't think they ought to have the vote in Switzerland, and he said it was irrelevant.) "What about myself then?"

' "A taste for abstract ideas is common among people under twenty. It wanes. It is not difficult, as you will learn, to find readers; it is dangerously easy to find disciples; it is extremely hard to find anyone you are personally attached to who will care two hoots about your work."

'I thought then of the wife, the difficult woman with the nerves, St-Jean was talking about, whose caprices and demands had made his life so impossible. Perhaps that story, too, was inaccurate. I hoped so.

'Constanza and I did not really talk about Michel. She had told me, quite sharply for her, to drop that silly name we used to have for him, the man of principle. When one morning she told me that they were going away, I can't say that it was a surprise. The way she put it was that Michel had very kindly offered to drive her to Paris, which she had never seen properly (Simon used to grumble so about not being able to take her because of the war). Did I think I would be able to manage for a while on my own? (with Mena, and Mr James in the offing).

'I didn't even want to ask anything. I only said, "Constanza, go; have a lovely time."

'Before they went off, Michel and I had a talk. He gave me the keys of the tower. "It's a good place, it's yours. Use it." Then he said, "You know we are going to get married." After I had congratulated him, I said, "You mean you asked her and she said Yes to you at once? She didn't say she wanted to wait?"

' "It was just a decision we came to. I believe it was your mother who said, Wouldn't it be the best thing?"

' "She asked you? Like the day outside Cintra's Bar?" I could not forbear to congratulate him once again.

' "As a matter of fact I'm afraid that we shall have to wait." He had neglected, he said, to press for the completion of certain formalities. "The issue seemed academic." To put it bluntly, he was not really divorced. It was a matter of time, most steps had been taken, "We are leaving St-Jean to avoid talk; we shall have to be reasonably discreet for the next few months or so."

'I said, "It will be good for her to get away from here. Michel, you are a responsible man." He said he hoped he was and I embraced him.

'After they had gone (they left one evening after dark, Constanza having said that there was one thing Michel refused to put on me— he will have to learn to be a bit less scrupulous, poor lamb— so that she would have to do it, and it was *not* to let on: "Tell our friends I've gone to Italy to look after my papa; as for Michel, he's God knows where, you don't know, it's nobody's business and they're used to his comings and goings." I said to count on it, what else?) So after they had gone I began to use the tower. I made myself the timetable you know. At first I thought about it a good deal, naturally, and the more I thought the more I liked it. I have a feeling it will do. I love Michel. I have a feeling that this time it will be all right for her. When she was younger she thought she knew what she was waiting for. Now in a queer way, a looking-glass way you might say, she seems to be getting it. One is always warned about the perils of wishing— perhaps Constanza won't be in trouble because she is not getting her wish literally. She used to be drawn towards political life, she dreamt of the English statesman, yet when Simon went for office she was against it. Isn't Michel a politician in reverse? His life is political theory, politics minus self. He has chosen obscurity? privacy? independence?

'Half her past life with Italians, half with the English, now it *will* be new ground as she has said. Michel's told me a few things about himself; he comes from a family of lawyers and administrators. There's always been land. His father and mother are dead. One brother is a *magistrat* in Paris, the other farms. (Experimental farming on Michel's persuasion and advice; it's not doing well and the brother is taking fright.) His sisters are married to the same kind of men. He, too, married a girl of his own milieu; they've been separated for many years. No children. A part of his inheritance has gone in a number of ventures; his books make about two and six a year. "Unlike Mr Crane's. I told her to think twice."

' "Then you haven't got a jealous disposition?"

'He said coldly, "Of all human failing jealousy is perhaps the most deplorable and most dangerous."

' "Not worse than cruelty?"

' "It leads to it."

'What else did he tell me about himself? When he was young he loved horses.

' "*La chasse à courre?*"

' "Jumping." "Do you mean show jumping?" "Oh, I gave it up ages ago." When I told Constanza, she who has a memory for these things said, "Good Lord, *not* M. J. Devaux who came over with the French team after the war?"

'So they have that, too.

'It is curious that it should have happened, that Michel came upon the scene the very instant she was really free for the first time in her life. I suppose from day to day Constanza always did pretty well what she pleased, but Anna was always there. "I don't think mama will approve of that." "I daresay mama will be glad." "They sent the bill, I must forward it to mama." That's all over. Michel thinks she will be in for a bad time when she realizes it. *He* will be there. It is a new life, nothing less. She has signed the long lease for the house inland, it will be for both of them, *Deo volente*, as she would say.

'When? I don't know. I pass by the house now and then but it doesn't seem awfully real to me yet. I've stopped thinking about that part of the future, I've stopped worrying about *her*. We can all start out now on our own.

'Michel wrote to me sometime ago— *not* from Paris— that they would be away a good deal longer than they originally planned, complications having arisen. Nobody except his lawyers and myself know his whereabouts or have an address and it might be as well to leave it at that. Constanza has added a scribble, "We've been running into a rather nasty situation. I keep telling Michel that nobody is in the slightest doubt that we've run off together, but the fact seems to be that as long as there's no actual proof, it can't hurt us. So, darling, keep mum about where we are. I know we can count on you. Let's pray we shall be back before you have read ten thousand books."

'So I will not tell— not even to you— in what country they are.

'When it's all done and Michel has made an honest woman of her, Constanza wants us to go to Rome, the three of us, and pay our respects to her papa. She says Michel and I will be able to sustain each other. For a minute I liked the idea, now I don't. Isn't it a bit late to acquire a family, that kind of a family? What could I say to my grandfather? Very likely he expects a *bambina*— even Constanza found they didn't speak the same language any more. Oh, I know the prince isn't a fascist, he's got nothing but contempt for Musso; Constanza says her father was never the man who had much faith in *any* trains running on time; but he is a man who can still get favours from the régime. It's different for Constanza, she's got so much affection for them. For me, it will be . . . awkward . . . unnecessary? And to think what it all meant to Anna.

'I don't want to think about that, I don't want to look at the actual scene, I've got over it, haven't I? . . . the way she died . . . and all that went before. It doesn't have much to do with me? Just because she brought me up. That was because of the custody. Very well, I loved her. I did do that. Now I want to get away from it, that is the truth. That is the reason I sent Mena away and kept Mr James from coming— I know it now, I can see it now, *this* instant.'

Flavia became aware of her voice and that it was loud, aware of herself on her feet rapidly walking the floor at first light.

'It was their story, everything in it seems to have led to the next thing— now it should have a stop! I want no more of it. I can become an English don and . . . other things besides. It is over, it cannot touch my life, it is not part of my story. Therese— *tell* me it is not?'

But Therese in the bed was peacefully lying asleep.

Flavia flung herself out of the room. For a minute she remained on the landing, shaking with humiliation and rage. Then she took refuge in Loulou's bathroom. Tears rolling down her face, she turned on the taps. She threw handfuls of Loulou's bath-salts into the hot water, then emptied the jar. There. A dash of eau-de-Cologne for good measure. Lying in clouds of scent in the sunken tub filled to the brim, that streak of equanimity she had asserted itself. She began to giggle; ruefully. And all of it in English! Poor Therese. Perhaps just as well? *Just as well.*

CHAPTER FOUR

Some Weeks

I

Is everything only what we remember it to be— neither more
nor less? Where, then, and when is truth? Does it take two to
tell it? Flavia herself that morning had slept late. And when
she had woken and eaten everything the femme de ménage
had left for lunch plus some extra eggs and some ham, she
was no longer certain what had taken place the night
before.

Can I have said all that? She did not actually remember
herself as talking the whole of the time— could there have
been silent passages when the words were only reeling through
her mind? And when had Therese dropped off? Had she
herself perhaps dropped off at one point? She was not able to
tell.

Nor Therese, too likely. Flavia was resolved not to ask.
That, never.

'You are late, coco, *à table*, you're going to have baked
pigeon tonight.' That was the opening of the following
evening, the evening to be faced. And when they were alone,
in the same room, there was no indication whether anything
at all had reached Therese's mind. Flavia, once more and
very firmly, told herself, *tant mieux*.

And after a week or so she found herself able to tease.

'See you tomorrow, coco?'

'How not? For dinner and bed. No extras.'

'I keep asking you to come out in the boat, you say you
have to work. What are you laughing about?'

Flavia kissed her hand. 'I will go in the boat. Tomorrow?'

That was not Therese's way to treat the sea. 'Tomorrow there may be mistral. Today is right.'

'I can't, it's my essay day.'

'You ought to have a holiday.'

'A holiday must be declared in advance, like a law.'

Flavia stuck to her guns and when she turned up next morning was told by the Loulou boys that she didn't know one wind from the other. No boats out today. Mama has driven to Toulon.

'To buy fish, papa is arriving.'

'He does eat a great deal of fish?' said Flavia.

'*Stupid*. He paints it.'

'Doesn't he do mostly portraits these days?'

The three little boys danced about her. 'Portraits of fish. Dead fish— *nature morte*, get it? When papa's away he paints ladies, at home he paints fish, stinking fish, rascasse, red mullet, sea spider, octopus, at night it goes into the icebox, table and all, it stinks all the same. It *de-com-po-ses*.'

Having gathered so much about Loulou's working habits, Flavia walked home by way of St-Jean. On the waterfront she ran into the most assiduous of her mother's winter acquaintances who greeted her with an exhibition of surprise.

'Well, well, our bookworm in person. In broad daylight what's more— and looking very charming in it too. To what do we owe the honour?'

'I'm having a holiday.' Flavia said.

'I fully understand: the day not being Sunday.'

Flavia gave him marks for memory.

'What excuse have you got to offer for not coming home with us for lunch?'

Flavia hesitated.

'Caught you. My wife's shopping over there, let's get out of the sun.' He steered her towards an awning. 'We can look at the ships from here.'

Albert Fournier was a slightly paunchy man, probably in his fifties, with silvery hair and a soft, handsome and not un-

intelligent face marred by a fatuous smile. He might have
been a minor orator, not quite in the senate, nor yet on the
stage, more likely at the Bar of some prosperous provincial
town; in fact he had made his early and relatively modest
pile in some wholesale business. He was a well if conventionally educated man, and a man of various interests and
hobbies. Flavia spent a not uncompanionable quarter hour
with him talking mast ratio and tonnage. He drank a *pastis*,
she a *citron pressé*. When Mme Fournier joined them, Flavia
rose and relieved her of her market basket; Fournier did
neither.

She was a plumpish woman, about ten years younger
than her husband and still moderately pretty. She had a fine
head of chestnut hair, protruding eyes and an upturned
nose; she wore patches of rouge on her cheeks, high-heeled
sandals (to Flavia's disgust) and a tight cotton dress. The
whole looked a good deal less awful than the parts. She, too,
greeted Flavia with exclamations and innuendo.

'So mademoiselle is no longer burning the midnight oil?
La vie de bohème seems to suit you, you're *en beauté, ma petite*.'

Flavia automatically scowled.

Fournier said, '*Bohème?* I'd call it *la vie de millionnaire*.'

'*Les artistes restent les artistes*,' said his wife.

Bouvard et Pécuchet, Flavia said, not aloud.

'A little bird tells me— oh, St-Jean is full of them— you
are dining every night at that great barrack of a house."

'*Peinture à l'huile— cuisine au beurre*,' said Flavia.

'*Comment?*'

But her husband laughed.

'And do you have any news,' she said— he gave her a
look, 'Oh, news, I mean new, you know——'

'Too much of it in the papers,' he said,

'Indeed,' said his wife.

'Which ones do you read?' said Flavia.

In her own house (a villa furnished to the last square inch)
Mme Fournier changed into a punctilious, even formal

hostess. She addressed her young guest with civilities suitable
for a personage of advanced years and uncertain appetite.
Just the simplest little *déjeuner à l'improviste*, you must excuse
us. May I persuade you— another morsel? I'm afraid there
isn't anything very exciting to follow. Flavia responded like a
well-behaved little girl. Fournier, more relaxed himself,
observed them with detachment. When he had had enough
he said, '*Ça va*, Rosette,' and started a conversation.

It was an ordinary conversation, not an interrogatory; for
the first time since Flavia had known the Fourniers, they did
not try to draw her out. If they didn't keep off personal remarks at least they asked no questions; personal subjects
were ignored or dropped. They did float up (because they
were avoided?). Mention travel, and it led to a woman
travelling alone; lending a novel, to a circular room full of
books— there was that underswell.

Fournier talked to Flavia about her own reading; she
must promise to come back soon, they told her, they were
expecting a houseful on the *Quatorze Juillet*, nephews and
nieces, young married people, *des universitaires*, they will be
interested to meet you.

Flavia had a sense that they were trying to flatter her,
butter her up; she didn't like it, she didn't like the Fourniers
enough. She felt vaguely uneasy, wishing she had not come.

One of their nephews, they told her, had just got his
degree in agronomics, he was going to teach, he couldn't
afford to farm.

'I thought farming in France paid well?'

'For farmers perhaps,' Fournier said, 'not for young men
with theories.'

'You need a fortune to farm with those, some people have
all the luck. Well, live and let live, that's my motto, isn't it,
Albert?'

'As long as you can see them doing it, *ma chère*.'

Just when Flavia felt that she could decently leave, her
host said that he would like to show her something.

'Oh, Albert, you're not going to do that, she doesn't want to see your bricks.'

Fournier led Flavia through a back door to an outhouse. He opened the door to a large room completely bare except for a vast trestle-table that filled it from wall to wall. This table was covered with what looked like a toy village, or rather a toy landscape for there were rivers and hillsides and boundaries and hundreds and hundreds of minute patches of green in every geometrical shape and minute model manor houses and châteaux and farms. Flavia stepped forward, looked: looked at her host, looked at the toy landscape— it was a homemade, handmade relief map of the vineyards of France.

She ran a finger up the pale blue painted ribbon that was the Rhône, came to the Saône, touched the Côte de Beaune, the Côte de Nuits, bent to read the microscopic legends on the sign-flags, Corton-Charlemagne— Chambolle-Musigny — '*Oh, oh, oh.*'

'. . . and it's so . . . delicate. Oh. . . . *You* made it yourself? It must have taken years and years——? Is it all there——? Is it accurate? Is it complete?'

He said it *had* taken years. He was still making corrections; he was doing his best to keep it up to date.

'May I?'

'What, my dear?'

'Look at it?'

'You are looking at it.'

'I mean longer . . . slowly.'

He showed her the cases with other small flags on pins: these he used in the autumn to mark the beginning of the vintages, and the card-index where he kept the regional weather reports year before year.

Flavia said, 'It must be a bit like . . . being a don.'

He handed her a magnifying glass. The sign-flags showed the average annual yields. Chateau Branaire-Ducru 100 tonneaux. Giscours 20 tonneaux. Lascombes 35.

'A tonneau is four hogshead, isn't it, about twenty-five gallons?'

When she did leave Mme Fournier was on the front doorstep. Flavia thanked her. 'Now you promise to come again?' 'I will.' 'To meet our young people.' 'The young people?'

As Flavia was about to trot down the drive she told herself, The world is not full of bugbears. Next moment she nearly tripped over her espadrilles, the lacing had got undone; as she was stopping to tie it again she heard Mme Fournier's voice, always strident, from inside.

'First time that thing's been of some use!'

And his voice now, too, angry and loud, 'Rosette— one day I will strangle you.'

'Unless you have a stroke first, *cher*.'

'One thing, I'm not going to help you use that girl.'

'Suit yourself. I don't think I'm going to need you.'

                                  II

For Flavia these were social days. Days of social thin ice. Or not? There was no one to ask. One evening Loulou had arrived. He looked almost exactly (had kept up looking?) like the full-length self-portrait of some twelve years ago. The stance, so rugged, so burly, so male, little-boy male; the scrubbed primary coloured clothes, the cotton trousers with the buckled belt, the brilliant shirt, the rolled up sleeves. And the head, the solid round head with the thick short hair, the smooth round face with the innocent look, the sturdy look, the poet's look— the sad, slanting eyes.

He seized Flavia by the shoulders and shook her, looked into her face and bellowed, 'So that's the little girl who reads Voltaire at the bistro.'

She grinned at him. She felt, it did happen to her with strangers, immediate sympathy: she liked him.

Loulou charged up to each new arrival, thumping and hugging in a demonstrative greeting. That over, the vitality seemed to go flat; he remained a centre, yet had little else to say. Good to see you, Loulou—— Tell us, Loulou—— Well then, Loulou——

Dinner was served. The host filled glasses, made a show with the carving things, held out his plate. Flavia saw that he ate and drank very little.

'How was Cap-Ferrat?'

'Hot.'

'How was Venice?'

'Hotter.'

'How is Fabrice?'

'Bearing up.'

'How is Marie-Rose?'

'Carrying on.'

'Have you finished her?'

Loulou made a gesture, 'Finished . . . Who ever does? Except that fellow Van Dongen.'

'But you sold it, Loulou?'

'Sold it. The viscount paid in advance.'

Therese said, 'He brought the photographs, *c'est une belle toile.*'

Paul said, 'She's right, it's a good Loulou, even a spectacular Loulou.'

'Oh, shut up,' Loulou said. His own words were *taisez-vous*, which was more gentle and sad.

Flavia, in two or three minds, looked on. The painter——? *L'uomo simpatico*——? Therese's husband——? What do married people tell each other? Is it . . . am I, worth telling about? What does he know, what does he think? What does she think for that matter? Is it better or worse or nothing because I am a woman? Here they are— their words, their faces, but what, oh what, goes on behind people's skulls? And here are *my* words and face.

'Yes, thank you. I will, thank you. Go to Toulon to

the *bal musette*? All of us? Too late? Yes, oh no, I'd love to.'

'Loulou is tired,' Therese said.

'No more than usual— we're all tired— the whole world is tired. Not that one,' he pointed at Flavia, 'that's not her problem yet.'

Manners are supposed to help carry things off. But what kind of manners? What is the code? Is there a code for this? Constanza says that the novel plays such a part in shaping social behaviour. Perhaps the novel has not caught up?

'What are you giggling about, Flavia?'

'Aspects of the novel.'

They went in two cars, Giles' and Therese's, Loulou's Buick being turned down as too showy for the quarter. But the Bugatti is even longer, said Flavia, look at the bonnet. That's all right they told her, everyone loves a sports car.

Loulou danced twice with Flavia, once with Therese and twice with Jeannine and sat down for good after that; Flavia danced also with Giles, with Paul and with Therese who was able to show the steps. Therese danced also with Bobbie and Paul; but most of the time the women in their party danced with the men who between dances stood watching against the wall. Many of them were sailors.

Therese had explained the rule here that a girl must either accept to dance with everyone who asked her or not get up at all. The band was two accordions and the tunes were *chaloupés* and *javas valsées*, penetrating, jerky, fast, and they were danced with extreme devotion and virtuosity. The dancers did not speak. The place smelt of caporal tobacco and hot light bulbs. There were a few wooden tables and benches and those who occupied them drank *diabolo*, white wine clouded with *crème de menthe*. The men against the wall drank little or nothing, and the most serious devotees danced chiefly with one another. Therese was much sought; one time the other couples stopped and fell back, and she and her partner, a slight man with a pock-marked face, received a solemn ovation.

On their way home they first dropped Jeannine. Loulou flung his arms about her and kissed her lovingly on the mouth. '*Ah, la belle fille——*'

'Hurry up, Loulou,' Paul said, 'we still have Bobbie and Flavia.'

On her own doorstep Flavia, relieved to know the form, returned Loulou's kiss with pleasure. Turning away she called, '*Ah, le beau garçon——*'

For the second time that month Flavia slept late. When she got to her desk she saw that it would not do; it was not an essay day but at that rate there would be no essay to write; she had not done her week's reading. She cut out her morning bathe, cut down her luncheon to minutes, stuck to work till the end of the afternoon (Concentrate, Don't stop: if Michel can do *his* kind of reading in an open car in the street . . .). She could not keep from the house on the bay but went late for a brief evening swim and, elated with resolution, left soon after dinner. Loulou saw her to the gate. He did not kiss her good night. It flashed through her, He only kisses in public.

By the end of the next day Flavia had caught up with her work.

'Where are they? Where's Loulou?'

'Loulou is trying to paint.'

'Trying——?' said Flavia.

'They've had a row,' said Jeannine.

'Oh.'

'Therese doesn't want him to go off to paint the Belgian ambassador's wife.'

'Belgian minister's wife,' said Giles.

'Don't spoil Loulou's fun.'

'Why doesn't she want him to?'

'For one thing she thinks he needs a rest and the children will be very disappointed.'

'And the second thing?'

Jeannine shrugged.

Giles said, 'The whole set-up is not for her.'

'Loulou wants her to go with him,' said Jeannine.

'Can you see her?'

'Therese could go anywhere,' said Flavia.

'Indeed,' said Giles. 'Anywhere she wants to. She doesn't want to.'

'Loulou is a very attractive man— he *is*, isn't he?'

Giles laughed. 'How would I know? Don't you know for yourself, Flavia?'

'Oh, I do think so, I want to know if he's considered so?'

'He *is* considered so,' said Jeannine.

'By the Belgian minister's wife?'

'I shouldn't be surprised.'

'And is he . . . fond of her?'

'Loulou's fond of everyone.'

'You mean, not *really* fond?'

'Quite.'

'Except Therese,' said Jeannine.

'Ah, yes, except Therese.'

'So it isn't that she . . . objects to?'

'Therese and Loulou,' said Giles, 'have been married a long time. They understand each other.'

'I see,' said Flavia. Presently she said, 'Then why did they have a row?'

'She thinks it's bad for him to go up there, the North, he really hates that country——'

'The country of his youth,' said Jeannine.

'But he was born in Rumania— Larousse says so? I thought that is why his long name ends in ov.'

'His father and mother immigrated when he was two. They came to France to find work.'

'In a cable factory and the mines.'

'Did Loulou wish they'd come and settled here in the Mîdi instead?'

'They would have starved in the Mîdi.'

'Are his parents alive?'

'Very nicely set up, thanks to Therese.'

'And now he goes back to paint the Belgian ambassador?'

'Therese feels that it's, well, unnecessary.'

'At any rate she wants him to work less hard.'

'To work *less*. She thinks they don't need all that money.'

'But she spends it,' Jeannine said. 'Therese is insanely generous.'

'But she doesn't *like* money and she doesn't like him to like it. She doesn't want Loulou to want the things he wants: for her it's a weakness, Therese is a moralist——'

'A moralist somewhat disguised,' said Jeannine.

'Not an obvious one, but mark you, Flavia, a moralist.'

'Yes,' Flavia said, 'a moralist at the core—— I think I know someone else like that.'

'You must have had a full life?'

'Oh, I suppose in a way I had.'

'Therese, I went to a party last night.'

Therese absently but kindly said, 'Good.'

'A *soirée*: young people, dozens of them.'

'Very good.'

'There was peach cup— that was very good; and we played guessing games and I won three times and later on they rolled up the carpet— figuratively— we just went out on the terrace and turned on the gramophone and danced.'

'You enjoyed that, coco?'

'Quite.'

'Therese, I'm going dancing again tonight.'

'Splendid.'

'I've taken to it.'

'What, coco?'

'Dancing. It's conducive to thought.'

Therese let that pass. Then, waking to responsibility, 'You are *not* going dancing in Toulon?'

'Nothing like it. I told you— paper-games first, *young* people, students, they're all going to be professors and head-mistresses the day after tomorrow.'

These members of her own generation, give a few years, were undeniably pleasant, serious, clever. A long chalk from resort children. A long chalk, also, it would appear from their aunt, Rosette Fournier. There were the agronomist nephew and his wife who was already a schoolmarm, two younger brothers, one having finished his *philo*, the other his *service militaire*, a niece who was at the Sorbonne and her fiancé reading economics at the university of Rennes. They were staying in the house and were joined almost daily by a number of their friends on holiday on the coast.

Articulate, easy to be with; filled with ideas and knowledge; nor could anyone say that they were a bad-looking lot, the young men got their sun-burn, the girls were pretty and well-turned out. Surely they *must be* interesting? Flavia enjoyed the paper-games and, as she had said, the dancing; she went nearly as often as she was asked (Better not hang about too much in the house on the bay); she enjoyed the company . . . moderately. Not one of them struck her fire. Recently we have been learning that young animals, puppy dogs, even a giraffe, brought up exclusively by humans will be unable later on to identify themselves or establish emotional contact with their own species. Thus Flavia was unable to feel a sense of kinship with people who were not decisively older than herself, who were not real grown-ups as she still called them.

On one occasion she caught her host's eye. He responded. 'It's still here. I keep it locked up these days.'

'You think I might——?'

'Slip out? Come along then. No, I tell you what, I am going to show you the place where I hide the key. Then you can go by yourself whenever you want to.'

'How kind,' she said, 'how kind people are trusting me with their keys.'

So sometimes she would sit out a dance or two by herself in the outhouse, by the Gironde, by the Garonne, in the Haut-Médoc, the Graves, Entre-Deux-Mers. She wondered if her father had ever been there? really been there, in the flesh?

One night after shuffling absently through a foxtrot, Flavia was walked a few steps into the garden by her partner and given a kiss, she quite cheerfully accepting this custom of the country.   *Bocca bacciata non perde ventura.* . . .

Two dances later (had word got round?) another partner, it was the philosophy brother— or could it be the soldier brother?— kissed her. Unlike Loulou, this young man did not stop but began to kiss again. Flavia stepped back smartly. In a clear voice she said, 'What's all that about?'

The young man faltered, but managed, 'If you'll only let me show you——'

Flavia looked at him, but it was too dark for him to see her face: she had to add, '*What* do you think you are doing?'

'*Eh, ben*— I thought— I——'

'You don't want to go to bed with me?' Flavia continued in ringing tones.

The young man faltered again.

'No, you don't. You hardly know me, you know nothing about me, you don't like me enough. I don't like you enough.'

The young man had recovered enough to sulk. 'Oh— *L'amour.*'

'We are not talking about *l'amour*,' Flavia said, keeping the stern face he could not see. 'I'm talking about liking people, liking them enough to be friends. Going to bed with one's friends doesn't matter; but one's got to *be* friends.'

'Quite a speech,' he said.

'I'm not unsurprised myself.'

The young man said, 'You are a funny sort of girl.'

Flavia still wonderfully cool, said, 'That's as may be. Now if you wanted to sleep with someone just to find out about it, I can understand that, but surely you are . . . beyond that stage?'

For the first time, the boy laughed, 'You're right there.'

'So why don't you go and find a girl you really like and who likes you very much.' She added kindly, 'It shouldn't be difficult for you, you are good-looking, aren't you? There are plenty of pretty girls just now, the beaches are full of them.'

'I was out dancing again last night.'

'Did you enjoy yourself, coco?'

'I did rather. I found I had a code.'

'What did you say?'

'A code of behaviour.'

'You are hopeless. But what were you doing?'

'Dancing at the Fourniers.'

'The Fourniers? Have you been going *there*?'

'About three times a week. But you knew?'

'You didn't say so.'

'You didn't ask me.'

'I don't ask you where you are going, coco,' Therese said.

'True enough,' said Flavia. 'Anything wrong with my going to the Fourniers?'

'None of my business.'

'But you don't like it?'

Therese admitted as much.

'*He* isn't so bad, you know, I could tell you something about him——'

Therese dismissed them, '*Ce sont des bourgeois.*'

There were too many angles to that. Flavia remained silent.

Presently Therese said, 'Come out in the boat with me.'

'Tomorrow?'

'Yes.'

'What about the mistral?'

'There won't be mistral. We are going to the islands.'

'A picnic?'

'We'll take one.'

'The boys will like that.'

'The boys are not going.'

'Who is going?'

'You and I.'

It was a clear day. They sailed, they landed, swam from rocks in clear water. They found a place in the shade to take their bread, fruit and wine.

'Does anyone come to this island?'

'Only the shepherd and not this time of the year.'

The afternoon was hot and still; timeless. Flavia said, '*E poi* non *se muove.*'

Therese said, '*Comme j'aime ce pays.*'

Presently Flavia said, 'I did miss you so.' Therese said kindly, 'So did I, mon coco.' And added, 'Don't worry about things, there is nothing to worry about.'

'Very well then, I shan't.' To herself she said, I trust you. And then, quietly, intensely, 'I do like you, Therese, I like you very much.'

Therese touched Flavia's cheek, '*T'es un brave cœur.*'

Oddly moved, oddly comforted, Flavia said, 'Oh, I do hope so.'

They saw the sky. Time to go? They went into the sea once more, then ate the last of the fruit. As Therese untied the boat, Flavia said, 'I would like to come back here.'

Therese said, 'Oh, you will.'

'Loulou has put off his journey.' The engine was on now and they were running smoothly towards the mainland.

'He is not going to Belgium?'

'He is going to stay here for a while.'

'Oh, Therese, I am glad. That was what you wanted, isn't it?'

'He needs the rest.'

'Will he do a . . . still-life?'

'Possibly. One doesn't ask Loulou about his work.'

'Therese— I am fond of Loulou.'

'He likes you, too.'

'Up to a point?'

'Oh, you know what Loulou is, he needs a hundred people.'

Presently Flavia said, 'Doesn't he come out with you, doesn't he come to the island?'

'He's never been out in the boat. He hates the sea. Some people do.'

'The boys don't, they're going to be sailors. Do they mean the navy or having their own fishing-boat?'

'At the moment Pierrot wants to be captain of a transatlantic liner and the twins are going to be purser and head steward.'

'The Loulou gang.'

Therese said, 'Life is not going to be easy for them, an artist's sons. They are giving Loulou the *Légion d'Honneur*, you haven't heard? It's going to be announced in the autumn.'

'May I congratulate him now? *Tiens, Monsieur est décoré!* He'll have a red ribbon to his buttonhole— but he doesn't wear a coat, what will he do? Can you wear *le ruban* on a shirt? But I do say good for France to honour artists.'

'Loulou has a dress-coat,' Therese said in an expressionless tone.

'Therese——' Flavia had been exercised by this. 'You believe you never tell me what to do, and then you are suddenly shocked. Like by my going to the Fourniers. I think you are right. I've never felt . . . comfortable with them, and I think I had a kind of lesson, I'm going to stop going to their house. Oh, not rudely suddenly, just less often, tapering off.'

Therese thought, then committed herself, 'That would be my instinct.'

'Agreed then, no more *soirées*. Yet I still don't understand *you*— remember when you put a stop to my having dinner *Chez Auguste*?'

'Oh, that.'

'You mean it didn't matter? It mattered less than the Fourniers?'

'It wasn't suitable.'

'That's exactly what you said. Now you tell me that the Fourniers are bourgeois, well, *Chez Auguste* wasn't *that*.'

'Nothing to do with it,' Therese said. 'It wasn't right because of what people might say— seeing you there night after night eating alone, they might have said you had been abandoned.'

'*What people might say*— from *you*? Now isn't that bourgeois?'

Therese said, '*Mon petit*, the people who talk don't matter, I wasn't thinking of them, I was thinking of your mother, of what they might be saying about *her*.'

'Isn't that precisely what the bourgeois do— thinking of their mothers?'

Therese said with some ferocity, 'They think of themselves.'

CHAPTER FIVE

Friday   Saturday   Sunday

I

The car that drew up outside the villa at sunset was of an obsolete make, long in the bonnet, high on the wheels, cared for, faintly absurd, the kind of car that nowadays would be called vintage. Flavia, looking from an upper window, saw it, saw it on the exact spot where she had first seen Michel, experienced confusion, incredulous joy, a pang. Then she perceived Rosette Fournier, who normally drove a Peugeot saloon, in the passenger seat.

Flavia pulled on the clothes she had been about to change into and ran downstairs. Mme Fournier was still in the car, she called out that she had only come to deliver a message. Flavia approached.

Rosette Fournier was not alone, next to her at the wheel Flavia saw the clear-cut profile of another woman. It was a classic profile, with the smooth texture, the pure line, of an artefact, finished, perfect, austere. Set against the high side-window of the open car and the evening sky, the effect was extraordinary, the portrait, Flavia thought she saw, of Isabella d'Este.

Ought to be scolding you, Rosette Fournier was saying, the way you've forgotten us— well, here I am with an olive branch——

The stranger at the wheel turned her face, Flavia saw grey eyes, deep-set and large, the small full mouth boldly designed, the helmet of burnished curls.

Rosette Fournier in unwontedly off-hand style said, 'Flavia— Andrée.'

The stranger directed a look of open interest upon her. Flavia gravely bowed.

— A little party— just a few friends— we are counting on you— tomorrow——

They were gone. Flavia managed to recall that she had been asked to dinner and that the time was eight. She believed that she had accepted.

Several times that evening at Therese's house, Flavia was on the point of saying, Rosette Fournier turned up with an apparition— who can she be? Or, The Fourniers have got hold of a rare bird, you know. Each time she felt that she could not say it.

II

The stranger stood in the Fournier's drawing-room in a simple white dress and some jewellery. Practically a tennis dress, Flavia noted with approval, having no idea who had made it, nor indeed that it was made, nor how much it must have cost. The stranger was neither short nor tall, and very thin, with a figure of the 'Twenties, slightly spidery, ineluctably elegant. Her skin was honey-coloured and, except for having probably retraced her mouth and eyebrows, she wore very little make-up for the time. The age that Flavia gave her was Constanza's, perhaps a few years more.

Fournier, having greeted Flavia, led her forward, his wife called out in her sharp way, 'They *have* met.'

The stranger held out her hand with a brief unseeing glance, then turned to resume a conversation.

It was a formal French dinner-party: best china, a second maid to wait at table, three wines. The stranger sat at her host's right. Flavia, from her distance among the hoi polloi, observed that only Mme Fournier used her Christian name, everybody else, including the host, addressed her as Madame. The atmosphere— at least until the second course got going

— was stilted, the elder generation on their best behaviour, the younger, if a shade sceptically, following suit. The stranger was talking, the voice was metallic and occasionally high: The tone, Flavia thought she was able to discern, was wordly: a worldly French voice.

Animation gained, everybody began to talk, Flavia could no longer hear; she only looked.

Her neighbour, after helping himself well to leg of mutton as the vast dish had at last come round to him, said (confirming her), 'Our guest of honour is a real *femme du monde.*'

Flavia clamped down on herself. No pumping, no questions. Nevertheless it was not too dishonourable to keep this line of conversation from fading out, so she said, 'You don't like them?'

'Frankly— no. I admit that Tante Rosette has produced a wonderfully decorative specimen.'

'Decorative——?' said Flavia.

'Precisely. The surface is all right. But you don't want to have to look at a woman too much— it's too romantic.'

'Perhaps it is that,' said Flavia.

The burgundy was going round.

'Well at least we've got this beano thanks to her— Aunt's been planning it for weeks, ever since she heard that this lady might be coming down here, you'd think she were dining the *Prince des Galles.*'

'She is not staying at the house then?'

'Gracious, no. At the hotel at Bandol. Aunt knew her at school; Aunt went to a posh boarding-school— only for a year or two— and she likes you to know it. It seems that this Andrée woman was the star turn there, won all the prizes, played all the parts, set the fashion or whatever it is they look up to at those girl schools, you should know.'

'I do not,' Flavia said firmly.

The stranger was talking with vivacity; she was eating little and without attention; her wine-glasses were untouched. The pomegranate mouth still glowed impeccably, the sculptured curls lay smooth; people were beginning to look flushed, she remained a fount of coolness.

'Mademoiselle Flavia——' her neighbour said.

'Flavia.'

'Then you do like me well enough——?'

'I loathe being called Mademoiselle.'

'Because you can't wait for the time when you'll be a married woman?'

Fournier, who was keeping an eye on their end of the table, called, 'Look after young Flavia's glass— she likes her tipple.'

The young man complied.

'I wonder why she came, though?' he said, '*she* doesn't look as if she needed a free meal. It couldn't be for my uncle's charms, or could it? Aunt hasn't let on much about her chum.'

No questions. Not those sort of questions. *Not* like the Fourniers.

'I gather though that she's not exactly a woman without a history— I daresay Aunt exaggerates— and rather at a loose end at present.'

There was champagne with the ice-pudding. Flavia and the young man gulped their first glass.

'Flavia,' he said, 'I do like you— may I? I've been thinking of what you said the other night, about being friends first. It means you are not to use people, doesn't it?'

The stranger had not once glanced in their direction.

'You think we could be friends? At least try to be friends——?'

'What were you saying?'

The men rose with the ladies. Coffee and liqueurs in the drawing-room.

'I'll have some brandy, please,' Flavia said.

The stranger had been settled on the sofa. Glass in hand and very quickly Flavia walked across the room and took the still empty seat beside her.

'Madame . . .'

But it was the stranger after all who began the conversation.

'Yes, do come and talk to me,' she said in English.

'Strike me pink,' said Flavia.

'I've heard so much about you.' She vaguely indicated the room at large.

'Good, I hope?' said Flavia.

'Oh, *only* good.' The stranger's smile was not easy to interpret. Contemptuous? plain cynical? cool, amused? 'What else? You live alone, you are industrious, you are well-read, you are a gourmet— as I can see.' It was fluent educated English and the accent had only a trace of French as well as a trace of English nanny.

Flavia took a swig from her balloon glass. 'I am rather fond of decent brandy.' In point of fact she had hardly tasted any before.

'Tell me about yourself,' the stranger said.

Flavia did. 'History is going to be my subject— modern history—— Of course it's a frightfully easy degree, but it happens to be what I'm most interested in' (even as she was uttering the words she was aghast), 'that, and literature naturally, and political journalism.'

'You are so right,' the stranger said, always with that look of persiflage upon her face, 'there is nothing to a degree, unless you are a complete clod, I got mine for a bet——'

'No——?'

'At Aix university.'

'You mean that you are . . . you are——?'

'Nothing at all, thank God. I told you I did it for a bet.'

'What was your subject?'

'I've forgotten.'

'But it is true?' Flavia said. 'The degree?'

'Yes, oh, yes. But you mustn't be naïve. It doesn't suit you. It doesn't suit young people. Go on, tell me more.'

'Well, you see, it is now more than ever that practising

politicians need the help of disinterested trained his-
torians——'

'My dear, *not* about your ideas, about your circumstances—— they appear to be more unusual.'

Flavia taking her own line said boldly, '*I* would like to
talk about *you*.'

'Have you anything original to add to the subject?'

Her eyes on the stranger's face, Flavia said, 'Nothing
original, I'm afraid. I could quote, though; there's a choice
of sonnets.'

'No, thank you.'

Flavia said, 'You seem to enjoy neither poetry nor ideas.'

'Oh, quite.'

'What do you enjoy?'

Again the stranger's expression was not easy to interpret.
'People,' she said.

Presently one of the young men came to Flavia 'We want
to dance, we need support, Aunt Rosette is against it, won't
you go and ask Uncle Albert?'

Flavia looked helpless.

'Don't you see,' the stranger said, 'she doesn't want to
wheedle your Uncle Albert into winding up the gramophone,
she wants to sit and talk to *me* like a civilized person. Go
away.'

When the drink tray came round again she accepted a
glass of fresh orangeade. Flavia had just sense enough to
refuse to have her glass refilled.

'Don't you ever——?'

'Drink? No. It makes one miss so much.' She looked about
her. 'This party.'

'You mean that you . . . enjoy being the only sober person
here tonight?'

'The only *entirely* sober person. Oh, I think we ought to
except our hostess,' she added with a curious air of satisfac-
tion, 'Rosette knows how to keep a clear head, a remarkably
clear head.'

Flavia managed to monopolize the guest of honour for the rest of the evening. When there were signs of breaking up, she said, 'Let me take you home.'

The stranger gave her a look. 'Towing my car as well?'

Flavia hung her head. 'I meant in a taxi.'

'Cruising in the olive groves, no doubt, at twenty-five minutes past midnight?' Flavia looked deflated. The stranger ceased to rub it in. 'May I take *you* home?' she said.

Flavia meekly followed, She sat wordlessly, gazing at the profile of the woman at the wheel. The drive lasted only a few minutes. Getting out, Flavia said dully, 'Thank you very much for giving me a lift.'

The stranger said, using French, '*Merci pour la bonne soirée.*'

III

Next morning Flavia did not sleep late. She woke early stabbed by wretchedness. As the high points of last night's blustering and boasting passed through her mind one by one, she groaned aloud. *Oh, God.* And sticking to that sofa! The Fourniers must have been mad— I have ruined their party. Why did they let me?

Veritas? Another recollection— *oh.*

She will never want to see me again. I cannot bear seeing her again.

At the moment Flavia could not bear herself. She ate some breakfast. Work was out of the question, she could not think about it; she did not dare go to the tower, she felt she had damaged something: loose talk means hubris.

She hung about the villa. The day being Sunday there was no femme de ménage; there was also nothing to do.

Presently she heard a klaxon, two slight short blasts like a morse signal— the stranger: Andrée, in person. For a moment Flavia believed that she had come to scold her and cringed. Pulling herself together she went out.

'Hello, good morning, I've come to give you a driving lesson. Not an unuseful accomplishment for people who want to see ladies home.'

Flavia said with a certain dignity, 'I'm under age for driving. And I want to apologize for last night, I made an awful ass of myself, I am sorry.'

'My dear, you made my evening— that ghastly gathering — don't give it another thought.'

Flavia said, 'You are too kind.' In the disenchanted mood of that morning it went through her: She is not. Whatever she is, she is not that.

Something made her say, 'The Fourniers took a great deal of trouble.'

'They certainly did.' She gave a hard look at Flavia and said in a hard tone, 'Now you're not going to break a lance for Rosette Fournier? You are not going to tell me that you like her? You know perfectly well that you don't. It's not your milieu, neither yours nor mine, so don't let's pretend.'

'But you went there?'

Andrée brushed it off. 'As one does. I went. You went. We're quits. Only don't wax sentimental over their hospitality, just thinking of it gives me indigestion. And now aren't you going to ask me in?'

Flavia opened the gate. 'It's a beastly place.'

'So I can see. You chose it, I presume?'

Flavia did not answer.

They went into the dining-room. Flavia saw Andrée glance at the square of oil-cloth off which she ate her meals.

'And you also pursue your studies in the *salle à manger*?'

'I don't work in the house, I don't work here.'

'Where do you work?'

'In a place someone lent me,' Flavia said with a closed face.

Andrée let it pass.

Flavia took the chance of changing the conversation. 'Are you going to stay here long?'

'I don't expect to.' Her voice had become fuller. 'I'm here to do a job.'

'Didn't you say you did nothing?'

'I do give that impression, don't I? I turn my hand to a job now and then.' Again that elusive air of enjoyment. 'Call it a mission.'

'A secret mission?'

'Of course. I'm staying as long as it takes. I'd give it a week; the inside of a week.'

Presently she said, 'Now I mustn't keep you, I only sought you out in your lair because this benighted village boasts no telephone, one has to be one's own messenger— well, as they say, *on est jamais mieux servi que par soi-même*. Will you come and have dinner with me?'

Flavia said, 'If you really want me to——?'

'Now you are forcing me into the most obvious remark of the week: I only do what I want— within our poor human limits. Tonight, then.'

'Tonight?'

'I told you there isn't much time. Eight-fifteen, shall we say? At my hotel?'

Andrée reversed the great car with a minimum of effort. 'I have a suite, if it's a fine night— it's never anything else in these damned summers down here— we'll dine upstairs on my balcony— much more romantic, don't you agree?' That was her parting shot.

Flavia spent most of her day puzzling about the stranger.

It crossed her mind that she might be a woman spy— like Mata Hari. She dismissed the thought as childish.

IV

There was a half-bottle of champagne in an ice-bucket and two glasses. Flavia, though glad to see it, felt obscurely affronted. Not as if it were Mr James giving a treat. This is out of place, not a . . . true gesture.

'Help yourself. Only one and a half drops for me.'

Flavia did as she was told; then tried not to drink too fast.

Andrée handed her the menu. 'Order our dinner.'

With a revival of pleasure, Flavia took it. 'Now, then——'
It was an international hotel menu of the kind Flavia was familiar with from her grandmother's days, impressive enough though the variety of dishes would exceed the variety of tastes. Perhaps Andrée was not aware of that? Yes, of course she must be, only she didn't care, she looked down on food: there was no fun in it.

Flavia put the menu aside. 'But you won't enjoy it.'

'Very likely not, but that doesn't dispense me from taking nourishment at regular intervals, nor other people from cooking and serving and ordering it for me.' She refilled Flavia's glass. 'Now go and choose a dinner for someone who is not interested in food— it's not the last time that is going to happen to you, my dear.'

Flavia gave her mind to it.

When the waiter came, Andrée referred him to her.

'You are putting me through my paces,' Flavia said evenly.

She ordered consommé madrilène, sole florentine and framboise nature.

'Quelques pommes vapeur?'

'No potatoes.'

'Une salade?'

'No salad.'

'A little chantilly with the raspberries?'

'No cream.'

'Very good, mademoiselle. Et comme boisson?'

Without a glance at Andrée, Flavia took the wine-list. 'Half a bottle of number 32, cooled,' 32 was a dry Graves, 'and a bottle of Evian water.'

'Coffee?'

'We'll ring for coffee.'

'Your French is not bad,' Andrée said when the waiter had gone.

Flavia gave her a somewhat grim look.

'You mustn't make faces at people, my dear; you look like a dog that's baring it's teeth. Drink up, finish your bottle.'

'No thank you,' said Flavia.

'My dear, not dog— bull-dog.' But sensing perhaps the hostility in Flavia, she added, 'I tease too hard— forgive me.'

Her eyes on Andrée, Flavia said, 'I cannot . . . understand you.'

'You do drive one into uttering banalities. *Is* it usual to understand anyone— I'm not even referring to my enigmatic self— at one's second meeting?'

'Fourth meeting,' Flavia said.

Andrée took that one in.

They sat down to dinner.

'I asked for it,' Flavia said, 'the teasing and all, after the way I pretended I could get you a taxi.'

'That was charming of you— it showed such a chivalrous nature. You are half Italian, aren't you?'

'Quarter.'

'How is that?'

'Too complicated.'

'But there is an Italian grandfather?'

'Yes.'

'Who is quite ill?'

'No,' said Flavia, 'I mean yes.'

'Read any good books lately?'

Flavia laughed.

'At least you are not stupid,' Andrée said.

'Nor are you.'

'Pour me some Evian.'

'Has anyone ever told you——'

'Probably.'

'Has anyone done your portrait, I mean a modern painter?'

'Others are hardly available,' said Andrée.

'Have you never thought of Loulou? I think Loulou could do you— he's very good with eyes.'

'Ah, poor Loulou. He does everybody nowadays. Oh, I forget you know him— and that extraordinary wife of his.'

'Therese *is* a truly extraordinary woman.'

'My dear, how loyal, how English!' Then, suddenly, brutally, 'Do you sleep with her?'

Such was Flavia's pride in the fact that she answered smugly, 'That is my business.'

Andrée said, 'I thought so.'

Flavia did not speak.

'A vastly overestimated pastime, or isn't that what you call it? Perhaps it still has the charm of novelty?'

Flavia still said nothing.

'Do you loathe me?'

Flavia nearly answered, I do, I do loathe you. But would have had to add, A part of me does. Instead she said, 'Your bark may be worse than your bite. I hope it is.'

Andrée seemed delighted. 'You've only had my bark; so far.'

Presently, as if seized by sudden revelation, Flavia put down her knife and fork. She said in a neutral voice, 'Why do you bother with me?'

'What an elegant way of putting it.'

'I bore you, I could only bore you.'

'On the contrary,' said Andrée.

'I am nothing.' Flavia spoke with both humility and coldness. 'I have no . . . merits yet; and what I want to be would be nothing to you.'

'How can you be so certain?'

'You are not interested in anything I'm interested in.'

Then Andrée saw that Flavia was near tears.

'If I told you that you had a good many things I am interested in?'

'I wouldn't believe you,' said Flavia.

'*Don't underrate yourself.*'

Flavia looked up.

'I have a pretty good idea of how you see me.' Andrée's voice had changed to a lower key, that air of persiflage was gone. 'I can almost read your thoughts— yes, you are transparent, my dear— has it occurred to you that what you see and hear, my bark, might be a façade? You are a very intelligent girl and you have read a great deal— no, I mean it; one thing you can't say is that I have been trying to flatter you— but you don't know everything, you don't know the French, the real French (though the Fourniers are quite an example of one kind), you can have no idea of what life among us is like, the attitudes, the demands; if you like, the values. You have no idea, have you, what my life's been like?'

'No,' said Flavia.

'In a hard school, a façade is a protection. The favourite French façade is bonhomie, that perpetual guzzling: *la chaleur des après-diners*, and the *couchage*. Well, that doesn't happen to be my style, my choice of façade. The pursuit of good living is not the innocent thing you would like it to be, my dear; you weren't born in time to watch my compatriots during the war, the energies they put into it, the boys dying *Pour La Patrie* while the family at home fought about *L'Héritage* and assured the survival of *La Bonne Cuisine*.

'Don't think I'm anti-food as such. That was quite a nice dinner you ordered, though you needn't have been quite so Spartan— I'm glad to see you've allowed us some sugar with these raspberries— I appreciated your, nuance of *not* having the fish just grilled.

'To return to myself, to my particular *egotissimo*. If I appear, let us say, disenchanted, it is because I have reason to be. My life——' Andrée appeared at a loss for a word.

'Your life has not been happy?' said Flavia.

'If you wish to simplify.' And then, 'God, how I hate talking this way.'

'Not happy,' Flavia said, 'when you are *so* beautiful?'

'Am I?'

'You are too beautiful,' Flavia said in a heart-broken tone.

'Too beautiful for what?'

'For everyone. For me. More beautiful than anyone can bear.'

Andrée, in her other manner, said, 'Looks are useful.'

'Don't,' said Flavia.

In the full, serious voice again, Andrée said, 'I told you I tease hard. And not only the young. I'm known to speak harshly to my contemporaries. New friendship does not come easy to me, I feel compelled to play it rough at first— your idealism, for example, I had to find out whether it was capable of standing up; testing and teasing, for me, are a kind of initiation——'

Flavia, sitting very still, was not sure if she could trust her ears.

'We all have reticences, they take different forms. What are yours? I can tell you: you will talk about your ideas, you will not talk about your feelings.' She looked Flavia full in the face, 'I do not mean your feeling for me, though you have hardly talked about that either. I mean *is* there nobody you are fond of? (Except Madame Loulou.) Are you a misanthropist, or are you an orphan? Come on, any brothers or sisters?'

'Not really.'

'A father?'

'My father is dead.'

'I thought your mother was divorced.'

Flavia looked taken aback.

More gently, André said, 'You see? You don't talk about her.'

When Flavia offered no help, she continued, 'You *see*? Perhaps it's just because you don't like her? More daughters than would admit it hate their mothers.'

Flavia put her hands under the table and crossed her fingers.

'Or is it that you think so highly of her that you can't bring yourself to cast her pearls before swine? That would be your English side coming out; I rather prefer you when you are being Italian. Or it might be that you don't want to talk about her because there is something to hide?

'Now before you go on presenting that blank face to me, think for a moment. My dear, you are on the young side— I am only stating a fact, the kind of fact the world sees— to be living in a kind of bachelor's establishment, so naturally one asks oneself where is that mysterious lady, her mother? Why has she gone away? Your treating the question as if it didn't exist is no help to you, no one ever got away by playing the ostrich.'

Flavia said, 'But surely the Fourniers must have told you?'

'Of course they have! You can imagine how fascinated Rosette is by everything a woman like your mother does; but that needn't mean that there's much truth in what she tells one.'

'Quite,' said Flavia.

'So I can't say that I *know* where your mother is or why she left.'

'Why should you want to know?'

'You are an extraordinary girl— quite insensitive in some ways. If you don't get it, there's nothing for me to add. Here I am talking to you about myself— a thing I assure you I very very rarely do— while you are shrinking from making the slightest personal communication to me. It isn't encouraging,

is it? It isn't even friendly. You are treating me as if I were
another Rosette Fournier.'

'Oh, no.'

'Oh, yes.'

'I am sorry. I suppose I have been beastly. I didn't mean
to.'

'Never say that, it's the feeblest excuse, like a housemaid
after breaking a vase. Either mean it, or don't do it.'

With some effort Flavia said, 'I don't want to talk about
my . . . about our . . . family affairs at the moment. . . .'
With reluctance she added, 'There are reasons.'

Andrée gave her a half-smile. 'Am I to take that as a sign
of your confidence?'

'It wasn't much.'

'As a reward you may change the subject.'

'Any good book lately?'

'*Point Counter Point— Contrepoint* as we had to call it in
our rigid language— for the third time I might add.'

'*You* read Aldous Huxley?'

'He's not a monopoly?'

'You said you didn't like ideas.'

'I like his about people.'

'I think he knows everything,' Flavia said. 'There is no
one like him. Have you read all his books?'

'Most of them.'

'So has my mother, though she does not put him as high as
I do.' Then she took another step forward, 'What would you
say were your political views?'

Andrée gave her a look of not unbenevolent irony. 'In the
narrower or the broader sense?'

'Both.'

'Well, none in the first: the more respectable French don't
go into politics.'

'I heard that.'

'Those who care about keeping their hands clean stay
away, though we are apt to follow a general in a crisis. In the

second: the obvious views, you could fill in the form for me. We're in a mess and nothing is going to pull us out; I am not a socialist; I'm not impressed by your little man in Rome; I don't like ultra-nationalists (I'm not one of those who'd follow the general); I think there is something to be said for constitutional monarchy but in France that cause is as dead as mutton; I have not much faith in the League, nor in democracy as an up-to-date technique of government. Call me an enlightened defeatist if you wish.'

Flavia nodded. 'Then you *are* for clearing up the mess if we could, you *are* against——'

'Dictators and war. I am on the side of the angels— that's what you wanted to be reassured about?'

'Yes,' said Flavia.

Presently she said, 'I know I haven't earned another turn, all the same may I ask you a question, a semi-personal question?'

'I won't guarantee an answer.'

'Your degree?'

'What about it?'

'It's been puzzling me. You said that you got it for a bet, well a bet is usually something like swimming in the North Sea on Christmas Day, I mean something sharp and brief, while working for a degree, however brilliant you are, takes years. You have to keep on, it's a way of life, and *not* being interested all that time— I can't see it.'

'All right,' Andrée said, 'I don't mind telling you. It was a half-truth. I did it for a bet— with one of my uncles, his side being that I wouldn't stick to anything— and because it seemed as good a way as any of getting away from home, but I was *not* uninterested and I have *not* forgotten my subject.'

Flavia was listening.

'I rather liked the work— it was not all easy, I had to make an effort, quite an effort, at times; but less than most, I knew I was good at it.'

'Exceptionally good?'

'Since you ask, and since we're talking for the record: Yes. They told me I had an academic future, a considerable future.'

'But——?'

'I gave it up. I didn't go on. There are other ways, you know, for a girl to get away from home.'

'Didn't you want . . . the academic future?'

'The intellectual side was all right. It was a kind of exercise, like a perpetual crossword, rather more rewarding. It's not bad to succeed, to excel, and it's always satisfying to solve a difficulty. It might have done. Work is a good deal less boring than doing nothing at all.'

'What went wrong? You weren't sent down?'

'Indeed not. *I* backed out; you might say, I ran. What was wrong? *The life.* My not being a man. My dear, don't talk to me about an academic career for a woman. A female don! She really hasn't much choice, there's the glorified schoolmarm; there's the brave little woman who tries to be a good wife and housewife, and I daresay mother, as well, and makes a point of her pretty clothes; and there's the bluestocking, the eccentric and frump, the mathematic's dean who doesn't know which side her tea-cup is chipped. As for the wining and dining don, you won't find *her*, she doesn't exist, and if she did the men wouldn't have her. Talk of segregation— you will sit with the men all right, you will sit round a table with them talking examination papers, you won't be at the table when the decanter goes round.

'French universities are bad enough, English are ten times worse. They sent me to Cambridge for a couple of terms— that's where I first realized I must run— I don't want to blaspheme about one of your famous institutions so I shan't tell you the name of my college though you're longing to know— the girls in their bed-sitters, the cocoa-drinking, the tittle-tattle, the atmosphere of heartiness or domesticity in the combination-room—— But, my dear, it must be getting late and here I am telling you things that you know as well as I do.'

Flavia looked at her watch. 'It's a quarter to two.'

'It can't be?' Andrée said. 'How flattering for both of us. But you are cold?'

'I don't think so,' Flavia said.

'You're shivering.' Andrée touched her arm. 'Chilled to the bone.' She went indoors and returned with an enormous, rough-looking navy-blue sweater. 'There, put that on at once— catch it.'

Flavia gave a gasp of surprise. The sweater was as light as a puff and as smooth as a bird to touch.

'Keep it,' Andrée said. 'It suits you, go and look at yourself. I'm giving it to you.'

'*Oh, no?*'

'It's yours. It's an Hermes.'

'The messenger of the gods?'

'The shop.'

A minute or so later Flavia said, 'Time for me to go.'

'How? How did you come? I should have asked.'

'By the bus. I'm going to walk.'

'All of twelve kilometers? I'm going to drive you home. That's to be our custom.'

They went by the sea route; the night was clear and calm. They sat side by side in silence.

Outside the house Andrée turned the car; as Flavia got out, she did too. 'Good night, Flavia.' She kissed her on the mouth. It was a chaste kiss. Flavia's heart turned over.

For a long time she stayed outside keeping from sleep to hold that moment, hold it as being now, not letting it go to be yesterday, go into the past.

CHAPTER SIX

Monday Tuesday Wednesday

I

Next day was Monday. Flavia did not go to the tower. She did not go to the sea. She stayed at the villa waiting for the long car.

The sense of happiness had remained. At times she heard a voice clearly, She *cannot* mean it. Another voice answered, *Don't underrate yourself.*

The morning went. The afternoon began.

The sun-set hour. When it was nearly dark, Flavia gave it another ten minutes, another five; five more. Then she locked up and went to the house on the bay.

Although it was late, the Loulou boys were still hopping about.

'You didn't come yesterday.'

'She didn't come the day *before* yesterday.'

'Did you find somebody else then to give you your dinner?'

'*Maman* asked after you.'

'Papa asked after you.'

'Not today!'

'Today she must mind her step.'

'Papa is in a temper.'

'A *fil-thy* temper— he has thrown them all out, he has thrown them all out of the window.'

'Is something the matter?' Flavia asked.

'Fifty dozen tuberoses— five hundred tuberoses— five hundred dozen tuberoses— last night they went into the ice-box, this morning they were *brown*.'

'White into the ice-box, brown out of the oven, five thousand white flowers— they *stank*.'

'They stank worse than fish, worse than fish, five thousand francs worth of white flowers, five big pots of white oil paint——'

'Papa isn't shouting about the francs, it is the arrangement, the *flo-ral ar-ran-ge-ment*, he cannot paint fifty dozen white flowers when they are brown.'

'And stink.'

Flavia went up to the terrace and quietly took her place.

Therese greeted her kindly. Loulou was not there.

'*Monsieur n'a pas faim,*' said the maid who brought their soup.

There was little conversation, and presently the maid returned to say, 'Monsieur demande Madame.' Therese rose at once.

Paul said, 'It really is a disaster. He will attempt these monstrous huge things.'

'Loulou is in arrears with his dealer,' Giles said. 'This thing would have helped.'

'It wouldn't go by the square foot?' Flavia said.

'As a matter of fact it does. Contracts go by the *square inch*.'

'Hadn't we better leave?' Bobbie said.

'Therese would want us to finish dinner first.'

They decided to do that and leave afterwards.

At the gate Flavia said, 'Will he go to Belgium now?'

'Very likely.'

At the villa, she found a screw of paper in the flowerpot where she had left the key. Feeling quite sick already, Flavia undid the scrap.

> *Disappointed to find that Mme L. has stolen a march on me.* (*Again!*)

A.

II

The next morning too was wretched. When Flavia remembered that tomorrow was going to be her essay day she ran up to the tower to fetch some essential books which she set out with grim awareness on the dining-room table at the villa. She made a few attempts and found that she could not work, she could not even read.

What does one do, she asked herself. What can one do?

At 2 p.m., rather than face more questions from the femme de ménage, she ladled the food that had been left for her to eat into one bowl and carried it some way down the hill to a place where she knew it would be picked up by stray dogs and cats. Half an hour later she could hold out no longer: she drank a cup of coffee and two glasses of cold water, put some money in her pocket and walked into St-Jean. It was very hot. The port lay somnolent, the shops were shut. So was the post office. She waited outside in the street, shaking in anticipation of the telephone call.

Soon she was joined by a peasant woman dressed in black who told her that she was trying to get on to the hospital in Toulon for news of her son. As the woman spoke she cried. Flavia looked and listened as if to events taking place at one remove.

The woman pressed a paper into Flavia's hand. 'You are going to help me, the post ladies have no patience.' Duly the office opened. Flavia, none too practised herself, managed to get the number. It took time. She stood in a dark stifling cell, the woman mumbling by her side. 'You will speak for me,' she said. There was an answer.

Flavia whispered urgently, 'Whom do I ask for?'

'Rintini, Joseph.'

There was a wait and another voice and another wait. Then, 'There's been no change, you may inquire again in the evening.' Flavia transmitted, the woman cried some more and said, 'Go and ask what I owe them.' Flavia did. The woman counted out the sum conscientiously. Flavia said, 'I hope you will have good news this evening.' 'It's nothing to you,' said the woman.

Flavia followed her out of the post office. The air was cleaner, the heat different. She had been spared telephoning after all— she realized that she did not even know whom to ask for at the hotel in Bandol.

She walked on to the Fourniers' house, dragging every step. Constanza would have carried it off, casually, lightly: By the way your charming guest the other night— so stupid of me——

But when Flavia turned into the Fourniers' drive she saw that she had been spared that errand as well, for there, shining, immobile, unconcerned, stood the long car.

Her first impulse was to turn and flee. Then she saw that the verandah doors were open and inside in the shade on two wicker-chairs, talking earnestly to one another, were Rosette and Andrée. Flavia's second impulse was to flee.

Too late. She had been seen. She walked straight in, feeling she had never needed as much courage in her life before.

Madame Fournier did not open fire. She seemed to wait for an initiative from her friend. Andrée took her time. She looked up lazily then said in her cooler manner. 'Talk of mad dogs and Englishmen, how brave of you to go visiting at this hour, Rosette and I haven't stirred a finger for ages.'

Flavia could think of nothing at all to say.

'Albert and the others are out, he's taken them to le Lavandou for the day.' When this didn't lead to anything, Rosette continued, 'They'll be so sorry they missed you.'

'That's the remark *you* ought to have made,' said Andrée. 'Yes.'

'It's heat-stroke— Rosette, you'd better get her a long cool drink, go and make her some lemonade.'

Rosette Fournier got up to do as she was told.

'Well, big-eyes?'

Flavia said, 'I would like to speak to you.'

'Well?'

Flavia looked at the open doors. Rosette could be heard talking in the kitchen. 'Not here.'

Andrée shrugged. 'My dear, this is not my house.'

'Couldn't you leave?'

'Like that? With you? You *must* be mad. Besides I promised Rosie-Posie to stay for tea.'

Flavia turned away, took a few steps, came back and stood still: keeping her eyes on Andrée's face she said with complete intensity, 'I love you.'

Andrée from her chair said, 'Well?'

'Well?' Andrée said again.

Flavia said, 'I had to tell you.'

'And did. What next?'

'I am *asking you*— after this solemn declaration, what next?'

'I don't know,' Flavia said. 'Nothing.'

'Are you in the habit of making that world shaking announcement?'

'No!'

'Then since you appear to be singling me out, what do you expect me to do? Fall in your arms? Exchange rings? Are you sure you've got your first premise right? Aren't you going on from a mistake? We're of the same sex, let me remind you, we're not supposed to fall in love with one another. Most women's tastes are not as catholic as Therese Loulou's.'

Flavia, almost relieved to have reached as much firm ground, said, 'I didn't think you were . . . I didn't know about . . . your inclinations. I didn't feel . . . I almost knew it was not possible.'

'How sure you are of everything. But I'm not talking about *my* inclinations, as you call them. Of course you know nothing about them. Again unlike Madame Loulou, they are not generally known. What I was talking about are *your* inclinations and I would suggest that you know nothing about them at all.'

'But I do.'

'You are having the kind of crush that is natural in a girl your age, and if you hadn't been seduced by a certain person (whose name I shall not mention again since you dislike it so) that would be that.'

'No— no.'

'You have not reached the stage at which you *can* know. You've had no conclusive experience, have you? You haven't had an affair with a man— that's understood at your age— but have you had a feeling for a man?'

Flavia said, 'I don't think I connect men with . . . love.' Then she thought of Loulou and felt confused.

'So until you know a little more of what it's all about, don't expect me to take you seriously. A second point— impudence or naïvety? You come here to offer me your undying devotion while you have an entanglement with the lady whom we don't seem to be able to keep out of the conversation.'

'It has ceased to exist,' Flavia said grandly.

'Has it?' Andrée said. 'How very sudden.'

'I'd do anything you want me to.'

'That's what people *say*. Do you want me to take advantage of it?'

'Yes,' said Flavia.

'Don't wait for orders. It's up to you, it's always up to the suitor to present an acceptable brief. And now we've had enough of the subject.'

Flavia said, 'Your head seen against the white wall, it shows up the structure, I know now *whom* you remind me of, I saw it when I first met you, but could not place it, it's not a *literal* resemblance, it's something basic, you do look like someone I know.'

'Who is it?'

'It's a man. You have heard of him— *they* must have talked about him. Michel.'

Andrée said, 'Oh, yes, we've been told that before, people seemed to find it surprising. It isn't. Michel and I were cousins, not first cousins of course——'

'*You* are related to Michel?'

'Why not?'

'Your name, then?'

'Devaux of course.'

Flavia said, 'That's rather delightful. And now I do see— the car? Only that yours is a Panhard and his a Delahaye, the year must be the same. Is it a family taste?'

'A shared taste,' Andrée said. Then not ungently, 'I ought to tell you, they did talk to me about him, it can't be news to you what they are saying, that Michel has run off with your mother and that he wants to marry her. Which doesn't mean that I am convinced, I would never rely on Rosie-Posie's gossip alone.' And before allowing Flavia to indicate a stand, 'By the way what *is* she doing?' And suddenly in French, in a voice as shrill as a station-master's whistle, 'Rosette— come back! that lemonade must be getting hot.'

Flavia said quickly, 'You will let me see you again?'

'Very likely.'

'When?'

'Bull-dog. Tomorrow evening. I'll call for you— no, come down to the port and look for me, I may be there. If you've been good.'

III

Flavia walked away from the Fourniers' house seeing the next stage of her course.

She had never been to the house on the bay at that end of the afternoon, and found Therese abstracted and busy. She was taking crates out of her car; Flavia gave her a hand.

'He's started again and he's pleased about it,' Therese said. She had been to most of the early-morning markets as far as Hyères. 'Let's hope they will keep this time.' They had been advised not to keep them *too* cold and also to cover them with waxed paper. 'Now he has got fascinated by the paper as well, he's made it look like a field of bridal veils, but it's going to be difficult to keep it in place when we move it at night. You have no idea how heavy flowers can be.'

When they had finished unloading, Therese said, 'My coco, I shall be helping Loulou for the next week or two, I don't like leaving him much when he's working on those big things. Afterwards you and I will have a day on the island.'

Flavia said, 'I have to tell you something.'

Still preoccupied, Therese said, 'Yes, coco?'

After Flavia had stated, baldly, that she had fallen in love with someone, Therese gave her a look. 'Good,' she said, 'I hope it will go well for you.'

There was a pause while Flavia waited, half hoped, for the questions which she realized Therese would not ask; while Therese too, perhaps, was waiting.

When it was clear to each that the other would not speak, Therese said, 'But you don't look happy, my darling, that's often the way it goes. It's seldom easy and never for long. But one comes out of it. Is there anything I can do to help?'

'Oh no,' Flavia said, but had the grace to add, 'thank you.'

'We shall be seeing you at dinner presently?'

'I don't know,' Flavia said with open wretchedness, 'I don't think I ought to come so often now.'

Therese said, 'That is all right, coco, come when you feel you can. Well, *bon courage*, and good luck.'

Going through the gate Flavia nearly cried. She told herself, it would not really be doing something for Andrée if it did not come hard.

It was cooler and beginning to get dark. Flavia set out on an aimless walk. She remembered the early summer when she was really alone without anyone to talk to: how fast the days went, too fast. Now it was the hour when they brought out the *pastis* and big water-jug and lit the scented candles on the terrace above the bay and Paul and Jeannine and the rest of them were beginning to arrive and Therese was telling them what there would be to eat. Flavia longed to go back and slip into her place just as the soup was brought and hear them telling about Loulou's day. But she felt she was under orders (there was some comfort in that) to spend the evening in the wilderness.

She was headed towards Bandol but checked herself half-way and returned in a semi-circle. It struck ten o'clock as she walked into St-Jean. She was hanging about the waterfront when she heard steps behind her. 'Flavia— what luck!' It was the Fourniers' nephew. He looked flushed and pleased. 'Oh, we've had such a marvellous day, Uncle Albert took us to the Marine Museum and then we went on to collect sea-shells ourselves, he knew where to go for them, we found hundreds; and we had a lobster picnic. We only just got back, the others have gone home, I was stopping for cigarettes when I saw you. What a perfect end to a perfect day, come and have a drink with me, *please*.'

Flavia accepted.

'In the afternoon we went to the festival concert, the Bach violin and Schubert, that was marvellous, particularly the Bach, it made me feel one could *be* like that— you would know what I mean?'

The waiter, who was an Italian, remembered Flavia from old days. There was some long-time-not-see and he asked about her mother.

'What are you going to have?' the young man said.

'A brandy and soda, if I may.'

'Two,' said the young man.

The waiter brought two tall glasses and filled them a good way up with Courvoisier.

'*Whoa*,' said the young man.

'Your syphon's going to splutter,' Flavia said.

It did. The waiter looked delighted.

'*A la vôtre*,' the young man said before he drank. He took a long pull. 'Goodness, I was thirsty.'

Flavia took a long pull too.

'Do you realize that I haven't seen you for three whole days, Flavia? I've been thinking of you though. Today, too; how I wished you had been with me at the concert. And now — *here you are*.' He went on in a similar vein. 'But you are very silent tonight? I'm not offending you by what I've been saying?'

'Of course not,' Flavia said, trying to pull herself into the present.

He began talking about the state of the world, saying that he hadn't even looked at a newspaper all day, when one was enjoying oneself one too easily forgot everything that was not on the personal level: and yet how desperately the economic situation was deteriorating everywhere week by week, it could not end well, it might lead to anything. As for the French government, the French general public for that matter, 'It hasn't hit us yet, so nobody cares. I bet you and I, Flavia, are the only people in St-Jean who have heard of *The Economic Consequences of the Peace*.'

Flavia entered the conversation sufficiently to say, 'Heard; not read. Not yet.'

'One of the things I like you for,' the young man said, 'is that there is no pretence about you. French girls are always out for something. With you I would feel I had an ally.' That's what a man needed in his life and work, a friend, an ally, not an idol or a toy.

'Oh, quite.'

'But I'm talking too much— it's having you all to myself for the first time.'

An idea struck Flavia. *The conclusive experience*?— here it was. On a platter.

She got up. 'Shall we go?' she said.

'May I see you home?'

They walked up the hill side by side. When they spoke it was generalities. Flavia was thinking of her essay with a pang, and of the prep she had failed to do in the morning, the morn-

ing— could it be?— of this same unending day. She took
herself in hand, the essay she told herself firmly had to be
shelved: one step before the other.

At one point she stopped in her tracks.

'You know—I feel awfully light-headed.'

'The air——?' he said with some concern.

Flavia almost giggled.

They dragged their steps as they approached the villa.
Flavia was thinking of the monstrous mass of tuberoses now
reposing inside that vast refrigerator under their paper veils.
She wished it could be dear Loulou.

Onward Christian soldiers.

Outside the front door he kissed her. She did nothing to
help and nothing to hinder. She hoped he would go on. He
did go on. She said politely, 'Would you like to come in for a
last drink?'

She unlocked the door and they stepped inside. She said,
'I usually don't turn the lights on when I come home at
night, it's a habit I have. Is that all right?' Then, still in the
tones of an uncertain hostess anxious to do well, she said,
'I have a room upstairs.'

If the young man was surprised or taken aback, he did not
show it. He was twenty-two or three, he was French, and to
him also the encounter may have appeared as something
handed on a platter.

To Flavia like that other first time it was both half-known
and startling. Memories of her grandmother's judgements
obtruded themselves and she closed her mind against them.
Her own refrain went: This is not for me.

The young man said, 'Are you sure you're all right?'

Meekly, Flavia said, 'Would you do something for me?'
Indeed.

'Would you get me something to eat? I think I'm going to
faint, I'm so hungry.'

Reassured, the young man became almost gay, 'Let's go
and raid your larder— let me cook you my scrambled eggs.'

'You won't find a scrap in the house, all the food . . . well, it's gone. Shall I tell you a secret? I've had no lunch and dinner.'

So he took her down the hill again. When they got to St-Jean it was only a little past midnight and the cafés were still open. The young man ordered two large ham sandwiches and Flavia devoured them while he drank a glass of beer. 'Thank you,' she said, 'that *was* kind of you. And now don't dream of walking me home again. No, don't. I insist. I'm used to being on my own and you've had a long day.'

Baffled or relieved, the young man let her go.

IV

Flavia got up next morning when the alarm clock rang: Andrée in the evening; meanwhile an honest day's work (for a change).

She went to the tower and buckled down. Bull-dog is who bull-dog does. To her tutor she wrote a frank if casual note apologizing for not sending an essay this week. She had slipped into doing no work for some days, would he look at it, please, as a kind of holiday— after all she had not had one since they had started on the course— she hoped she would be able to do better again next week. When later on she went down to the sea she felt almost as cheerful again as in pre-Andrée days. Had she been asked that minute what her exact feelings were, she might have said, I have done what I can for Andrée; if she's going to blow cold again, if she doesn't want to see me any more, *vogue la galère*, I shall have to survive, I shall. I always knew that she was not going to stay— perhaps I'll be better without her.

Yet had the question gone on, And what if she does not turn up on the waterfront tonight? The answer would have been, Ah, *that* would be unbearable.

Flavia was there so early that she ran into Therese in the little square where people left their cars.

Therese took in Flavia's gleaming silk shirt and eager face. 'You're looking very nice, coco,' she said. She noticed the new sweater Flavia was carrying and praised it generously. 'You know where that exquisite wool comes from? It is very rare.'

Flavia said, 'I got some work done today— I think I'm going to be all right.'

They were still talking when Andrée was there. Andrée saw Therese, and Therese saw Andrée.

She walked up to them with a kind of swagger. Flavia saw a curious look pass between the two women— defiance? on Andrée's part; stony anger on Therese's.

'*Bon jour*, Andrée.'

'*Bon jour*, Therese.'

They did not shake hands.

Therese pushed a basket into Flavia's arms. 'Take it to the car for me,' she said. It was an order— a rare thing from Therese— and Flavia could not refuse it short of gross discourtesy in public to an older woman and a friend. She was marched off under Andrée's eyes.

'I did not know Andrée was here!' Therese still had her Medusa face. 'Have you been seeing *her*? That is bad. How could you?'

Humiliated enough and ready to dig in her heels, Flavia said, 'What's bad about it? Do you mean her being connected with Michel?'

Appalled, Therese said, 'If you don't feel it——'

'Are you going to tell me it's unsuitable?'

'It is— and it is wrong,' Therese said majestically. 'Besides it's dangerous.' Softening a little, she said, 'Can't you see, coco, that she's an extremely dangerous woman?'

Flavia was infatuated enough to be taking this as a compliment.

'What *is* she doing here? Wherever she appears, she's up to no good.' Again more mildly, she added, 'I wish I could forbid you to go on seeing her.'

Flavia said, 'But you can't. I'm going to have dinner with Andrée.' Truthfully, superstitiously, she added, 'At least I hope so.'

Andrée, waiting in her car, asked with something short of her usual self-possession, 'What did that termagant say about me?'

Flavia thought, She's lost face because it has come out that she is on Christian-name terms after all with Therese. Relieved to be let off herself, she said lightly, 'Oh, a dire warning, you're bad and dangerous to know.'

'Was that all?'

Flavia seized the chance of teasing in turn. 'She didn't give chapter and verse.' In another tone, she said, 'Not that I would have let her.'

'How loyal, how British,' Andrée said and it sounded almost like approval.

After that everything between them became easy for the time being. Andrée without appearing to do so took charge of the evening. They drove a short way along the coast to a restaurant that was neither smart nor squalid, hushed nor noisy, and where a dinner they paid no attention to was served to them seemingly without any act of volition. They talked. Andrée appeared to have padded most of her edges; she was being considerate, intelligent, serious, talking like an elder person generous with knowledge to a younger one, and Flavia ceased to feel an absurd adolescent and a target. Andrée spoke of Saint-Simon and compared him to some English memoirists; she spoke of the astonishing variety of the classical French novel, *La Princesse des Clèves*, *Adolphe*, *Les Liaisons Dangereuses*.

Of the latter, Flavia said, 'I realize that it must be well done, but I couldn't bear it when I read it.' The duplicity and wickedness of Mme de Merteuil. 'It made me quite ill.'

Andrée showed a claw. 'Reality would make *you* feel ill.'

'Isn't Mme de Merteuil too bad to be real?'

'Possibly too much of a piece for modern fiction.'

They talked, inevitably, of Marcel Proust.

'Michel would never let me meet him,' Andrée said. 'He doesn't approve of satisfying one's curiosity or of seeking out the notorious. He doesn't approve of Proust either.'

'Surely not?' said Flavia.

'You haven't begun to know Michel. He's against rummaging in one's past— not that even he would use that term for *A la Récherche* though he really detests the style. Michel still worships Anatole France.'

'So did Proust,' said Flavia.

'But *he* didn't noticeably try to write like him.'

Then Andrée talked about Paris, where she lived.

A large carafe of wine was on their table and Andrée filled up Flavia's glass from time to time.

'I'd give a great deal,' Flavia said, 'to know about you, to know what your life is really like?'

Andrée's quizzical expression returned. 'Would you?' Then she veered; assuming her least play-acting manner, she said, 'I understand you, I also have that passion to get to know about people, to find out what's behind them, what they want, what they're after.'

'How much truth is there in the phrase, What makes people tick?' said Flavia. 'Does it mean that everybody has some definite thing that moves him?'

'Not one single thing— a clockwork isn't so uncomplicated either— a *combination*. Ah, yes, find that and you *can* make them tick. Or stop them from ticking.'

'I shouldn't like to be able to do that.'

'I told you,' Andrée said, 'you haven't enough stomach for the world. And don't think that being squeamish is a virtue in itself— there are many ways of doing harm.'

Flavia would have liked to hear more about this but Andrée was already on to something else.

'*Glissez, mortels,*' she said, '*n'appuyez point.*'

All in all it could be said to have been an amicable evening.

They had left the restaurant and were taking a few steps on the front. Suddenly Andrée said, 'Take me to the place you work in, show me your hide-out.'

Flavia manifestly hesitated.

'What's the objection?'

But Flavia was unwilling to express what she strongly if obscurely felt— that a matter of trust was involved. She said, 'You see I was given it to work and read in, not to . . . entertain.'

Andrée said reasonably, 'You're not being asked to throw a cocktail party. My dear, we have things to talk about and I don't expect to be here for very much longer— would you prefer us to trail off to my hotel or some public place, or to your frankly not very inviting villa? Surely the place you work in has a more civilized atmosphere? And I'd like to see it. Can't you take a friend, even if it's a recent one?'

There was nothing decently to be done and so with disproportionate reluctance Flavia took Andrée to the tower.

The key, here, was not kept under a flowerpot or stone but in a more foolproof and elaborate hiding-place. Flavia unlocked, let Andrée pass, preceded her to the top floor to light lamps.

'Civilized enough?'

Andrée stood in the round room looking at the books with a mixture of curiosity and distaste.

'You do know where we are? You know whose this is?'

'Knock me down with a feather, to coin a phrase,' said Andrée, 'it's his, it's saintly Michel's retreat. I've heard about it.'

Seeing it anew, Flavia said, 'It *is* something?'

'Oh, *very* comfortable, *very* sober, *very* insulated— I know Michel's taste in house furnishing. What's the rest like?'

'I don't use it, it's kept locked. I only come up here. That's where he works.'

'You admire him, don't you?'

'Oh— yes.'

'What do you admire about him?'

Flavia thought. 'Doesn't the whole of him strike one? His mind. His manner: so calm, so kind, so on top of things. His looks. Don't they show up what he is? . . . alert and benign — he is as good as he is intelligent. Like an . . . ideal judge. A young judge.'

'An ideal judge,' Andrée said. 'What flights of fancy. I daresay his brothers might accept that one.'

'Not you?'

'I'd rather take the law into my own hands.'

'*I* don't believe in that,' said Flavia.

'Meaning——?' Andrée said, not missing a thing. 'Meaning that all the same you *might* do so yourself?'

'I have done so,' Flavia said.

Andrée let it pass.

Flavia went on following her train of thought, 'I cannot see *him* doing even a disinterested thing if it went against a rule.'

'Not *he*,' said Andrée.

'He's so unlike anyone else.'

'And wants to be! He despises the human race and the combinations that make it tick; the human race in its present state, he'd qualify— he'd like to send us all back to nursery school— so *he* has to behave as unlike his fellow beings as he can.'

'Behave better? Isn't that all to the *good*?'

'That depends on how you count the cost,' said Andrée.

'But Michel is so very kind to the fellow beings.'

'So is the Seigneur supposed to be. With and without the capital S. You've heard him go on about those selective hierarchies?'

'I know he is fighting the mediocre common denominator

in politics and life, but isn't he personally an extremely modest man?'

'I would say he was too proud to put his light above a bushel.'

'*You* don't approve of Michel?'

Andrée played it lightly. 'The prophet in his own home as one might say—' She settled into the big armchair. 'There wouldn't be such a thing as a cigarette? I thought not. He doesn't even smoke.' She looked at Flavia. 'Oh, do sit down, or stand still, you make me nervous. You're too young to have habits. That's better.' She looked at Flavia again. 'Tell me, does your mother enjoy principles and abstract ideas?'

'Oh, yes, she does,' said Flavia.

'Really?'

'Not that she has so many herself— principles I mean— but they are essential with . . . when . . .'

'When——?'

Flavia said bravely, 'She looks for virtue in those she loves. It's in our family, we all do.'

'Tell me, is it true that Michel wants to marry her?'

'It is true,' Flavia said.

'There— you're on the defensive again.'

'I don't mean to. It's because— can't you see?— it's really not up to me to talk about their . . . concerns.'

'Their . . . concerns *are* being talked about. Do you prefer me then to get it all from Rosette Fournier?' Flavia hung her head. 'My dear, it is time you told *me* a little more about it. So Michel wants to marry her— what about your mother?'

'Oh, it's all right, she didn't even hesitate, she as good as popped the question herself.'

'Did she? You know that Michel *is* married?'

'Oh, that,' Flavia said, 'you must know that's just a technicality.'

'Is that how you see marriage?'

Flavia said with some spirit, 'That's how I see divorce. His ought to have gone through ages ago.'

There was a silence. 'I know,' Flavia went on, 'that people don't *like* a divorce in their family, but when you think that his has so long ceased to be a real marriage—— You haven't seen them together, Michel and . . . Constanza.'

'No, I haven't seen them together,' Andrée said. 'What is she like, apart from being keen on other people's principles? Albert Fournier says she isn't too bad-looking.'

'Did he put it that way?' Flavia said.

'Rather Southern? rather sultry? Correct my impression, I'm listening.'

But Flavia merely said, 'You will be able to judge when you see her.'

'Mule.'

Flavia relented. 'It just struck me, you and she have the same long eye-lashes, silky long, and so has Michel. That's a coincidence.'

'Any others?'

'You both have that golden skin, but yours makes one think of lovely geometrical planes, you're all bone, she's got bone too, but what one sees most is contour and colour— no, you are not remotely the same type, she could never be painted by a Modigliani or a Loulou, or a Piero for that matter, she is something between a Titian and a Gainsborough.' Having warmed to it, Flavia went on, 'And then *you* are so essentially neat, no, neat is too prosaic, you are so . . . *styled*, you look as though you had been *made*.'

'Whereas she?'

'Is more like flesh and blood,' Flavia said impartially.

Andrée gave her a look that she could not interpret.

'She's well-read, like you. Like you, she likes to tease and can be rough.'

'Tell me something about her life.'

'If you promise to go to sleep,' said Flavia. 'People get bored if you try hard enough to tell them how things were.'

'Haven't you found me rather a good audience?'

'At moments,' Flavia admitted, truthfully. She had no

desire whatsoever to repeat her own performance. The very brief account she gave now was selective— it referred to Anna but not to Anna's story; Rome was a place of origin; there was no mention of a Mena or a Mr James (Simon she could not entirely subdue), the prince was a bare name. Nevertheless the account glowed.

'You see,' she said, 'I had that winter with her.'

Thoughtfully, Andrée said, 'Do you think your mother cares two hoots about being married or not married to a man? From what you've been telling me I shouldn't think she did?'

'Odd thing,' Flavia said, 'I shouldn't have thought so either and now I'm convinced she does. She's never been one for *unnecessary* nonconformity and there's the Italian family to think of, but there's more to it. I believe she used to be so reluctant about marrying people because marriage *is* important to her, she's only been waiting for the right one.'

'So you think that she wants the substance *and* the form?'

'Oh, yes. The one would be less without the other.'

'And Michel?'

'He feels the same way. I saw how protective he is about her, and how could he protect her better than by being married to her. And don't you think, he'd like to score a happy marriage to set against the other one?'

'And you?' said Andrée, 'Wouldn't you rather keep her to yourself?'

'I want it for her, I want it very much.'

'For *yourself*?'

Flavia said happily, 'It would be quite wonderful, I should have a family to come home to in the holidays all my life.' She added quickly, 'At least for many many many more years than one can think of.'

'By the way,' said Andrée, 'leaving that rosy future aside, where are they at this moment?'

'I can't tell you that.'

'So they *are* together.'

'But you said you knew? Apparently everybody does.'

'Everybody *guessed*. Now you have told.'

'Only to you.'

'Yes,' Andrée said, 'only to me.'

'You are not going to *repeat* it?'

'I don't think I shall repeat it.' She looked hard at Flavia who as so often could not tell whether Andrée was serious or contemptuous or amused. 'But I would rather like to know where they are?'

Flavia was silent.

'They left France, haven't they? My dear, I thought that you and I had become— friends?'

'I've only got a poste-restante address myself,' said Flavia.

'But where? What country?'

Flavia began to count till ten hoping that Andrée would get on to something else.

'I bet you told *her*, you told your *belle-laide*?'

'I didn't even tell Therese.'

'*Even*.' Andrée's eyes flashed. 'You will do nothing for me— except spout fine words and declarations.'

'I would do anything for you,' said Flavia.

'Well——'

'Anything within reason.'

'More fine words.'

Flavia plunged. 'I did what you told me to— I've got it now. You remember? The conclusive experience.'

'What are you talking about?' said Andrée.

'I should be allowed to know about my inclinations now. I've had an affair with a man.'

'You had what?'

Flavia repeated her words.

'*When?* You haven't had the time.'

'Last night.'

'Say that again. And with whom, for heaven's sake? Don't stand there, tell me about it.'

In a reticent but factual way, Flavia did.

'So you and he went up to the villa? And then you went back into St-Jean again for supper? That was the only consequence you were bothering about?'

'Only I ate supper,' Flavia said.

'And what on earth made you do it?'

'You. I thought . . . I understood that you might like me better if I had experience, if I didn't have opinions about things I knew nothing about. . . .'

Andrée had begun to laugh. It was the first time that Flavia heard her do so. She laughed and she laughed, and she laughed again. 'You did *that* for me?'

'Of course,' said Flavia.

Andrée's control seemed to have gone. Flavia watched her with distaste and some alarm.

In her smallest voice, she said, 'Perhaps it was a mistake?'

When Andrée had recovered she said, 'And yet you will not tell me that simple thing?'

'It involves *them*. The other . . . last night, that was only me.'

'*Only you!* The dear little girl, Catherine the Great, isn't in it.' Before Flavia could find her bearings, she went on, 'Only what involves *them* is sacred?'

'Why do you want to know so much where they are?' Flavia said soberly.

'Why should *I* want to know where Michel is? You are being stupid and impertinent, you're beginning to irritate me.'

Still soberly, Flavia said, 'I've thought about it hard, do believe me. Belonging to Michel's family doesn't mean that you have to know where he is. My mother's aunts and cousins in Italy don't know where she is and I wouldn't tell them if they asked. Please, try to look at it the way I have to— you must know that it's an important matter because of Michel's divorce; if it were known, if it could be proved, that he is,' Flavia looked at Andrée and continued firmly, 'living with my mother, the divorce could still be stopped. You must also

know that there is a time limit and that it is nearly up. These
are critical days. If Michel had wanted you to have his address he would have sent it; he must have yours. Now don't
you agree? I have no right to go against what I must presume
to be his wishes?' She added, 'I'm sure it's only because of
safety in the smallest possible number, only his lawyers and
my mother's father have the address, aside from me, and I
only have it because they didn't like to leave me here without
one.'

Quite soberly too, Andrée said, 'I can follow your argument. As far as it goes. Now let me present you with another
one. Yes, I do happen to know that these are critical days.
Though that was not my subject at Aix, I've made rather a
point of knowing a certain amount of French Civil Law.
Assuming now that I was aware of one or two facts of which
you, my dear, could not be, assuming that I had something
of importance to communicate to Michel, would you still
stick to your stubborn refusal?'

'You mean that you do know something that may help
them?'

'Might that not be the motive for my request? Imagine my
being in a position to tell Michel something that he ought to
know— that may be vital for him to know.'

'Couldn't you reach him through his lawyers?'

'By way of Paris? When time may be of the essence? You
don't know what lawyers are, seldom a constructive force in
private affairs.'

Flavia said, 'Could you . . . would you consider sending
your message through me? Would you trust me with it?'

'As much as you trust *me*?'

'Oh, what ought I to do?' said Flavia.

'Follow for once the judgement of your elders. I know for
certain that your giving me Michel's address will make a
very great difference to the two of them. How will you feel
about that afterwards? Think for a minute.'

'May I have some time?'

'Six more rounds of the room? Go on.'

Presently Flavia said, 'All the same, I can't do it. I promised.'

'*He* made you do that?'

'He did nothing of the kind, he wouldn't even ask me.'

'So we promised mummy. And now we're more concerned with our little rules than with what's going to happen to mummy in the future. And *don't* make faces at me.'

Flavia controlled herself. 'It's not a rule, it's . . .'

'What?'

'A kind of instinct.'

'Do you believe in instinct? Your own instincts?'

'I don't *know.*'

Andrée said not unreasonably, 'Why not do as I ask you and let me look after the consequences?'

'You *may* be right,' Flavia said, 'that's the devil of it.'

Andrée said, 'Look at me— you don't look at me any more.'

With candour and concentration, Flavia did.

Andrée gave her a mocking, almost tender smile. '*Mon bel éphèbe——?*'

Flavia cried out, 'Your . . . looks have nothing to do with it. Should have nothing to do with it.'

'Haven't they, though?' said Andrée.

With a coldness, a remoteness, a knowledge, that seemed to have descended on her without volition, Flavia heard herself say, '*You are making a mistake.*'

An expression of open delight appeared on Andrée's face. 'Oh, but I court them, the way I play my game!'

'I don't know what you mean, I don't want to know.'

With an instant return to sweet reasonableness, Andrée said, 'Admitted that I've been trying to seduce you, doesn't that only go to show how desperate I am to get my way? Desperate to get my message to Michel? Well, it will be on your head.'

Flavia said, 'I'm getting confused, please give me time, let me sleep over it.'

'No, you may not. I've had enough of you. Who do you think you are? Let's have no more nonsense, miss— give me that address.'

'Please don't make me,' Flavia said.

'I am going to make you. I insist— or.'

'Yes?'

'I shall never see you or speak to you again.'

'Do you mean it?' said Flavia.

'I mean it.' Andrée got up and went to the door. Then in her full, sad, serious voice, 'Perhaps I shall regret it, more perhaps than you will ever know, you foolish girl. But I do mean it: if you do not give me my answer now, I shall have to go, for ever.'

Flavia said, 'Then you will have to go.'

'Is it over then?' Andrée said, turning away.

Flavia sat down in the chair beside the desk. She said slowly, 'It was over.' But Andrée had already left.

v

Flavia woke feeling sadder and wiser; such was her sense of escape, of relief, that she felt free to grieve.

She spent half of her morning crying. Crying for the stranger, crying for the lost face— She was so beautiful— crying again. And now for picking up the bits. The day was Thursday, the start of the academic week; Flavia combed her hair, washed her eyes and marched herself to the tower.

She let herself in, went up the stairs, set the shutters; she had meant to leave all behind but was seized then with the oppressive memory of Andrée in that room. She might have been present now. Still resolute, she turned to the desk: something was wrong, her books and papers did not seem to be in their usual place. They were still neat, aligned and stacked precisely, even to the point of pedantry, they were in perfect order, only it was an order that made no sense whatsoever, an order in which Flavia had not left them.

She felt fear. She opened a drawer: the same deliberate rearrangement of envelopes, pencils, pens. She opened the drawer where she kept the letters she received. They were there. Her tutor's in one bundle; the three thin sheaves, Mr James's, Constanza's, Michel's. On top of Michel's last a piece of paper had been clipped. It read,

Mission accomplished.   A.

CHAPTER SEVEN

Thursday

It was a quarter to eleven by her wristwatch and she ran all the way into St-Jean. There was a taxi on the front and she took it telling the man to drive her to the hotel in Bandol and be quick; she was still trembling. She was seen by Fournier, who was starting on his apéritifs across the road; he signalled the driver to wait and came over; putting his head into the taxi, he said without a greeting, 'If you want Andrée Devaux, you will find her up at our house.' He turned away before Flavia could say thank you.

Like the last time Andrée and Rosette were on the verandah. They were standing and Rosette was stuffing something into her bag. She did not look at Flavia as she came in. Andrée did.

'You brought my taxi, so you did manage to capture one. Such perfect timing— just what you need, Rosette.'

The taxi was turning in the drive.

'Tell him to wait.' Flavia made no move. Andrée gave a shout herself. She turned to Rosette. 'That's understood then, you've got it all clear?'

Rosette Fournier left them and was borne off.

'That came in handy, the post office shuts like a drum at noon sharp.'

'I've got to talk to you,' Flavia said.

'Suit yourself.'

Voices from the drawing-room, voices in the house. 'Not here. Privately.'

'As you please.'

'Follow me,' said Flavia.

They went through the passage and across the yard. Flavia, with Andrée's eyes upon her, looked for and produced the key to the outhouse.

'One of your hide-outs?'

Flavia shut the door behind them.

'There's nowhere to sit,' said Andrée.

Flavia pulled out the stool from under Fournier's filing cabinet. Andrée sat down fastidiously. She did not appear to see the toy landscape spread before them.

Flavia said, 'It is a hoax, isn't it?'

Andrée had a smile upon her face.

'You've got what you wanted, you are not going to . . . *misuse* it? It is all right?'

Andrée said nothing.

'You are not going to . . . interfere?'

Andrée said loud and clear, 'Poste-restante, Almuñecar, Alicante.'

Flavia put her hands over her face.

'Rosie-Posie is on her way with the telegrams.'

'Telegrams?'

'To inform the detectives.' Flavia made a move to the door. 'Stay— we know you're fast on your feet but you're not going to catch her up now. That's not the way to stop it. Besides there is much that I've been waiting to tell you, *much*.'

Flavia said, 'What is going to happen?'

'It's a tiny place— we looked it up— only one possible hotel, they should be able to get the evidence in no time. Waiters, chambermaids, you know. You've heard how these things are done?'

'And then?'

'In due course the evidence is going to reach the court in Paris who'll adjourn the suit for desertion by Michel Devaux *sine die.*'

'You mean that the divorce will be held up?'

'A way of putting it.'

'For long?'

'For ever.'

'My God,' said Flavia. 'Oh my God, my God.'

Andrée looked at her with detached interest.

'*You* are doing that?'

'With your help, and Rosie's.'

'Because . . . you are against the divorce?'

'Because *I* am against the divorce.'

'But, Andrée, it's they who count— it *cannot* mean as much to you.'

'That has been your view throughout our brief relationship. I am aware how consistently you've been disregarding my feelings and position.'

'Your position?'

'*My* position.' That mystifying look of near enjoyment Flavia had so often seen appear on Andrée's face now crystallized. She said lightly, 'I am Michel's wife.'

'Did you not know?'

'The technicality, the obstacle— the partner of the unhappy marriage.'

'The impediment he ought to have got rid of long ago.'

'You are looking at me with new eyes as they say— well, go on, do.'

At last Flavia spoke. 'Is it true?'

'Ostrich.'

'You didn't tell me.'

'*Was* it necessary? I thought we were introduced? Oh perhaps we weren't, careless of Rosie.'

'I thought she . . . the wife . . . I mean you were shut up somewhere?'

'*What* did you say?'

'They told us she suffered from nerves.'

'*That* is your crowning touch,' said Andrée. 'Well, you are going to pay for it. As for the rest. *Who* told you this rubbish?'

'As a matter of fact it was the Fourniers when we first met them.'

'*Le juste retour des choses d'ici bas.*' Andrée's tone had gone back into voluptuous nonchalance. 'Didn't I tell you never to rely on Rosie's information?'

'You told me you were his cousin.'

'And so I am,' said Andrée. 'One doesn't prevent the other. I don't think I told you one single straight lie (that would have been too easy). I made a point of always telling you the truth, the limited truth, shall we call it? I was sailing near the wind often enough— Oh, there were quite a few warning signals. You will see what I mean when you cast back your mind on our conversations as I am sure you will do a good many times in the future.'

'*If only* someone had *told* me!'

'I was afraid that Therese had. That was a nasty moment.'

'I'm beginning to understand,' said Flavia. 'Therese must have taken for granted that I knew who you were.'

'You did not pay much attention to her warning.'

Flavia said, 'Did you come here just . . . for this? Did you come on purpose?'

'What I do I usually do on purpose. (*Unlike* you, my dear.) If you mean, did I come here foreseeing our entertaining little game? I must say, no. *That* was sheer bonus. I came here in the hope of picking up a trail that would let me put a stop to Michel's divorce.'

'But why? For God's sake, why? You have been living separated from him for years. What difference can it make to you? I don't believe you even like Michel?'

'Like Michel? I? That failure? That self-righteous bore? They go on about how unhappy I made him, how wretched he was with me— well, I was wretched with him, *and* bored! Stuck with a man for whom nothing counts more than his own integrity!'

'You look disapproving? Time you were told a few facts of life, you slobbering little moralist. "Behave better?" ' she mocked Flavia's voice, ' "Isn't that all to the . . . *good*?" Time you learnt a thing or two about your own behaviour. I've been longing to tell you some-home-truths, God how fed up I was with having to flatter you. I know you had more rough than smooth— it wasn't what everybody would call flattery— I did it in my style; but wasn't my attention flattering enough? Pretending to take you seriously, listening to you, throwing you scraps about politics and Saint-Simon? "*Do* come and talk to me," ' she mocked her own voice. ' "*Don't underrate yourself.*" You fell for it, didn't you, you conceited little fool?

'You thought that I *chose* to talk to you, chose to spend evening after evening with you? The pretensions you have, I imagine you got them from your precious mother— what a pair you must make.' Andrée laughed. 'But I suppose you can't see yourselves as others see you? The adventuress, the divorcée— I hear your father couldn't wait to kick her out— without house or home or country.'

Flavia said, 'I'm going to hit you, I'd hit you if you weren't a woman.'

'You mean,' Andrée said, 'if *you* weren't a woman. You really must get these things straight. Society may accept women going to bed together, but *not* fist-fights, dear, ever. To resume, the divorcée with her young daughter to tout for her, or shall we call a spade a spade? Weren't you sent out to lure Michel into the parlour? Shall we say with her young daughter to pimp for her? A masculine role which for once you filled, while grandma— who appears to have been the one respectable member of the family——'

'Andrée! Stop it!'

'*You*— ordering *me*? Let me tell you something, little girl, you cannot. Because you cannot afford to. You are in my hands, your precious mummy is. These detectives are *my* detectives, I hired them, I pay for them, I can do with that

evidence whatever I choose, or *might be persuaded to choose*—
you are following me? I could change my mind. I am warning
you: be nice to me, listen to me; don't spoil my fun now,
don't interrupt my little homily.

'I see that you have understood. Hope springs eternal. It
was you who brought me here, who insisted on the tête-
à-tête. So here we are and you will hear me out. And if you
please, none of your canine scowls.'

'Blackmailer.'

'You *are* crude. I don't mind. The exercise of blackmail
isn't appreciated nearly enough, it's almost its own reward.
Provided you do the dirty work yourself; I never do it by
letters unless I can be certain of a *personal* follow-up.'

'Andrée,' Flavia cried, 'you are putting it on? Nobody *is*
like that.'

'Smile and smile and be a villain? Am I too bad to be
true? That's what we're being taught by modern literature.'

Flavia said, 'You are play-acting. You have been all the
time that I've known you.'

For a second Andrée showed anger, then she said, sounding as aloof as ever, 'And what difference would that make?
Since it's my play and I've forced you all to take a part
in it.

'Now where was I? Oh, yes, the respectable old lady who I
was told committed suicide more or less on your doorstep
after she had learnt about the goings-on.'

'*You are unspeakable.*'

'Feeble, my dear, feeble. But the verbal weapons against
the wicked *are* so limited. If I'm wholly wicked— have you
decided yet? Perhaps you will let me give you a resumé of
my side of the . . . campaign (I'm catching your stammer)?
You like dotting the i's, so I'll begin at the beginning.

'Well, I knew that *they* had been to Paris but wasn't able to
find out where they'd actually stayed; they had been seen
but nobody was going to swear to it, a conspiracy of loyal
friends no doubt. After Paris they appeared to have vanished

into the proverbial thin air. Rosie— faithful soul— wrote to suggest Rome. A blank of course. Then she tried to get it out of you, but you didn't respond. She urged me to come down myself and try my hand. Rosie thinks I'm irresistible because I have snob appeal for her; you'd have to be fairly expert about the social structure of our bourgeoisie to appreciate that point; these things don't export and wouldn't have cut much ice with you. At any rate I wasn't thinking of you at that stage— Rosie can't make you out and her descriptions weren't very helpful— I expected I would get a servant in your house to go through your desk for me. Then it turned out that there weren't any servants. I was told about the way you live. The Fourniers thought it was because your mother was hard up. They said that before the Loulous came and took you up you had to have your meals in the cheapest place, they were sorry for you about that: Poor girl, much too thin, if you give her an apple it's gone in two bites. And so your mother was after Michel's money.

'That was rather a laugh, it almost made me decide to let the divorce go through. You see, Michel must have come very near the end of his money. That side of the Devaux' have never been more than just well off (it's my people who didn't regard it as beneath them to go into industry who are rich), they have a good deal of land— they never sell— but they've always put more into it than they took out, and now that Michel is using the land as a guinea-pig there *is* nothing to take out. He's been involved in other enterprises, not commercial ones needless to say, and he's been quite remarkably unlucky. Add to it his habit of giving money away. All you have to do is to be a friend of his and ask him, he'll be too proud to refuse. They don't know how little he's got left nowadays, nobody knows about the lump sum he gave me. That was a private agreement preliminary to our first divorce; the one that didn't go through.

'It's a far more intolerable situation for a poor man to be *married* to the woman who expected his money than to have her merely as his mistress, she knows that she isn't stuck with him and so won't let him feel it so much.

'Luckily I made inquiries. The boot is on the other foot, the poor old lady so conveniently dying left a fortune. An American fortune, I'll have you remember, not the safest thing at the moment. All this is no news to you, but it was to me and I bet that I've got more information about facts and figures than you have— I've even seen her list of investments, an American Consulate is not the fortress people like to think it is. The slump is bound to get worse but for the present at any rate she could well afford to give you decent pocket money.

'Don't protest. What difference does it make to me whether she is stingy or has reasons of her own to keep you short. What interests me at the moment are her reactions when she finds out what Michel regards as legitimate expenditure. I wonder whether he thinks the time has come to build himself an electric brain. Perhaps he won't consider himself free to do so if they aren't married. I see that I will have to think again.

'To return to my narrative. I arrived; I saw you; I saw the way you looked at me. It wasn't the kind of appeal that Rosie had had in mind. But it was going to do.

'Well, that first evening was pretty uphill, your strutting and talking big at the Fourniers' party, you were absurd, you were pathetic, you were a colossal little bore.

'But we don't have to go into that now, I can see you are sufficiently aware of it yourself.

'Next night was our dinner on my balcony. I noticed that you didn't take to my nice *mise en scène*; you balked and were hostile and critical. That was when you first began to interest me. I had expected you to spill the beans after my first soft look and your third glass of champagne. You refused the latter and I couldn't bring myself to produce the first. I am a truthful woman fundamentally, I don't like playing parts that I despise.

'You were very much on your guard about being drawn out. Drawn out about *their* guilty secret (which you did not guard so well after all), you were ready enough to blab about your own. You longed for me to know about you and Therese, didn't you? Curious ambition, when you think that the only man or woman on this coast she hadn't slept with are probably Michel and me. Even if Loulou *is* impotent, need she be quite so promiscuous?

'Do I see you flinch again?

'So then I tried a tack or two to find out how far you could be led or pushed and in what directions. I realized just in time that you were slipping away. You were quite astute about one thing, you felt that I was incapable of being interested in you emotionally, you could not believe that my affections were involved (perhaps I haven't got any?), I might have been interested erotically, your instincts may have told you that this was not inconceivable, but there you were on most uncertain ground, as well as uncertain of yourself, and I did nothing to help you. (All that is of the past. Let it remain in the air between us.) I rather think that in your own heart you wanted your sentiment for me to remain platonic, if only to keep it apart from your easier encounters. You may have had a sound instinct (for an intellectual of the kind you imagine yourself to be, you certainly have a good many) as to what is possible at your age and stage. Very young people are perfectly capable of love, they are sometimes capable of a sensually adequate affair; they are very very rarely capable of managing the two together, the *whole* thing is too much for them. And there's something else I don't mind telling you about— to show you that I am neither unfair nor biased and only harp on your bad points— I want to tell you something about your looks. I can safely do so as I've noticed that you don't care about them yourself one way or the other, and I don't think you ever will. People can take or leave them as far as you're concerned; conceit or indifference it comes to the same. You

want to be liked for other qualities. So a compliment from
me at the point we have reached is not going to boost your
morale. Well, your looks, my dear, are charming; they're
not exactly conventional and I'm not going to predict what
they will be like in twenty years from now with your guzzling
all the way, but for the present they will do, they will do
nicely for any man, boy, or girl.

'I'm not digressing. I did have, I do have, an interest in
you, it's genuine— so that confused you too— it's not personal (I don't need you), it's a clinical, a general interest. I
told you that people are my main thing. I didn't want to
lose you for more than one reason and when I saw that I
was about to, I had to put on the kind of act I *dislike*, I
pulled out the organ stops and told you about "my life",
about the "façade" life had forced on me— mawkish rubbish, I did resent that.'

'You did not really tell me anything,' Flavia said, 'I
thought about it later, it didn't hang together.'

'The devil it didn't?'

'It wasn't about your life at all, it was mostly about French
attitudes.'

'You know,' Andrée said, 'I could almost like you at
times.'

Flavia said, 'I must ask you again: why don't you let
Michel go? Go in form? I still don't understand. What can
you hope to gain?'

'You have read enough to know about *l'acte gratuit*.'

But Flavia was intent on unravelling it along her own
lines. 'It isn't as if . . .'

'Say it.'

'As if he'd ever come back to you.'

'Are you *sure*? (Assuming that I wanted him.)'

'Yes,' said Flavia.

'So young and so untender. (That's what he once said to
me.) And what makes you so sure, my tactful one?'

'A man like him does not put up with what you are.'

'He did have to put up with it for a good long time.'

Flavia said, 'That was his tragedy.'

Andrée stood up. They were facing each other across the enormous table. '*Still* full of fine words? I haven't crushed you yet. You haven't heard enough home-truths. What about *yourself*? Do you think he . . . a man like him (an ideal judge!) will put up with you now? Do you think he could bear your association with me? Quite apart from its results. Won't he, won't *they*, look at you also with new eyes?'

Flavia brought out, 'I shall tell them exactly . . . what happened.'

'Yes——?'

'That you stole their address.'

'Crude, my poor child, crude. One would think you had spent most of your young life in a police court. In your story, your . . . confession (gracious, your stammer again) would you mention your own gullibility?'

Flavia nodded.

'Your . . . infatuation?'

'Yes.'

'Your running after me? Your refusal to listen to Therese?'

'Yes.'

'Speaking of Therese, does your mother know— *she* who's such a one for *les beaux garçons*— is your mother aware of your . . . deviationist tastes? Don't frown. I can use other terms, there is quite a choice, classical, medical, contemporary. Let's try if you've heard any of them.' She did. 'You don't like that one? Does your mother know that it applies to you? Answer me!'

'I don't think I knew myself.'

'Meaning, until Therese? I suppose you will have to include your association with the Loulou family in the tale you are planning to unfold to Michel? It won't be so easy.'

'*Not easy*,' said Flavia.

'But mummy will forgive you?'

'Andrée— Andrée, is there nothing that could stop you from doing it?'

'If I believed, for instance, that they'd be more unhappy married than not married. I *was* rather afraid that she wouldn't give a damn. Fortunately you took the trouble to reassure me on that score.'

'Is there nothing you would take in exchange? Nothing I could give you?'

'A bribe, dear?'

'Something you wanted.'

'What could *I* want?'

'Wouldn't you rather be free yourself?'

'I am free.'

'To marry again?'

'Marry the kind of man who puts up with what you say I am? You wouldn't mind that? My marrying some inferior Michel as long as I leave the original to your mama?'

'Isn't there anyone you want for yourself?'

'Oh, for a time. My . . . influence on people doesn't last as long as you might think. (Michel was rather unique in that regard.) Besides I don't care about domesticity, or respectability. It's I who don't give a damn; your mother's turned out to be the conventional one, not surprising perhaps when you consider her— let's not qualify— past. I know, rumour may exaggerate, she *couldn't* have had quite as many lovers, though she must be rather older than she admits to being.'

'Constanza! She who never dreams of lying about something like her age!'

'Ah— I *have* provoked you into using the sacred name.'

Flavia controlled herself.

'You are going to hear something else. You do know whom you are really in love with?' Andrée gave her a long look; in her softest voice she said, 'You are madly in love with *her*.'

After a moment, Flavia said slowly, 'Everything you touch becomes . . . hideous.'

'Or true? Oh, you do have no stomach for reality. You don't want to see yourself as what you are— *you*, who are worse than your mother.' Andrée's voice went up, 'Oh, I told Rosette, never fear, St-Jean will be ringing with it, the story of the man you dragged into your bed— you can't even remember whether he's called Marc or Charles— you little pervert, you cold-blooded slut, shall we talk about what you let him do to you?'

Andrée was pressing her hands against the edge of the big table, the part that represented the extreme south-eastern corner of France. 'Shall we name the rather . . . indelicate? things people do with each other for lust or for money, or conjugal duty or sentiment, and which *you* allowed to be done to you to please me? Of all the forms of prostitution yours surely takes the biscuit.' There followed a sequence of precisely phrased obscenities, 'And that was what you let him do? And that?'

Flavia had stopped her ears.

Andrée became shrill.

Flavia cried, 'But . . . you are raving?' She was shaking herself. She looked at Andrée with a sense of the ground giving way, of sliding into the past. 'You are like . . . you are like . . .' She did not finish the sentence, she did not say that she was hearing Anna.

Presently, and quite abruptly, Andrée stopped.

Flavia said, 'I must go now.'

Andrée once more in full self-possession asked, 'Go to what?' And went on, 'So *you* are sending a telegram? I can read your thoughts. But it's not going to be much use your warning them, my detectives will be on their way to Madrid now. By air. I daresay it'll take them another twenty-four hours on a Spanish train, but you don't imagine that Michel and Mrs H. will be able to cover their tracks after ten weeks in Almuñecar?'

Flavia said, 'You haven't really answered me: I would do

anything for you, anything in the world, if you will let the divorce go through.'

Andrée looked at her. 'What have you got to offer?'

'Nothing now,' said Flavia. 'But I would work hard, I could work for the future.'

'For my financial support? Supplementary income is always useful, though hardly an adequate inducement in my case. I'm rather well off, you know.'

'I might . . . become something.'

'And dedicate your Ph.D. thesis to me?'

'If I promised to keep myself at your disposal for the whole of my life, doing everything you told me— the bad things, too— if I promised to serve you, like a pact, you know?'

'Ready to sell your soul?'

'Yes.'

'Your proposal shows some insight. Yet, once more, too crude. Childish and crude. No, I do not need a sorcerer's apprentice. As for your future— that academic future!— frankly, I don't believe you've got one. You are a precocious puppy and you've got a good memory (too good) for parrotting what you've read and heard, but have you ever proved your worth in the slightest way? Have you tried? You haven't even sat for an exam; at your age people like Michel and I had got our *bachots— summa cum laude*, what else?— not that it means much, but since you do cherish these ambitions, it's rather essential.' Still leaning against the table, Andrée picked up a little co-operative winery off the Roussillon. She was speaking with the utmost deliberation and gravity, without any of the maniacal strain of a few minutes ago, putting behind each word a full and memorable weight of conviction. 'You haven't got what it takes— you are a flash in the pan— you think about doing things, that's all— you're a dilettante. You will never get a degree, Flavia, you will never be a fellow of your college. Never, do you hear me? Never.'

Even at that moment Flavia recalled the fact that she

had kept from speaking of the other thing, the secret thing, her hope one day to write.

She went round the table and took the winery out of Andrée's hand before it came to any more harm. She uncrumpled it and replaced it accurately. As she turned to the door, Andrée followed her.

'And what are you going to do with the sweater I gave you? Try to burn it? You'll find that stuff pretty hard to light. Throw my sweater in the dustbin? Give it to the femme de ménage? Such *common* gestures. Well, it's your problem, one of your *minor* ones.'

Flavia ran through the house, the verandah, the garden, at the gate Fournier's nephew stepped into her way. 'At last, I've been trying to get hold of you——' She ran on. 'I've got to see you, I've got to talk to you——'

'Not now, for God's sake, not now.'

CHAPTER EIGHT

Cornered

I

To Therese the essential facts were quickly told. She had no remedy, offered no consolation.

'*C'est mal*,' she said, shaking her great head, '*c'est mal*.'

Her soft word was for Flavia's mother. To Flavia protesting her initial good intentions she said with final sternness, 'That was no excuse.'

II

During the days that followed Flavia did not stir from the villa except for a walk after dark. She remained in her room in the mornings sequestering herself from the femme de ménage, pleading a bilious attack through the door, feeling as sick as she said. The rest of the time she spent pacing the floor downstairs: recapitulating. Her most concrete reflection was, If only it were still eight days— nine days— ten days ago.

Twice the Fournier nephew called. He knocked at this door and that, called her name under windows, walked round the house, while she lay low till he went. The second time he left a note which she destroyed unread, feeling that she could not bear communicating with him again in any form.

One day she found two letters in the box. The first was from Mr James and it was post-marked Rome. It was a long letter containing many sheets of fine rapid script, requiring

more than one reading to take in. Mr James's first paragraph revealed that he was in Rome, had travelled to Rome:
the prince had had a heart attack.

Not the most serious kind, he reassured her at once, then a
few lines farther down the page appeared to contradict himself. He had set out from London, the letter went on, as soon
as he received the news, Rico after all— though nobody ever
seemed to remember that— was one of his oldest friends, his
earliest friend in Rome; moreover he had realized that Constanza must have been sent for and that in the circumstances
she might be alone. This indeed had proved to be the case.
Here followed particulars about trains, arrivals and de-
partures; Flavia skipped these for the present. On another
page she found (some passages stood out more legibly than
others),

> ... end of an epoch ... at least so it is to me ... sad to
> think that you, dear girl, will never have known. ...

It was over then? The prince——? And here,

> ... glad to learn that the government have promised a
> safe-conduct to your mother ... no attempts while she
> is here to bring her to book for her political peccadil-
> los ... last illness of a parent still respected in Italy
> ... grateful the régime ... not entirely dehuman-
> ized.

So the prince *was* dead?

But no,

> ... tenderly and competently nursed by Giulia ...
> fully conscious ... great pleasure in your mother's
> presence ... oppressive ... writing to you in the very
> *salotto* dear Anna used to ... still remarkable how un-
> inhabitable the house became after she left. ... My
> hotel room ... stifling ... Santa Maria Sopra Minerva
> ... to be near ... a seven minutes' walk ... the
> Corso ... the scirocco. ... Never known Rome so
> empty ... one used to be away ... season of *saturnali*
> ... *ferrogosto* ... evening in Trastevere with one of

your great-uncles-in-law. . . . Rico . . . almost cheerful . . . apparently improving every day, although he
himself . . . quite certain of a second attack. Curiously
enough everybody else here expects this, too . . . according to the doctors nothing in the clinical condition
to justify . . . of a far less serious nature than my own
two years ago . . .and here I am to tell the tale (for the
time being). . . . His sisters . . . your mother . . . Giulia
. . . dissolving into tears . . . Italian women . . . extraordinary the way she becomes one of them here . . . so
much stoicism . . . open emotion. . . . She wonders,
she speaks of it, whether her true life and lines may not
have been to have remained here . . . 'They plucked me
from my father' . . . They did that! But true lines? I,
who saw her in those years before the war in London. . . . Now, such certitude of death . . . to her— you
know her— it is the final point: *Extinction* . . . with it
goes, when does it not? a part of her own life. . . . Too
much in one year. . . . Michel Devaux . . . glad to
have had a glimpse . . . between trains . . . saw him off
while your mother was taken straight to the palazzo.
And now an almost unbroken paragraph,
    . . . best for her to go through it in that ritual way to
which she was brought up. Alassio seems to haunt her
all the more because she was not there . . . decided not
to send for you, dearest girl, and I agreed with them . . .
too late for you to meet your grandfather at this stage
and much too late for him. How I wish you could have
known him as I did, young Rico at Castelfonte . . .
coming in from riding. . . . That was his home, his and
Constanza's. It was Anna and I, the barbarians from
across the sea, who had the love for Rome. That was *our*
home!
    By the way, I am afraid there is the bad news that
Castelfonte is now lost, that no-good brother of hers
(much in evidence at present snivelling away in the

family circle) has already pocketed millions and millions
of lira from some nefarious concern that plans to turn
the place into a casino cum resort with bungalows on the
hills; nothing but an equivalent number of millions
would make him change that tiny, greedy mind.

Flavia put down the sheets. The prince ill, getting better,
or not better; Giorgio about to succeed; Constanza in Rome;
Michel also in Rome, but apparently gone again. She was
seized by hope. Recounting days and dates it became certain
that they could have, that they *must* have, left Spain before
the arrival of the plain-clothes men. She was shaking, she was
levitating with relief— then the record in her mind played
clearly,

> *You don't imagine that Michel and Mrs H. will be able to
> cover their tracks after ten weeks in Almuñecar? Waiters,
> chambermaids, you know. You've heard how these things are
> done?*

And yet, and yet? They might conceivably have had
Flavia's own telegram in time to make the waiters and the
chambermaids promise not to tell. She could not see Michel,
she could see Constanza doing this and doing it successfully—
a conspiracy of loyal friends, a conspiracy of loyal servants.
The world was still like that, the world was not Andrée's.
The hotel register? One can tear out a page when nobody is
looking and burn it, and Flavia could see her mother doing
this as well.

She sorted the letter into order and began carefully now at
the beginning. Constanza, she found, had arrived at Roma-
Termini eighteen hours after Mr James's own arrival. He
had met the train and she had been taken immediately to a
waiting car. Mr James had hung back while she and Michel
Devaux said good-bye. Afterwards the two men had walked
to the Grand Hotel where Mr James had given Devaux
breakfast. They had sat about for a couple of hours until it
was time to go back for the Paris train.

Devaux told me about the manner of their leaving

Spain. They drove to Murcia where they caught a
train that took them up the coast, They were obliged to
leave his car and books in the small place by the sea
where they had been spending the summer. [Here
Flavia groaned] and he appears to be anxious about their
fate; your mother's effects— you know how light she
travels— seem to have presented less of a problem. At
Valencia they were able to change on to a faster train
which reached Barcelona at four o'clock the next
morning, and from there they boarded the through
carriage to Genoa at noon. In fact, Devaux managed to
get her here most efficiently and considering that he
would not allow her to fly by a Spanish line with the
minimum of delay. Your mother, as you would expect of
her, took the heat, fatigue and various discomforts of the
journey with complete cheerfulness and I am sure that
she was looked after by him *à merveille*.

Mr James went on to say that he concurred with Devaux's
reasons for not hanging about in Rome.

He told me the nature of the business that was awaiting
him in Paris and he had that look upon his face of a
man who expects to come prancing back with a marriage
licence in his pocket. What do I think of him? I can
hear you ask the question. I've been told that you and
he have taken much to one another, so what you would
enjoy to get from me would be enlargement rather than
plain confirmation. Well, what can I tell *you* who have
spent weeks with him after my mere two hours of
wandering in public places? They were, I can say, well-
spent hours, I taking in (with such attention: we hope
so much for those we love), he laying himself open to be
taken in. He showed a simple joy in finding himself with
an old friend of your mother's, treating me quite un-
selfconsciously as one in *loco parentis*. (Like many people
who set out on intellectually original lines he has a
yearning for the traditional human ties.) I was charmed

— how could I not be?— by so much grace of manner covering so much quality. He has what is well-named *une grande gentillesse*, that rare compound of patience, sensitiveness and great kindness. That he has a mind, you know; I would also guess that he has an ample reservoir of will, and that he is using it in what many people would regard a negative direction. The *forte* he has chosen is detachment and uncompromisingness. He is fastidious and does not conceal it, and the consequence of that is that he stands aside. There is an aura of defeat about him, his ideas are not likely to find echo or approval in his lifetime (if ever), and she has talked to me a little, only a very little, about the extreme moral and emotional strain he was submitted to over a long period in his private life. What impressed me about Constanza and Devaux— though, mind you, I only saw them together for a matter of minutes— is that they are less like people about to strike out together than like two people seeking rest. What we must hope for is that in due course they will be able to do the first after having found the second. Only the future can tell.

For the time being he has let himself become dominated by a set of prescriptions as how to regulate his conduct, some of them on the stiff-necked and quixotic side (a French agnostic intellectual with a non-conformist conscience is a force of nature, so far I had not been able to study one at close range); his standards of probity, responsibility and industry appear to me to be not short of the fantastic although, if personally idle, I do not belong to a generation that could be called permissive.

Your mother tells me that he refuses to verify any bill presented to him on the ground that to question the honesty of those one deals with is in itself a dishonest act. I asked her if this applied to bills in restaurants, and she said it did. 'Can you not stop him?' 'I don't think that I want to.' She also told me that if he does discover some unreliable or dishonest act— one must wonder by what process?— his disapproval and rejection are absolute and formidable. It *is* a change for her, drawn as she used to be, I think I can say this to you without undue disrespect to your unusual, talented, and unusually unscrupulous father, to men with a strain of the opportunist or the buccaneer. Never to miss a pleasure in life at whatever cost to someone else was an almost philosophical concept with Simon; with Devaux, it is to do one's duty at whatever cost to oneself, and he always sees his duty clear— which is of course more clearly than one's duty ever can be seen. Oh, he has his faults, or if you prefer, his dangerous qualities.

Constanza sees them but— most unlike her— refuses to comment. It was Anna who wanted people to be what they were not, her daughter, never tried to change (or hold), she saw her loved ones plain; *but* she talked of what she saw, she judged them. She judged Simon to the point that he turned away from her in order to regain confidence in himself. Now she is determined not to judge Michel Devaux.

Not even his political ideas. I can see that she is not at ease about them, about the long view he is taking. I, more frivolously, must confess to being charmed by his pessimism which I find refreshing in contrast to the half-baked nostrums so solemnly propounded by the run of the high-minded. Devaux's theme is the spoliation of our environment on this planet by increasing population and rash use of new technologies; his nostrum, to *by-pass* greed, ignorance and lazy lack of foresight (Giorgio multiplied by myriads), unlikely to be changeable on a mass-scale in the present context of society, by excluding them from public administration and decision-making. He believes that this could be managed by selecting our custodians by 'objective' tests— no believer he in universal franchise!— even by breeding them to specification like so many queen bees. He thinks that this may be possible, if not acceptable, in the near future. *Not acceptable.* Hence the pessimism. The old old problem, how to effect desirable changes without employing undesirable means tied to the most basic problem of it all, desirable to whom? Devaux would say that as one must choose for children why not also for the remaining high percentage of the insufficiently mature (detected, no doubt, by more tests)? His world *is* Utopian, and Quality, not equality, is the dream. It all has little connection with any extant political right or left, to the extremes of each he has in turn been accused of belonging; his own dimensions, I should say, are severely vertical: from high to low. For one of my age, it is an exhilarating spectacle to see a man go so slap against his time. Your mother, I am sure, would like him to be less detached about the Bolsheviks and Fascists and the menace of that odious man in Germany, her point being, as it has always been, that it is upon us now to get people out of Siberia and off Mussolini's islands and to stop rearmament (in my view mutually exclusive undertakings) rather than shudder at tomorrow's ravages.

Flavia laid down the sheets in dejection. She had barely taken in what she was reading, none of it was now capable of firing her. Nevertheless, after a few listless minutes, she resumed.

The next paragraph did nothing to lift her spirits.

Needless to say that we did not go into all of that at Roma-Termini (I have glanced since at his books and had various conversations with your mother), what we talked about, apart from the house they hope to furnish in the South of France and a tower of his that he intends to make over to you, was the boot-black and the traffic policeman's gestures and Italian cooking. He told me that Constanza cooked for him in Spain. He literally couldn't swallow Spanish food, he quakes when he talks of it. It isn't because he is insular, it is more complicated than that; he does not like French cooking either but that, unlike the Spanish oil, appears to be a moral issue. He regards food as *le vice français*— in many ways he is one of nature's Protestants— so he was perfectly happy with your mother's pasta. (Neither she nor Rico ever properly appreciated Anna's house-keeping, that was left to me, and later on to your father.) Constanza made it herself, what's more, that pasta, rolling it out, getting food for her man for all the world to see in the kitchen of that Spanish inn.

Why am I writing to you at such length? Well, for one thing your mother has asked me to do so— you know what *she* is about letters— 'Give her my love, tell her about everything.' She is concerned about you. 'Do you think Flavia is all right?' I told her I was certain that you were, chasing no doubt a hundred hares. (Did you not make it clear to me, dear girl, when you last wrote, that you had no wish for company?) She spoke to me of the curious feeling she had when she passed along your coast in their train: it was early morning and she kept looking out of the window and for a few seconds she could see the bay of St-Jean. 'What is Flavia doing at this hour— is she in the tower, reading? or perhaps swimming in the very sea below? It was a queer feeling, I had that impulse to wave to her, and yet it was so remote, so inexorable, I might as well have been up in the aeroplane Michel wouldn't let me take.'

The morning, the time (if the dates worked out were right) when Flavia was weeping for Andrée, and Andrée was in the tower.

So you see, dear girl, that telling you 'about every-thing' means a good many touches here and there. It is a long time since you and I talked together and it may be a longer one before we shall again. There are one or two things I should like to say to you, convey to you— I must try. I wish we *were* talking, though it is not that I lack time, your mother spends hours sitting with her father, and even if it were not for this confounded heat my time for running after the sights of Rome is past. I should have been content— more content!— never to have seen Rome again. What one has loved, one possesses. Return won't do. It is unnecessary. The reality is too strong as well as too diluted by material cares and impacts. I always felt that Anna's mourning for the City was mistaken; how I wish that she had been able to realize that it was hers. I do not expect you, my child, to follow me here. When one is young one needs the experience, the whole of it, in the round, in the flesh, not the imprint of it or, as it might seem to you, the shadow. When one is young one cannot imagine, literally not imagine, the changes that will overtake one's spiritual digestion; one cannot see a future different in kind from the present, one can only see an extended now. It is later, when one has *become* different— and how much so— that we may be able to see (if we have taken care not to forget too much) the then *and* the now; and perhaps that double vision is the enrichment, the only one, that old age brings us.

Don't be impatient. Do I appear to be talking about myself? Perhaps what I am trying to impress on you is that when you yourself will have reached the stage— as people of talent and imagination will— at which you can see both the now and then, it will matter immensely what the quality of the *then*, your present now, has been. Beware— I don't think I need to tell you, perhaps I am trying still to tell myself— beware of allowing it to go meagre by failing to feel and to record. Train your memory, on all levels. The worst we can do towards the past is to let it go by default.

Again I wish that I were talking to you instead of writing and could be helped along by your questions; letters are soliloquacious work. But there it is; and forgive the trouble that you will be having with my handwriting— one is not getting younger. I am not brave enough, you will notice, to say *I*.

Perhaps I am affected by the spectacle of my friend Rico's illness, a man my junior by nearly a decade. Rico has given up. He reminds me of nothing so much as a passage of Trelawny's about Shelley bathing in the Arno (you will recall that the poet could not swim): having plunged in and sunk instantly to the bottom, he lay on the river-bed 'extended like a conger eel, not making the least effort or struggle to save himself'.

Here Flavia cried again; not for her grandfather whom she had once been able to see so vividly and who was becoming more and more implausible to her, but for herself; for her isolation, her own inability to struggle— What *can* I do?— to save them, to save herself. Mr James's letter, including her so naturally, brought home the sense of her own exile; for her, the events described could not be taking place in the same world and time; she felt insulated from them, as insulated as Constanza must have felt when the train had swept her past the bay, they had no present reality for one so far from grace.

That she herself might move did not occur to her; if there was impulse to hurl herself into Constanza's presence, it was paralysed by a sense of the impossible. She was not able to believe in herself, in Flavia, passing the gate of the dark house in Rome waiting for death, bearing her tale.

Presently she went and warmed herself a little food. She ate; then cried again. She told herself, speaking aloud in the old habit, I am losing grip. But the answer was only a quiet yes.

Dully she returned to the one task on hand. She unravelled another passage of the letter. It contained no fact of material or immediate reassurance. It was about Constanza.

You will find her changed. How can I describe her? Acquiescent? Placid? Rounder? Were it not for hubris I should be tempted to put down serene, or an even simpler word. Older? Yes, older. She has entered another phase. (The last time I saw her was a year ago almost to the day at the time of her flight with Lewis Crane.) Now it is as if she had laid aside half her brilliance and half her will and her immense claims on life like so much ornament (and armour—Anna is no more), almost as if she had deliberately dimmed herself. Perhaps she knows that by making oneself less one may be able to give more.

If she seems muted— oh, very comparatively speaking— she also seems at peace. She asked me if I could reconstruct for her some wintry lines of Hölderlin's she once came across in a translation and which lately keep jingling in her mind, they go something like, Who has no house now/Will build nevermore. 'But I am building a house now,' she says. 'Aren't I?' She is certain that destiny— she won't settle for less— has presented her with Michel Devaux, her second chance, or third or fourth, whatever her reckoning, to make up for the mistakes and omissions of the past. One smiles, and fears. And yet— who am I to scoff when the name I so often gave her in my mind, the name I once heard Simon use in his way, lightly, was (*she* will not thank me for spelling it out on paper) a favourite of the gods?

It was almost with relief that Flavia turned to the second letter. It was from her English tutor an acknowledgement, presumably, of her apology for having failed to do the weekly essay, and she opened the envelope without interest or anticipation. The opening, 'You tell me that you have slipped into neglecting your work for some days and ask me to regard it as a holiday,' reminded her of the present identical situation: another note of apology was overdue. Ah well, it would have to be written; she felt nothing but reluctance at this demand on her to cope.

The rest of the letter was short and clear. The gist, set down in a large and well-shaped hand, sprang at her as it were from the single page: I am aware that for some months you have had no holiday, when most people would have had one. Was not that exactly what we had agreed on when we drew up your course? I was not in favour of the plan of your working on your own and without supervision. I am not saying that your work has not been quite satisfactory so far, however, you have too much ground to cover and too many gaps to make up to be able to afford any slackening off if you want to take the examination in October. You cannot afford to in terms of sheer time. I am surprised at your having apparently lost sight of this fact. Perhaps you will decide to work in England, or to postpone your going up for another year?

Flavia had felt that nothing more would be able to touch her; now she found that it was not so. That blow reached her more swiftly, more directly than any of the others and it collapsed her last defences. For some time she remained in the same place, the same position.

There followed days and nights when waking or under shallow sleep her mind was a passage through which there marched, unhaltably, a succession of set words; unceasingly, the three records turned and turned: Andrée speaking in all the modulations of her moods and voice, now Mr James, now the unseen man in England whose approval and support had been one more illusion.

The villa was the last house on the hill, once or twice Flavia heard sounds that might be of approaching wheels—Someone to come for me. Constanza has never been the mother who was suddenly by one's side. Anna is dead. Therese! (She prayed for this.) But the sounds always stopped short below.

She was still able to conceive of one way back, the beginning of a way back, to write step by step, truthfully, of all that happened, a long letter, a difficult letter; a letter difficult to begin. Flavia put it off from day to day.

III

One morning she heard a klaxon, two light short blasts like a morse signal. She went outside. It was the long car. It was, once more, Andrée. She looked gay, composed, crisp. There was luggage on the back seat.

Flavia wondered whether she was in fact delirious.

Andrée spoke. 'I am not a ghost. I've come back. I've changed my mind.'

Flavia only stared at her.

'Cat got your tongue?'

Slowly, Flavia said, 'You have changed your mind . . . it was only a nightmare?' She said it as if she were still talking only to herself.

'Don't rush to conclusions. I've changed my mind about not needing *you*. I find I want my sorcerer's apprentice. I've missed you. These last days have been dull, there isn't much point in the game if you've got no one to talk about it. I realized how good an audience you are, one of my best since Michel. You and he have that in common— you're vulnerable.

'So I came back to fetch you. Hop in, off we go.'

Flavia said, 'You want me to go away with you?'

'You heard me. You're not being very bright this morning.'

'For long?' said Flavia.

'A day? A week? Ten years? The timing will be tricky.'

Flavia said nothing. Andrée looked at her with interest but made no comment.

Flavia got a hold on herself. 'If I come with you will you let them have the divorce?'

'Horse-trader. Well, I might. I'm not saying I will and I'm not saying I won't. Let's see how we get on, let's see what value you're going to give.'

Flavia said, '*I don't want to go with you.*'

'There's my bull-dog. I thought we'd lost him. Please yourself. Here's your chance, not a good one mind, but the last. So go and make yourself presentable, comb your hair, put on some of your *pressed* pants. Take a bag.'

Flavia went into the house to do as she was told. Andrée followed her.

'Pack some of your nice shirts.'

Under Andrée's eyes Flavia put a few things into a case.

Mr James's letter was visible on a table under a stone for paperweight. If Andrée saw it, she said nothing.

Twenty minutes later they were on the road. As they entered Toulon, Flavia said, 'May we stop please so that I can get some money?'

'Money where?'

'From the bank, I've got a box.'

Andrée said, 'Apprentices need no money of their own.'

'Please,' said Flavia, 'I'd rather.'

'Thinking of your return fare?'

Flavia touched her pocket.

They did not stop at Toulon.

They took the inner road. Presently Andrée said, 'Want to stop for lunch somewhere?'

'No, thank you.'

'You'll find some biscuits and an orange in the back.'

'No, thank you.'

Andrée herself did not say much. She drove fast, though not excessively so, and with concentration.

Flavia looked at the quattrocento profile by her side and the beauty of it that was always there, and looked away again. She thought, If we had a crash that would be a solution. But the road was reasonably wide and straight and Andrée's driving was not of that kind at all.

Andrée said, 'When we were young, Michel and I, we and all our friends were coached by a man called Raoul who was a pro and an ex-rally-driver. None of us would have dreamt of taking out a real car just on our official *permis de conduire*, we all put ourselves through Raoul's drill. He made us practise cornering on a skating-rink and we had to learn to change gears without using the clutch. I can do it to this day. But what Raoul was really fanatical about was safety. When you are at the wheel, he told us, it's just as if you were handling a gun: you are responsible, you are in charge. The whole of the time. If you're below par or worried about something you're not fit to drive and you *don't*. He terrorized us. You can't imagine what it was like turning up at Raoul's after one'd been out dancing all the night.'

Drawn into it without her will, captivated by the sheer pleasure of human conversation, the sweet reflection of past ordinary life, Flavia said, 'You must have enjoyed it, it sounds such fun.'

Andrée answered in the same simple spirit. 'Oh, it was. We worshipped Raoul, we were all car-mad at that time and his training was really wonderful, you can still know a Raoul driver anywhere. Michel was his star pupil, but then he had a natural bent for it. Some day I must tell you about Michel aged eleven and the Hispano. Do I see two and a half inches of shade?'

They stopped and parked the car off the road. As they were sharing the fruit and biscuits under a pine tree, Andrée said, 'So don't expect me to drive myself over a cliff, if you want to get rid of me you will have to do it yourself. I don't think that you'll get off, your motive wouldn't be moral to the jury. It wouldn't be the guillotine, though, on account of your age.'

'I would not try to get off, I wouldn't put them through the horror of the trial. Besides——'

'What?'

'Can one live after one has killed someone?'

'So you *have* thought of it,' said Andrée.

'Yes,' said Flavia.

'A fit beginning for our little outing or lifelong ménage or whatever it'll turn out to be.'

'I didn't think you'd mind.'

'Your telling me? Or your putting poison in my coffee cup?'

'I couldn't do that!'

'What can you do? May I ask?'

'Oh,' Flavia said, 'it's all a fantasy.' And, driven on by her need to talk, 'Suicide as well. I know that.'

'Isn't that a mercy?'

'No. Only knowing that a door is locked.'

Andrée took her in with that open interest she so often showed.

'I could shoot you, perhaps, from quite far, without really seeing you, as they must do in wars.'

'Conditions somewhat difficult to reproduce?'

'When you think of it,' Flavia said, 'some people you see walking in the street must have killed that way.'

'And live on.'

Flavia said miserably, 'It's horrible, I find it horrible, even now.'

'Except for the result as far as I'm concerned, you could bear that? You can hope for that?'

'If you were dead all would be as before.'

'I wonder,' Andrée said.

'Not all. But much.'

'Isn't that a criminal wish?'

'I suppose so.'

'Then aren't you a murderer at heart?'

'Yes, that too,' Flavia said with such despair that Andrée was moved to say, 'I think we've gone too far, both of us. Come on, let's move from here.'

They drove through the Forêt du Dom. There had been forest fires that week and the air still smelt of ashes and charred wood and the heat was very great. When they came to the turning for St-Tropez, Andrée did not take it. Ten minutes later they stopped at Beauvallon. 'I much prefer Ste-Maxime,' she said, 'but this is the one hotel this side of Monte Carlo that's got a suite.'

She seemed to be expected. The manager took them upstairs and saw them in. There was a spacious bedroom with a vast brass bed and several windows shuttered against the sea, a small sitting-room and off it a narrow second bedroom. It was in that room that Flavia found herself; a boy brought in her suitcase, propped it on a stand, saluted, left and shut the door.

She had her watch. The time was ten minutes past three in the afternoon.

She took her things out of the suitcase and arranged them in the cupboard and in the cabinet de toilette. She had brought no book. She sat down on the bed.

Some time later there was a knock at the door, another bell-boy bringing a bottle of Evian water on a tray.

Flavia began to pace— five steps from door to window, five steps back. When she became too dizzy she sat down on the bed again.

No sound came from Andrée's quarters.

Except for these constraints time in that room was not very different from being alone in the villa.

In the evening there was another knock, a chambermaid this time, Madame is expecting Mademoiselle downstairs for dinner.

The dining-room was lit up but not crowded. Andrée was at a corner table in an open french window. She was wearing a white linen dress and a coral necklace. 'They're having a bad season,' she said, 'the slump is beginning to tell in places like this.'

Flavia took her place opposite.

'Have an apéritif, it'll do you good.'

'No, thank you. It won't. Do me good.'

'Ah?'

'I found that out. Not even wine.' She could not stop herself from going on. 'Perhaps it only works when . . . all is well.'

'Not the general view.'

'I know,' Flavia said solemnly. 'Another resource that I haven't got. My father used to say that it pulled him through anything.'

'Tell me,' Andrée said, 'after I left, the week I was away, what did you do?'

Flavia told her.

'You didn't go to see Therese again?'

'With their worrying and busy with Loulou's painting and Therese finding me so bad? How could I?' She spoke without disguise; it was the candour with which one soul in hell might address another. 'Therese feels I've let her down.'

Andrée listened; her expression was not unkindly.

Flavia went on. 'I can't talk to her, words don't get to her.' And suddenly she told about the time when she had talked all night.

'You don't choose your audience wisely,' Andrée said.

'Therese isn't interested in what people tell about themselves, she believes in what she sees, she believes in deeds.'

'So you think she's dropped you?'

'I love Therese. I shall always love her.'

'Your loyal friend.'

'Loyalty does matter a great deal to Therese.'

The waiter came hovering again. 'Yes, give her some more,' Andrée said to him. 'Eat up, you need it, you're getting to look like that boy in the story-book who refused to eat his soup, made of nothing but match-sticks.'

Flavia's eyes filled.

'Would it surprise you to hear that there isn't much love lost between Therese and Michel? She has no use for him, he is too finicky for her taste. And Michel, well, he doesn't like that world, Michel's no Bohemian, he won't stand for sloppiness in any form, don't make a mistake about that because he occasionally goes about in mechanic's overalls. I was told that when you first saw him you took him for a taxi-driver?'

Flavia was going to say, How do you know? and who told you? but checked herself. She had learnt how much Andrée enjoyed these minor moments of omniscience. 'There is nothing . . . sloppy about Therese and Loulou, you can't know them, you always misjudge her. You said that she is promiscuous, it isn't like that at all. Friendship is the great thing with her— between friends everything is natural, do you see?'

'I see,' said Andrée.

'Isn't that as it ought to be?'

'*Ought*,' Andrée said, 'is not *is*.'

When they had finished their dinner they went for a stroll on the beach. After that they parted for the night in the stiff little sitting-room upstairs. 'You must ring for your breakfast in the morning,' Andrée said. 'Ring for anything you want.'

Inside her room Flavia found that she could sleep. She slept well. She woke early and her head felt clear. She looked about her and out of the window on to the well-kept, dreary hotel garden, and the situation seemed unreal to her. Unreal and silly. Unreal and ominous. She told herself that she could run away.

Instead she washed and dressed and got herself ready for the day. Nothing happened. At last she rang for some tea. The idea that Andrée was paying for everything bothered her. With the tea, brought by yesterday's boy, came a copy of the *Figaro* and the *Continental Daily Mail* and a couple of uncut French novels. Flavia drank her tea, then paced or sat. Below, people were coming out carrying golf clubs or bathing things. Flavia wondered if it would be all right for her to go

out. But that meant going through the sitting-room and she
decided to stay put.

She had a second shower-bath in the cabinet de toilette.
Every now and then she admonished herself to think hard
about Andrée's behaviour, about what to expect and what
was expected of herself, but she got nowhere. She felt confused and she hated Andrée too much. Everything was
distorted. The hating would not subside and she nourished
it with invented circumstances causing Andrée's deflation
and defeat.

At noon she was summoned into the presence. She responded with near eagerness.

The whole of the time that Flavia spent at Beauvallon was
divided in that way. The hours in the room, the hours of
waiting, uncertainty, total disoccupation; and the actual encounters, the reality, always in a cooler key, not lessening
aversion and uncertainty, yet bringing interest, relief, a
curious appeasement.

As soon as I'm with her, Flavia warned herself, I eat out of
her hand. But the next time it was the same.

On a drive they took on the second day, she was nevertheless able to move to an offensive. 'Andrée, what am I supposed to do? What do you want of me?'

'Didn't I tell you?'

'You proposed a bargain, you didn't name the price.'

'The bill comes at the end.'

Flavia was on to that quickly, 'The bill for letting them
off?'

'You're so impatient. Don't start on that subject. Just do
as you're told— it won't be for long now.'

'But I am *not* told.'

'The perfect apprentice guesses.'

'I am not your apprentice, you are not teaching me your

skills and secrets, You are only . . .' it came to her then, 'you are only a puppet-master.'

Andrée looked at her without displeasure.

'Oh, you've been very considerate,' Flavia said. She thought of the polite knocks at the door and the books and the mineral water always replenished. 'And you don't blow hot and cold any more,' (again that compulsive candour), 'you don't say . . . unforgivable things, you are civil all the time, as if I were a real guest.'

'Some things need never be said twice. Yes, civil, that is the word. This round, it's going to be that: civil.'

'But I don't know what it's all about— it frightens me— why do you want me here?'

Andrée said in her light voice, 'Why not for companionship? a sparring partner. Can't we leave it at that? Don't think you're the only one who is ever alone.'

That evening Andrée said, 'Your mother is in Rome, I mention it in case you haven't heard. Your grandfather is quite ill.'

'Had they——?' Flavia said. 'Were they——?'

'Yes, they were gone. When the detectives got there, they'd left forty-eight hours before. The evidence was all over the place, books with their names in them, clothes, he'd even left his car. The Delahaye isn't exactly mass-produced.' Flavia remained dead-pan and she went on. 'That car. He's going to have more trouble. The triptych was run out— they're impossible in Spain about such things— they were going to impound the car. I had that fixed. I wanted the detectives to drive it back to France; they refused, said they couldn't touch Michel's property, they weren't bailiffs they said, their job was matrimonial offences. Sticklers. I think I will send a chauffeur out and have it taken over the border for Michel. You think he will appreciate it?'

And as Flavia still did not respond, 'They found a telegram, signed by you, in a pigeonhole down at Almuñecar.

That, too, came after they were gone. The detectives grabbed *that*. Text ludicrously mutilated— you ought at least to have used French, they make less of a hash of another Latin language, and I could have put it shorter— still, it might have served as evidence of . . . your good intentions.'

Flavia said, 'You mean my telegram's been put in a dossier?'

'No,' said Andrée, 'your telegram has been destroyed.'

At their next meeting she let fall a warning. 'I think I told you that I made a point of not telling you a single straight lie? That was while you were in the dark as to my identity. Now that this particular card is on the table, we shall play it differently.'

'And may I lie, too?' said Flavia.

Andrée considered this, 'Why not? If you *have* something to lie about.'

On the third day Andrée sent a message regretting that she was unable to join Mademoiselle for luncheon, would Mademoiselle proceed alone.

That evening Flavia asked point-blank, 'Have you made up your mind— will you let Michel off?'

They were in the stiff sitting-room, Andrée on the upright sofa, Flavia leaning against the back of a chair. Andrée got up and used the house telephone to order *citron-pressés*. They came fairly quickly. Andrée told the waiter to leave the tray. She cut and squeezed one of the lemons and filled up her glass, she seemed to want to underline the point of not making Flavia fetch and carry. 'Help yourself,' she said.

'Why did he marry me? Have you ever asked yourself? Would you like to hear our story? Why did I marry him? He was madly in love with me, which won't surprise *you*. I was far from displeased. Michel then was not so dusty either, everybody thought the world of him. He had an exceptional academic record and he had had a very brave war— he came back with so many medals that they forgave him the anti-war pamphlet he wrote and published; he'd only have to choose his career, they said. *And* he was so handsome. Well, he is still, but you cannot imagine what he was like then. It was just after the war and young and whole men were rare, women used to stop in the street to have a second look at Michel. It was also the time when the country was beginning to discover *le sport*, and there he was back from horse-shows in Rome and Madrid and Brussels having won all those prizes for France. Michel on a horse, I must say, was a lovely sight. People were mad about him, M. J. Devaux was a kind of god. (That was one of the reasons why he gave it up so soon, he couldn't stand the publicity.) I was never much a one for horses— I don't seem to get very far with them— but I travelled with Michel a few times, to Budapest, to Brioni, I was his fiancée and we were fêted everywhere. There was a certain quality about it all then, an elegance, in those first free years of peace. Tennis was my own line. I was good at it, really good, Suzanne says I once took a game off her (I did take more than one off Señorita Alvarez). I didn't push it, what with the training and being told I would have to put on some weight and muscle, per- haps someone ought to have made me a bet. I played the tournaments a bit though, Michel played too— he wasn't bad either— he and I used to do mixed doubles. People looked twice at me as well. Oh, we were quite a couple!

'The ball, as they used to say, was at our feet. I was al- ways fond of that saying although one only hears it about people for whom things did not turn out that way. Then, everyone was for us. We basked in approval. To our families nothing could have been more fitting: he was considered brilliant, so was I; he would have solid property, I would bring ample cash; we were supposed to share the same interests; if I was older than girls of our milieu are when they marry it was thought right for Michel to have a wife with a mature mind and nearer his own age; but what counted in their eyes above all else was that we were cousins— of a suitably remote degree— for a Devaux can do no better than marry a Devaux. We are a family with a long record of achievements and responsibilities, which I daresay stands for more in the world today than a moth-eaten Italian title.

'Oh, I wanted him all right, it suited me. Even Michel's being so much in love; it's not a bad thing in the man you're going to marry, it will make it all the easier to lead him, or so I thought. (I am not infallible.) For the time being we enjoyed ourselves, Michel's not solemn; we had fun.

'We moved about a good deal but Paris was where we were both living, and you know, or perhaps you don't, how that can be. In the evenings one drove out into the country to have dinner or dance in the banlieu— in our beautifully made fast cars and there seemed to be no one on the roads except people like ourselves and our friends. I gave Michel a second-hand Hispano Suiza— an Hispano of a good year— for an engagement present. It wasn't a thing people did but we were not conventional in that way. It was the most sentimental present I ever gave, and he loved it; we both did. We got on. We didn't know each other at all well then— we'd never played together when we were children or anything like that; we met, as it happened, in somebody's château in the depth of the winter of 1919. It was a hunt ball and Michel's party was late. I've never seen so much snow. He came in, you know in that light way he moves, I didn't know him from Adam but he had hardly greeted his hostess when he was by my side. He kissed my hand (as I wasn't married yet men didn't do that, at least not in public) and he said, '*Je crois que nous soyons un peu cousin.*' He told me later that he knew I would be there, and that he had seen me before, at a theatre in Paris, it was at a Bernstein *première*. Michel could have great charm.

'I didn't keep him dangling. What I wanted was a partnership, and that postulates equality, not coquetry. My idea was that, together, we could make ourselves quite a place in life. He had everything, I thought, except the ruthlessness. I didn't think he would really prevent me from using mine. I wasn't so aware of all those ethics, or rather I took them for conventional ones, family ethics, what they call *une conduite honorable* is a fetish with that kind of French. Michel himself appeared to be a rebel all right. (He is, of course, but in such an eccentric and exaggerated way.) Then, we all were.

'Freedom was the great thing, and it meant freedom from almost anything pre-war— patriotism, family life, making money. We decided not to marry for some time. Neither of us wanted to settle down; we were doing a hundred things at once and none of them was playing house. He was definite then that we ought to have no children, no more cannon-fodder. Many of our friends felt the same way, no children for this world until we've changed the world. Not even children of the quality ours were bound to be. It suited me down to the ground. I have no disposition towards maternity whatsoever, the whole business rather revolts me. (What irritates me perhaps most about you is your devotion to mama.)

'Another thing we were down on was sexual fidelity. Jealousy was possessive and therefore disgusting like hanging on to armament shares. Goodness knows, I gave Michel no cause, anyway I liked him better than anyone else I knew. But there was a girl, very young and pretty, sizzling with life, whom Michel had had a brief affair with just before we met. Nothing serious, nothing tragic, she slept round a great deal, with artists and writers mostly, and didn't care a scrap, we three met often quite amicably, but I think she and Michel still had got something for each other. I managed, well, to turn her head. I did it chiefly to tease Michel, but when he found out, as he was almost bound to do, he was very angry indeed. Men don't like that kind of thing, and *he* certainly doesn't. Naturally he said it wasn't jealousy, that it was the spirit, *my* spirit, of the thing that disturbed him. I told him he was absurd. That wouldn't do at all— when he is angry, which isn't often, he is pretty formidable. He doesn't say *much.* . . . It took quite a time to make it up; he never forgot it.

'I was cool, cooler perhaps than Michel would have liked, but then one was that way at the time. Coolness meant style, *tenu,* the one indecency people were afraid of was showing sentiment.

'That did not mean you were allowed not to have any. Michel, for all his cynicism about the human race, was full of affection for his friends; he wanted everyone he knew to have *bon cœur,* though he was apt to choose them mainly for intelligence. They had *that,* Bertrand . . . Gaston . . . Drieu . . . They were full of bright plans— don't think it was all horse-shows and dancing— though none of us including myself realized how far Michel's plans really went. It wasn't merely total disarmament and changing the parliamentary system, he wanted to change the texture of life, private as well as public. He believed that it should be tackled from two ends, education and the management of our natural resources. And by changes in education he didn't mean something like switching from dead languages to commercial German, he meant a radically new physical and emotional training, babies brought up without fear, that line, and smaller cities, universal birth control, forests in the deserts, tropical agriculture to improve the food supply, and the whole of it run by a supra-national administration and unarmed police. He spent all the money he could get hold of on homework: laboratory research (on a tiny scale, inevitably) and he and his friends formed a little new party, we have so many of them, they come and go. Michel didn't even want to be elected, he only wanted a platform from which he could make himself heard, so he went about quite valiantly sticking up posters and making speeches.'

'Did you go with him?' said Flavia.

'Everyone had a rather spectacular wife or fiancée, and we tagged along. We were quite a circus. But the party fell to pieces even before they started disagreeing about scope and means. Michel was the worst public speaker I have ever heard.'

'He was?'

'He didn't get stuck, and he wasn't long-winded. In fact he spoke in shapely fluent sentences and to the point. It would have gone down at the *Institut de France*. It did not at the café de l'Univers at Le Mans. And they had been prepared to like him because of the sports' page. We would write in some introductory chaff and a bit of local colour, Michel refused to use our stuff. He was not a demagogue, he said. We tried to laugh him out of it. We couldn't. He laughed with us, but he wouldn't be budged.

'After that had fizzled out, he decided to become a publisher. Of educational and political material. That failed too. We were married by then.'

'Yes——?' said Flavia.

'There is not much else to say. We nearly weren't. I saw that Michel would have liked to call it a day— release me from my word, or the other way round— I wouldn't let him; for a woman that situation always looks like a defeat. So he did his duty as I saw it.'

Flavia said, 'What had happened? What had gone wrong?'

'We had got to know one another.'

'That was all?'

'That was all. The rest you can imagine.'

'No,' said Flavia. 'Yes.'

'One day we knew what not to expect.'

When that had sunk in, Flavia said, 'But you stayed? You did not leave him?'

'Oh, we were tied in so many ways.'

Presently Flavia said, 'It doesn't explain everything, it doesn't explain about you.'

'I was not explaining,' Andrée said, 'I was talking about the past. The past is short, we got landed in the present.'

'You hadn't come to that yet.'

'Hadn't I? The foundations of it. Life with Michel was no help. I fell short of something he wanted from me, or imagined of me, one day he ceased to be interested in me as an individual or in my emotions. He endured them. My presence made no impact; except to hurt him— that I was always able to do— but he never gave way. Can you wonder that now and then I endeavour to remind him of my continuing existence?'

After a pause, Flavia said, 'I wish you had not brought me into it. I am out of my depth.'

'You were in it from the time your mother was in it, from the time they saw each other; from the time you saw me.'

Flavia said, 'Is there never an escape— from the minute you are born?'

Andrée in her other manner said, 'There can be. A matter of timing.' Then, '*Who* sought me out in the Fourniers' drawing-room? Remember?'

She held out her glass, 'Make me another *citron-pressé*.' Flavia complied and also gave herself a large glass of ice and soda-water.

'Tell me, my dear, have you written that letter you talked about? The letter "telling exactly what happened?" '

Flavia hesitated.

'Have you, or haven't you?'

'Not yet,' said Flavia.

'*Not yet.* Never say that you haven't had your chance. So as far as you're concerned there's been no communication— they are still in the dark?'

'They do know, then?'

'He does. He knows about my foray in Spain. He must wonder who was the informer.'

Without warning Flavia burst into tears.

Andrée sat waiting as people do when the curtain goes down briefly.

Flavia brought out, 'Am I unfit to live?'

Andrée said, 'Let us not exaggerate.'

'It is what *you* think of me.'

'You are as fit to live as the next person— if you lower your sights a little.'

Flavia said, 'It was my fault.'

'Would you say so? One might say that you have quite a case.'

'Do I have a case?'

'Don't *you* know?'

'You left me no choice but to take you to the tower. Did you not?'

'I left you no choice?' Andrée said. 'Very likely. Only you can tell, *only you can tell*.'

'I?'

'Only you, Flavia.'

Flavia said, 'Do you realize— this was the third time since I've known you that you called me by my name.'

'I realize.'

'It meant nothing the other time.'

'And when was that?'

Flavia said bravely, 'When you were the stranger, when you kissed me that night outside the villa.'

Andrée stood up, holding Flavia's eyes, she said slowly, 'And did I use your name in vain, *mon bel éphèbe*?' and they were in each other's arms.

A few seconds later Flavia broke away. She cried out, 'But I *still* hate you!'

Andrée withdrew to the window. She stood still for a time. When she had recovered, she spoke, 'That will have been almost my last lesson. Yes— you hate me. One can. Physical passion is not as delicious dix-huitième as you like to think it is, it has little to do with friendship, moral worth, choice

or will; it is not cosy, easy, reassuring, debonair. It is——
But need I go on?'

Flavia stood before her struck and trembling: she need not
have spoken.

When they met again, at luncheon the next day, Andrée's
surface was perfect. She appeared, perhaps was, gay,
interested in outside things, almost joyous. Flavia, who had
an idea of how much Andrée gloried in her control displayed, tried to match the performance. Their table was on
the terrace under an ample awning, the day was as sunny as
all the days had been but that noon there was an agreeable
breeze; the waiter rolled forth the hors-d'œuvres. Andrée
insisted on their having wine. The food at that hotel, though
Flavia would not allow herself to notice it, was excellent, the
cold straw-pale wine in the thin clear glass looked charming,
it was a setting for well-being.

Again Andrée fell back on reminiscence. She, too, seemed
to have a need to talk. 'I haven't told you yet about the little
boys and the motor car. Well, one holiday Michel was asked
to stay with a schoolmate of his, some people called Barraton
who had a house not far from Chantilly. So Michel arrives at
the station and is met there by his chum who says, '*Bon-jour,
tu as fais bon voyage?*' They shake hands. French boys are
mandarin with each other on such occasions. They were all of
eleven, the two of them, you can see them very neat and
trim with their clean haircuts and knickerbockers and well-
pulled stockings. Outside the station waits the family Hispano, chauffeur standing by. Little Jacques Barraton opens
the door, makes a bow to Michel and says casually, 'Want to
take the wheel, Devaux?" Michel bows back, says, "Just as
you like," and steps in. Jacques gets into the passenger's seat,
the chauffeur puts on his cap and gets in at the back. Needless to say, Michel had never driven a live car before; (as it

was he was hard put to touch feet to pedals) though of course he had practised on stationary ones and in his dreams ever since he was six years old. He slips into gear and off they go, the chauffeur, if you please, on the back seat with folded arms. Michel drives the blooming great thing all the five kilometres, or whatever it was, to the house without a swerve or hitch and pulls up in front— the Barratons were on the doorstep— switches off the engine, does another bow, "Thanks, Barraton, runs beautifully, doesn't she?" '

'True story?' Flavia said. Food and drink had lifted her morale.

'Literally.'

'It's a sweet story.'

But Andrée had already suffered one of her quick reversals. 'It's a horrid story! Stupid, conceited little boys, those awful Barratons letting their brat drive that car as a matter of course, they might have wrecked it and served them right, the little beasts.'

Flavia was sure then that the control must have been a performance; she had never seen Andrée so nervous.

Quite soon she said that she could not stand the luncheon clatter any longer. 'We can have coffee upstairs.'

They went, and as Flavia wanted to withdraw as had been their custom, Andrée stopped her. 'No, stay with me, I don't feel like being by myself.'

The coffee came. 'No— not on here, stuffy little room, in my room, at least we'll have more air.'

Flavia had not been inside Andrée's bedroom since the day the manager had shown them in. Again it was shuttered and in semi-darkness. Andrée did not sit down; like Flavia, but unlike herself, she began to move from place to place, touching objects here and there.

She said, 'I almost regret having brought you here. When I went to fetch you and saw you come out of that villa I realized that you needed no further rubbing in. Ah well, too late now.'

Then, unaccountably, 'One has to go through with difficult things— we all pass through bad moments.'

After that she had nothing further to say.

The house telephone rang in the sitting-room. Flavia made a move but Andrée had already gone. She heard her say, 'Ask him to come up, please.'

Andrée returned, leaving the door open. They heard someone enter the sitting-room. Andrée seized Flavia by the arm and pulled her to sit beside her on the bed; she called out 'I'm in here!'

A man stood in the door, there was light behind him, it was Michel Devaux.

The coldest voice ever heard fell into the silence. 'You have sent for me?'

'I sent for you— and you came. I believe we have matters to discuss.' The bravado was in the tone but it had worn thin.

The room was still unlit but by now he had seen Flavia.

Andrée went on, 'But first I must ask you to remove . . . this. I may like being run after, but there are limits, aren't there? Isn't she rather *your* responsibility now?'

He said, 'Get out of here.'

Flavia was unable to speak.

The same voice, 'I shall see you later at St-Jean.'

Andrée said, 'She's got some luggage.'

'That can be seen to. Go.'

It was only when she was standing on the highway that Flavia remembered that she had no money. Little matter: One only has to keep on putting one foot before the other, like this and like this again; and so at a moderate pace, steady as a sleep-walker, she started on the road home, if it was that.

An hour or two later a car pulled up beside her, one of the many that had stopped to offer the lift that she did not take.

She walked on. The car remained: Michel opened the door,
Get in.

After a time he said, 'Your mother is in Rome. I shall join
her there tomorrow.'

'Michel——'

'Michel——'
'Don't tell me about it.'
'Michel—— I must—— You must——'
'We will not talk about it. We will not talk about it, ever.'

An Ending

Constanza and Michel Devaux never married. During the years of their life together they neither apologized nor explained. They furnished the house at St-Jean-le-Sauveur as they had planned and when it was finished moved into it together, Michel keeping the tower for his writing retreat. They never called themselves anything other than Mrs Herbert and Monsieur Devaux. Whether their situation made a difference to their lives is not possible to say. They were accepted everywhere they cared to go, and by Devaux's family with some reservations. The prince died soon; Constanza in no case would have been affected by any attitude of the new head of the house, her brother. She cut herself off from Italy. In a measure she also cut herself off from England, but that might have been because her interests were no longer centred there.

Flavia first procrastinated then gradually gave up all idea of an academic education or career and spent many years in an eclipse of relative idleness and dissipations. She began a habit of moving about a good deal; her basic home, however, remained her mother's house at St-Jean even after she had contracted what was looked on as a wasteful if not scandalous marriage to a man twice her age, a homosexual, of undoubted brilliance and initial talent, who drank too much and was then already an established failure.

When National-Socialism came to power, Christian— that was the man's name— who knew Germany became one of the earliest Cassandras of the régime and Flavia put her energies into the same cause. Here she had her mother's approval and support. Flavia's own heart was in it; at the same time this, too, could be seen as one of the excuses for retardation and by-passing obligations nearer home.

Constanza ceased to be well-off. Anna's money after holding up so many years against so many inroads finally did not long outlast her lifetime; whether due to the depression or Devaux's management on which Constanza insisted, it diminished annually by leaps and bounds. Flavia gave up a regular allowance and earned some money by reading for publishers and translations. During that time she did practically no writing of her own and the little she produced, a few book reviews, some political journalism, was adequate— no more— and derivative.

Flavia's relations with her mother were never other than affectionate, but they had changed. Too much had come too suddenly and when they met again at the end of that summer they found it no longer possible to talk in their old way. Left to her own impulses Constanza might well have liked to ask some questions, even so she might have feared to seem to probe or blame; her daughter had turned alien to her in some aspects, as incomprehensibly as her own mother had in some of hers. Michel's interdiction and Flavia's loss of self-confidence each played their part. Michel consistently acted as a friend and a companion to the girl: the atmosphere in the house at all times was immensely civilized, but Flavia who had heard his other voice, could not detach her consciousness from what might be beneath the surface. She felt herself, mistakenly perhaps, to have been judged, not heard. She continued to admire much about Michel but was never at her ease with him again. A good part of her waking life was spent with Christian and his followers at parties and in cafés. For a long time she held the hope that one day, when they were both older, Constanza would be able to hear, and she to tell, the truth.

* * *

After Munich, Constanza and Michel shut down their house at St-Jean and went to Paris where they camped in Michel's old flat waiting on events from which he could no longer feel aloof. Flavia moved to London. Her intermittent existence with Christian had foundered; partly on the irreducibly square streak in her own nature. They were amicably dissolving the marriage and Flavia had gone back to her own name. At that time she was regaining a balance and also beginning to buckle down to sustained work.

In 1940 after the German break-through, Constanza and Michel stayed on in Paris until a date in June when they decided to join the exodus, gain a southern port and make their way to England. They were ready to leave in several cars with Michel's lawyer brother and his family. What kind of a place Michel Devaux would have taken in the Free French movement, or how he would have made out with its leader, we shall never know as he did not get there. At the last hour he received a message from his youngest brother who was still in his house in the country. Andrée had arrived, placing herself under his protection. Andrée, it was known, had publicly and insolently unmasked a German agent during the recent phony war, as well as indulged in some merciless leg-pulls with some prominent French Nazi sympathizers; she was a marked person (as it turned out, both the names Devaux and Herbert had got on to Gestapo lists), in danger, and a risk as well as an embarrassment to the rest of them. The brother and his large household were preparing to be off as soon as possible and put some distance between themselves and the advancing German armies. What added to their troubles was that things down there were already disorganized: most of their vehicles had been requisitioned, the remaining ones were wholly inadequate, Andrée had lost her car, there was no petrol. They implored Michel to come at once, while the going was good, to take charge and cope with Andrée's evacuation. They reminded him that he was the head of the family; the other obligation was not expressed in words. Michel and Constanza did not want to leave one another. Their decision— it was always said that it was made by both— was that he had to go. So at Fontainebleau they went on in different directions, he driving off alone, Constanza going on with the family party. They had a rendezvous at Bordeaux, and if that failed a later one in London.

On the second day out, low-flying planes again machine-gunned the crawling queue of vehicles on the road and the men, women and children who tried to take cover by the sides; and many people, Constanza among them, were killed. So the favourite of the gods died in a ditch after all.

Michel remained in a remote part of unoccupied France for the rest of the war. He did not join a maquis, but personally at great danger to himself sheltered and assisted a number of individuals of all nationalities and races. Few people ever heard of his activities; there were later on even rumours of collaboration. Andrée who had managed to keep moving between the two zones under a cover name was decorated both by the French and the British.

Flavia has often come near to absolving herself. At such times she seeks to answer one question— did she or did she not suspect from the beginning who Andrée really was? She goes over those days again hour by hour, word by word, and always comes to the conclusion that her mind had been in fact a blank: She knew nothing. It is then that she hears Mena's remembered voice, 'Anna opened a door and saw . . . in the long room at Castelfonte . . . she shut the door and walked away and came in again from the other side of the house, a smile upon her face.' And she wonders.

If you would like to know more about Virago books, write to us
at 41 William IV Street, London WC2N 4DB for a full catalogue.

Please send a stamped addressed envelope

VIRAGO
Advisory Group

Andrea Adam	Zoë Fairbairns
Carol Adams	Carolyn Faulder
Sally Alexander	Germaine Greer
Rosalyn Baxandall (USA)	Jane Gregory
Anita Bennett	Suzanne Lowry
Liz Calder	Jean McCrindle
Beatrix Campbell	Cathy Porter
Angela Carter	Alison Rimmer
Mary Chamberlain	Elaine Showalter (USA)
Anna Coote	Spare Rib Collective
Jane Cousins	Mary Stott
Jill Craigie	Rosalie Swedlin
Anna Davin	Margaret Walters
Rosalind Delmar	Elizabeth Wilson
Christine Downer (Australia)	Barbara Wynn

Book Tokens

Give them
the pleasure of choosing

Book Tokens can be bought
and exchanged at most
bookshops

Other VIRAGO MODERN CLASSICS

Other VIRAGO MODERN CLASSICS

ELIZABETH von ARNIM
Fräulein Schmidt & Mr Anstruther
Vera

EMILY EDEN
The Semi-Attached Couple &
  The Semi-Detached House

MILES FRANKLIN
My Brilliant Career
My Career Goes Bung

GEORGE GISSING
The Odd Women

ELLEN GLASGOW
The Sheltered Life
Virginia

SARAH GRAND
The Beth Book

RADCLYFFE HALL
The Well of Loneliness
The Unlit Lamp

WINIFRED HOLTBY
Anderby Wold
The Crowded Street
The Land of Green Ginger
Mandoa, Mandoa!

MARGARET KENNEDY
The Constant Nymph
The Ladies of Lyndon
Together and Apart

ROSAMOND LEHMANN
The Ballad and the Source
The Gipsy's Baby
Invitation to the Waltz
A Note in Music
A Sea-Grape Tree
The Weather in the Streets

F. M. MAYOR
The Third Miss Symons

GEORGE MEREDITH
Diana of the Crossways

EDITH OLIVIER
The Love Child

CHARLOTTE PERKINS
  GILMAN
The Yellow Wallpaper

DOROTHY RICHARDSON
Pilgrimage (4 volumes)

HENRY HANDEL
  RICHARDSON
The Getting of Wisdom
Maurice Guest

BERNARD SHAW
An Unsocial Socialist

MAY SINCLAIR
Life and Death of Harriett Frean
Mary Olivier
The Three Sisters

F. TENNYSON JESSE
A Pin to See The Peepshow
The Lacquer Lady
Moonraker

VIOLET TREFUSIS
Hunt the Slipper

MARY WEBB
The Golden Arrow
Gone to Earth
The House in Dormer Forest
Precious Bane
Seven for a Secret

H. G. WELLS
Ann Veronica

Also of interest

THE LOVE CHILD
by Edith Olivier
New Introduction by Hermione Lee

At thirty-two, her mother dead, Agatha Bodenham finds herself quite alone. She summons back to life the only friend she ever knew, Clarissa, the dream companion of her childhood. At first Clarissa comes by night, and then by day, gathering substance in the warmth of Agatha's obsessive love until it seems that others too can see her. See, but not touch, for Agatha has made her love child for herself. No man may approach this creature of perfect beauty, and if he does, she who summoned her can spirit her away...

Edith Olivier (1879?-1948) was one of the youngest of a clergyman's family of ten children. Despite early ambitions to become an actress, she led a conventional life within twenty miles of her childhood home, the Rectory at Wilton, Wiltshire. But she wrote five highly original novels as well as works of non-fiction, and her 'circle' included Rex Whistler (who illustrated her books), David Cecil, Siegfried Sassoon and Osbert Sitwell. *The Love Child* (1927) was her first novel, acknowledged as a minor masterpiece: a perfectly imagined fable and a moving and perceptive portrayal of unfulfilled maternal love.

"This is wonderful..." — *Cecil Beaton*

"*The Love Child* seems to me to stand in a category of its own creating...the image it leaves is that of a tranquil star" — *Anne Douglas Sedgwick*

"Flawless — the best 'first' book I have ever read...perfect" — *Sir Henry Newbolt*

"A masterpiece of its kind" — *Lord David Cecil*

THE SHUTTER OF SNOW

by Emily Holmes Coleman
New Introduction by Carmen Callil and Mary Siepmann

After the birth of her child Marthe Gail spends two months in an insane asylum with the fixed idea that she is God. Marthe, something between Ophelia, Emily Dickinson and Lucille Ball, transports us into that strange country of terror and ecstasy we call madness. In this twilit country the doctors, nurses, the other inmates and the mad vision of her insane mind are revealed with piercing insight and with immense verbal facility.

Emily Coleman (1899-1974) was born in California and, like Marthe, went mad after the birth of her son in 1924. Witty, eccentric and ebullient, she lived in Paris in the 1920s as one of the *transition* writers, close friend of Peggy Guggenheim and Djuna Barnes (who said Emily would be marvellous company slightly stunned). In the 1930s she lived in London (in the French, the Wheatsheaf, the Fitzroy), where her friends numbered Dylan Thomas, T.S. Eliot, Humphrey Jennings and George Barker. Emily Coleman wrote poetry throughout her life — and this one beautiful, poignant novel (first published in 1930), which though constantly misunderstood, has always had a passionate body of admirers — Edwin Muir, David Gascoyne and Antonia White to name a few.

"A very striking triumph of imagination and technique... The book is not only quite unique; it is also a work of genuine literary inspiration" — *Edwin Muir*

"A work which has stirred me deeply...compelling" — *Harold Nicolson*

"An extraordinary, visionary book, written out of those edges where madness and poetry meet" — *Fay Weldon*

PLAGUED BY THE NIGHTINGALE

by Kay Boyle
New preface by the author

When the American girl Bridget marries the Frenchman Nicolas, she goes to live with his wealthy family in their Breton village. This close-knit family love each other to the exclusion of the outside world. But it is a love that festers, for the family is tainted with an inherited bone disease and Bridget discovers, as she faces the Old World with the courage of the New, that plague can also infect the soul...

Kay Boyle was born in Minnesota in 1902. The first of her three marriages was to a Frenchman and she moved to Paris in the 1920s where, as one of that legendary group of American expatriates and contributor to *transition*, she knew Joyce, Pound, Hemingway, the Fitzgeralds, Djuna Barnes and Gertrude Stein: a world she recorded in *Being Geniuses Together*. After a spell living in the bizarre commune run by Isadora Duncan's brother, she returned to America in 1941 where she still lives. A distinguished novelist, poet and short-story writer, she was acclaimed by Katherine Anne Porter for her "fighting spirit, freshness of feeling." *Plagued by the Nightingale* was first published in 1931. In subtle, rich and varied prose Kay Boyle echoes Henry James in a novel at once lyrical, delicate and shocking.

"A series of brilliant, light-laden pictures, lucid, delightful; highly original" — *Observer*

"In delicate, satirical vignettes Miss Boyle has enshrined a French middle-class family...The lines of the picture have an incisiveness and a bloom which suggest silverpoint"— *Guardian*